Riding School

Samantha Alexander lives in Lincolnshire with a variety of animals including her thoroughbred horse, Bunny, and her two kittens, Cedric and Bramble. Her schedule is almost as busy and exciting as her plots – she writes a number of columns for newspapers and magazines, is a teenage agony aunt for BBC Radio Leeds and in her spare time she regularly competes in dressage and showjumping events.

Riding School

Three Girls, Three Ponies, Three Exciting Adventures

SAMANTHA ALEXANDER

MACMILLAN CHILDREN'S BOOKS

*Samantha Alexander and Macmillan Children's
Books would like to thank all at Suzanne's
Riding School, especially Suzanne Marczak*

Jodie
First published 1999 by Macmillan Children's Books
Emma
First published 1999 by Macmillan Children's Books
Steph
First published 1999 by Macmillan Children's Books

This three-book edition published 2001 by Macmillan Children's Books
a division of Pan Macmillan Limited
20 New Warf Road, London N1 9RR
Basingstoke and Oxford
www.panmacmillan.com

Associated companies throughout the world

ISBN 0 330 48359 5

Text copyright © Samantha Alexander 1999

The right of Samantha Alexander to be identified as the
author of this work has been asserted by her in accordance
with the Copyright, Designs and Patents Act 1988.

3 5 7 9 8 6 2

A CIP catalogue record for this book is available from the British Library

Printed and bound in Great Britain by Mackays of Chatham plc, Kent

Contents

Jodie

Chapter One

"Mum, stop fussing!" I snapped as my stomach somersaulted with a fresh wave of nerves. "Honestly, I'm not an invalid."

The car jerked to a halt outside the high wrought-iron gates and I immediately unfastened the seat belt. An oblong wooden sign swung in the breeze: BROOK HOUSE RIDING SCHOOL. The B in Brook had cracked and all but peeled off.

We'd arrived. There was no turning back now.

"For heaven's sake, Jodie, you're lucky to be alive." My mother touched my arm as if to hold me back. "Aren't I at least entitled to worry?"

"I'll be all right." I fixed a grin on my face and reached for my lunch box and grooming bag on the back seat, avoiding her eyes. "Trust me, I'll ring if anything goes wrong. But it won't. I'm fine."

Her face showed her concern, but she let her hand fall and shooed me out of the car, trying to hide the raw panic which consumed her at the mere mention of horses.

"Mum, I've got to do this." I squeezed her hand

and tried to smile reassuringly. "By myself, I've got to prove . . ."

"I know, I know, go on, get out of here." She waved her hand dismissively, staring straight ahead. I stepped out of the car and slung the grooming bag over my shoulder.

"Jodie?"

"Yeah?" I hovered by the half-open door, feeling like it was the first day at a new school.

"Just be careful, that's all your dad and I ask."

"It's crazy! Half the eleven o'clock ride have cancelled, there are no rides tomorrow afternoon . . . At this rate we'll be shut by the end of the week, never mind the end of the year."

"Sssh," another voice chipped in, "there's someone there."

I knocked on the office door and felt a flush of embarrassment creep up my neck. It was so obvious I'd been listening. The door swung open to reveal two girls, one sitting behind a desk, about my age, with thick black hair, the other tall and pretty, perched on a filing cabinet, swinging her legs which were dazzling in bright yellow jean jods.

"Um . . ." I hesitated. "I'm looking for the owner. I was told to come . . ."

"She's not here!" the dark-haired girl fired back. There was no mistaking the irritated tone in her voice. "What do you want?"

"Um, I . . ." I could feel my hands starting to sweat. "I'm the new girl. I was told to be here by nine."

"Oh great, that's all we need." The dark-haired girl slammed the diary shut with unnecessary force. "Look, I don't know what Mrs Brentford's told you but we don't need any more helpers." Disappointment crashed around inside me. I'd been waiting for this day for two and a half years.

The pretty blond girl shifted uneasily, shooting critical looks at her friend. "Why don't you hang around for a few hours?" she suggested hesitantly. "Now that you're here, I'm sure we can find something for you to do." I just wanted the floor to open up and swallow me. The tension in the room was unbearable. "I'll show you round." She jumped off the filing cabinet, pulling on a pair of riding boots.

"Well, if you're going to hang around," the other girl sniped, "there are twenty-four hay nets that need filling. I'm sure Sophie will show you where they are."

"Take no notice of Kate." The other girl took my arm and guided me towards the first row of stables. I instantly liked her warmth and her easy way of talking as if she'd known you for ever.

"Kate's really bossy and it upsets most people. She's got an uncle in Hong Kong who owns race-horses and he's buying her an Arab for her fifteenth birthday. I think it's gone to her head. But she's all right mostly."

We stopped at the first stable which said Rocket above the door. Most riding schools display the names of their horses so people coming for rides can find their mount. A 14.2 chestnut with a squiggly stripe down his nose stuck out his head and nuzzled Sophie's pockets.

"Rocket's really fast and a good jumper," Sophie explained. "Everybody wants to ride him." My hand trembled as I reached out and touched a horse for the first time since the accident. He rubbed the top of his head against my hand and it felt soft and familiar. The smell of hay and leather and horse enveloped me and my eyes filled with tears as emotion threatened to take over.

"Are you all right?" Sophie suddenly looked really concerned. "Only you look as if you've seen a ghost."

"Oats are a traditional feed that can make ponies very excitable. True or false?" A plumpish girl in multicoloured leggings and an "I Love Milton" T-shirt darted out the question as soon as we walked into the saloon.

"False." Sophie rolled her eyes at me after deliberately giving the wrong answer. "Emma talks non-stop and has the attention span of a five-year-old." Sophie bounded forward and pulled the copy

4

of *In the Saddle* out of her hand. "She also has an obsession with a pony called Buzby who would have a criminal record and an IQ of zero if he were human."

"Don't be a pig." Emma grabbed for the magazine, hurt flickering over her face.

"Oh Emm!" Sophie read the quiz. "You haven't even got one of these questions right!"

Sophie and I had just spent an hour trudging around with a leading rein class, walking stubborn ponies through heavy sand. The instructor, who worked part-time, kept losing her temper and didn't seem the slightest bit bothered when one of the smallest riders got caught on a bramble and was nearly pulled out of the saddle.

Sophie had giggled and desperately tried to lead a piebald called Foxy. I was leading a gorgeous little Connemara called Blossom who quickly learned she could lean on my arm. The boy who was riding her kept kicking me in the back when I didn't run fast enough so I was quite pleased when Blossom eventually tipped him off.

"If I have to prepare to trot and trot on one more time," I groaned, "I shall go mad."

Sophie shot me a quizzical look and then pulled me over to a corner by the window on the pretext of looking at riding hats. "Listen," she said, "I couldn't help noticing your leg."

"What?" I yelped, immediately on the defensive.

5

"If you've hurt yourself, you shouldn't be running up and down like that. Don't let Kate bully you."

"I'm not. I mean, it's just a sprain." All the old feelings of humiliation rose up and I had to take a deep breath to get a grip. "I'm fine," I lied. "As I said, it's just a sprain."

"Are you a horse-brain or just a beginner?" Emma plonked herself down next to me and bit into a banana and peanut butter sandwich.

"Um, neither really." I felt my spirits hurtling to the ground. My first day back at riding school wasn't meant to be like this.

The saloon was a converted stable with western-style louvred doors and a long table in the middle. There were posters of horses everywhere and piles of bags and riding gear in the corner. It smelt of dust and desperately needed a good clean.

"So do you own a pony or what?"

Emma didn't stop talking for one second, mainly about Buzby who she obviously worshipped, and about the other girls in the yard. Every muscle in my body ached. I was completely out of shape and had never worked so hard in my life. Kate had pushed me from the start, rattling out orders to do all the jobs that everyone hated. Scrubbing mangers, sweeping the yard, levelling the muck heap, cleaning horse rugs. I'd put up with about all I could take. Brook House had to be the worst run riding school in the whole country. It was a nightmare.

"Take no notice of Kate." Emma dropped her voice and leaned close, seeming to tune into my thoughts. "She gives every new girl a hard time – it's like her own personal initiation ceremony." Emma wrinkled her freckled nose and glanced around as if to check Kate wasn't there.

"Oh," I murmured, relief flooding through me. "I thought I was the only one she didn't like."

"Jodie, Jodie, where are you?" Kate's deep authoritative voice bellowed out from behind the door.

"Speak of the devil," I groaned, wanting to dive under the table for cover. "Doesn't she ever give anyone a break?"

Kate marched in through the louvred doors just as Emma dropped half her sandwich on the floor.

"Oh, you're in here. I might have known." Kate eyed the mess with a look of disdain. She had a way of tucking her dark hair behind her ears and sticking out her chin which made her seem ultra-important. "Frank needs tacking up," she ordered. "And while you're at it, you can give him a good brush." There was still no sign of Mrs Brentford or of Sandra the (full-time) groom, and the riding instructor had disappeared on the pretext of picking up her cat from the vet.

Frank was a part-Shire, gentle giant with feet like

breeze-blocks and a really gormless expression. He looked after the novice adult riders who were either terribly nervous or fancied themselves as a Frankie Dettori. Even if a bomb went off, Frank would still have a one-paced plod. According to Sophie nobody liked tacking him up because the saddle was so heavy and you had to stand on a bucket to reach his back.

"Yes sir." I saluted Kate's departing figure. One more order and I was going to tell her where to go.

The tack room was up a flight of stone steps above the stables. There were neat rows of saddle racks and bridle hooks with a horse's name next to each, and various bandages, boots and martingales thrown all over the place. Frank's bridle was in pieces on top of his saddle and I only needed one guess as to who had undone it.

I picked up the headpiece and browband and methodically fitted it back together, remembering to keep the bit the right way and the noseband on the inside of the cheekpieces. It would take more than a dismantled bridle to catch me out.

Voices in the stable below drifted up just as I looped the reins through the throat lash.

"Do you think she knows what she's doing?"

It was Sophie. Without a doubt. I stayed absolutely still and recognized Emma's voice mentioning Buzby. They can't have realized I was still in the tack room.

"Don't tell anyone," Sophie said in a hushed whisper, "but when I showed her Rocket she nearly freaked. I thought she was going to burst into tears. And when I suggested we rode bareback to the field she was petrified. I don't think she can ride."

White-hot anger mixed with bitter resentment boiled to the surface. How dare they talk about me behind my back? I thought they were decent – I thought they were possible future friends.

Grabbing Frank's saddle and bridle, blinded by tears, I stumbled for the door. I didn't notice that the reins were dangling down.

"Watch out!" Kate looked up from the yard just as I lost my footing. My knees buckled and I tipped forward but I couldn't right myself. The steps swirled into a blur as a sudden needling cramp shot up my left leg.

There was nothing I could do. My whole leg had seized up.

The saddle crashed downwards pommel first, stirrups flying, as I released an arm to grab for the handrail. The noise was horrendous. It crashed down each step, scuffing on the rough stone, bruising from the sheer force. It could have been me.

Kate moved forwards in slow motion, her wide, horrified eyes never leaving the saddle. After what seemed like minutes it bounced off the last couple of steps. I heard a sickening crack as the wooden tree under the leather snapped in half and it rolled limp onto the concrete.

"What have you done?" Kate ran forward and then shrank back from the misshapen heap as if it were a dead bird. Sophie and Emma dashed out of the stable, open-mouthed with shock. At least they'd noticed that I was doubled up, clutching my left leg and trying to drag myself down the steps on my bottom one at a time.

"It's ruined . . . You idiot!" A wave of anger darkened Kate's features.

But it was too late. I'd had more than I could take.

"Don't say a word," I hissed, halting halfway down the steps and gritting my teeth to keep a brave face. "You can stick your stupid riding school, and all your lousy jobs. Even convicts wouldn't want to work here. It's the unfriendliest place on earth." I was really buzzing now, letting it all rush out. "I thought horsy people helped each other. Well all you lot do is snipe and pick holes in people. You're pathetic, all of you, and it's no wonder nobody rides here. It's a shambles. It's the stables from hell, it's . . ."

"Have you quite finished?" Kate glared at me, her eyes wide.

"No, I haven't," I yelled. "Not until I collect my stuff and get out of here. And good riddance."

I made a superhuman effort to drag myself up

and then limped across to the saloon feeling their eyes boring into my back.

Inside, I slammed the door and then leaned back, my breath coming in short gasps. I closed my eyes and slowly slid down the door, wrapping my arms round my legs and burying my head in my knees. Hot tears trickled down my cheeks, followed by rasping sobs and long shudders of emptiness.

I'd waited for this day for so long. After the accident the surgeon had told my mother that nothing could be done and most of the nerves in my leg had been damaged. Two six-hour operations followed. I'd smashed my lower leg in seven different places. The surgeon was nothing less than brilliant. I couldn't move my toes for over a year but I had a superb physiotherapist who I worked desperately hard for. Over my bed was a picture of a chestnut Arab and it was the driving ambition to ride again which kept me going.

Brook House Riding School was meant to fulfil that dream. It had never occurred to me that it might not be like my old stables. I'd thought that I could slip back into my past life. But that wasn't meant to be.

The only thing I was sure about at that moment was that I'd never come back to this riding school. Not in a thousand years and not if they paid me a million pounds. Not ever.

Chapter Two

"There are two girls to see you." Mum pushed open my bedroom door completely ignoring the *Do not disturb* sign. "You never told me you'd made some friends." She practically pushed me off the bed and started puffing up the pillows.

"I haven't," I snapped, trying not to show my red swollen eyes. "And I'm not here. Tell them they've got the wrong house."

I'd already spotted Emma and Sophie hovering in the driveway. They were still in their riding gear so they'd obviously come straight from the stables. Of course, my address and phone number were in the appointment book.

"I'm not going to start lying for you, Jodie." Mum straightened up, giving the room one final appraisal. "I don't approve of you riding again, you know that, and I don't know what's gone on today at the stables, but how many times have I told you, you can't run away from your problems."

"Millions." I stared out of the window, scowling.

"Well then, I'll send them up."

"Can we come in?" Sophie knocked nervously on my half-open door and peered round the gap. She was uneasy with embarrassment and Emma clung on behind like a scared rabbit. Despite myself I softened, just a little.

"Wow!" Emma caught a glimpse of my model horse collection and all her inhibitions flew out of the window. "These are so cool." She was at my dressing table in seconds admiring Black Beauty which stood a whole thirty centimetres high. I had fifty-two model and china horses and a miniature stable and paddock with jumps, which was balanced on my bedside table.

"Don't touch." Sophie followed Emma in, padding across the carpet in her socks. While they had their backs turned I hastily shoved a photograph of me riding into my chest of drawers.

"Nice bedroom." Sophie gazed at the horsy posters which were all of famous showjumpers. Underneath, I'd marked in the date, place and rider's name as well as the horse. She squinted slightly and I guessed what she was thinking. I didn't have the usual twelve-year-old's bedroom. Everything was impeccably tidy. Like my dad, I'd always needed everything to be orderly, and after the accident it had become essential to have everything in its place just so I could function.

"Um, we're really sorry about earlier." Sophie fidgeted, twisting her ring round on her middle finger. "Nobody meant to upset you."

"If it's about the saddle I'll pay for the repairs." I tried to make my voice as cold as possible. I didn't let on that I hadn't got a penny to my name. I'd just have to get a job.

"No, no, it's not that," Sophie stammered, casting her eyes down. "Kate didn't mean to be so nasty, it's just that she's trying her best for the stables."

"What, by getting rid of customers?" I deliberately loaded my voice with sarcasm.

"No, it's—"

"Coffee!" Mum burst in with a tray of mugs and biscuits and I nearly died of embarrassment. "We've only been here three weeks." She started on our life story before she'd even put the tray down. "Most of the furniture is still in storage. I expect Jodie will be going to the same school as you in September."

"Mum," I hissed, breaking out in a sweat, "we're having a serious conversation here."

"Oh, righty-ho. Well, I'll just go and polish the bathroom tiles then." She winked at me as she went out and I caught Sophie smiling.

Dad was an engineer working in India for two months at a time and we'd moved to Limestone

Avenue so Mum could be nearer her family. My brother loved it because there was a bowling alley just down the road and a football pitch. I hated it because it didn't have a paddock and I'd left all my friends behind.

"Brook House is in trouble," Emma blurted out as soon as the door was closed. Sophie glared at her but she carried on. "Look, we might as well tell her," Emma insisted. "It's hardly a well-kept secret."

"Horseworld Centre opened about a year ago," Sophie said, taking over the story, "and it's taken all the business. They've got an indoor school and young flashy ponies and, well, Brook House can't compete. It looks unlikely that Mrs Brentwood will be able to feed the horses this winter. She's absolutely broke."

I remembered Horseworld Centre. There were big adverts in the evening paper but when I rang up to enquire, the lessons were expensive and they didn't let anyone help out.

"So why are you telling me?" I was trying hard not to look interested.

"Because we care about the horses." Emma was getting really passionate. "Because half of them are too old to start a new life and the other half are either too badly behaved or set in their ways. Rusty is ancient, Ebony Jane's taught so many people to ride she deserves a medal. Tinky wouldn't last two minutes in a new home, Monty is a crib-biter and Elvis and Faldo aren't even broken in yet." She was flushed and tears shone in her eyes. "They all love each other though. They're a family and they don't deserve to be split up. They'd end up at some horse market being sold for meat and we can't let that happen." She shuddered at the thought of it and Sophie reached out and touched her shoulder.

And I knew I'd been touched too – in my heart.

"Mrs Brentford's given up hope," Sophie explained. "She doesn't know what to do for the best."

"If the school closes down it will break her heart," Emma added, her mouth quivering.

"But I don't see," I said, slumping on the bed. "What can *I* do? Why are you telling *me* this?"

"Because we want you to join our gang." Sophie stared straight at me. "There are five of us – Rachel and Steph you haven't met. We're all determined to save the riding school."

"We were really impressed by all your hard work," Emma explained. "We call ourselves the Five Pack, and we'd like you to join us."

"And Kate's in agreement?" I asked doubtfully.

"Well, not exactly," Sophie hedged.

"She's been outvoted," Emma jumped in. "You don't have to ride, just throw in some ideas."

"It took us an extra bus ride and half Emma's pocket money to find you," Sophie pleaded.

I decided not to mention overhearing their conversation in the tack room.

"So, are you in or what?" Emma demanded.

"Have you any kind of a plan?" I asked.

"Nothing." Sophie shrugged. "We haven't got a clue what to do."

I reached out my hand. Emma put hers on top and Sophie placed hers on top of Emma's.

"The Six Pack," I said.

"The Six Pack."

"And I'll try not to freak out when I see the horses," I said, grinning.

Needless to say, they both cringed with embarrassment.

"This is Rachel, and that's Steph."

Sophie shuffled awkwardly as Steph barely acknowledged me and carried on tacking up a pretty grey pony called Monty.

"She can be a bit awkward sometimes," Sophie apologized, breathing a sigh of relief when Steph mounted and rode off to the manege. "I think she's got family problems. Monty's on part-loan at the riding stables but her dad wants to get rid of him."

"That must be awful." I really felt for her.

"Yeah, but Steph's not the kind of girl you can feel sorry for. She shuts everybody out, and to be quite honest, she thinks she's it."

All five girls were having an hour's group lesson with the instructor, Janice, in return for helping Sandra out over the weekend. I was dying to get up in the saddle but didn't dare try in front of everybody. Yesterday I'd taxed the wasted muscles in my calf and now I was suffering the consequences.

Rachel led out Rusty who was an ancient roan pony but with the sweetest face I'd ever seen. His thick tail fanned out behind and his eyes were hidden behind a thatch of black mane. Rachel tied it up in a bobble so "he could see where he was going".

Rachel was small with long brown hair. She was eleven and crippled by shyness. She wasn't unfriendly but when I tried to make conversation she blushed deeply and shot under Rusty's saddle flap to tighten the girth.

Sophie was explaining how to stretch one of Rusty's forelegs forward so as to even out any wrinkled skin caught under the girth. Sophie spoke gently and Rachel listened quietly, taking it all in. She obviously hadn't been riding for very long.

Rusty was the perfect beginner's pony and stood half dozing, as solid as a rock.

"Rachel lives near you," Sophie said, turning towards me. "Perhaps you could give each other lifts, organize some kind of a rota."

The colour drained from Rachel's face and a flicker of real fear filled her eyes. "Or perhaps not,"

I hastily added. Sophie and I shared a look, wondering what on earth had caused such a reaction.

"Don't start without me!" Emma charged up the drive clutching a pink and black crop and wearing an oversized T-shirt with a photograph of Buzby printed on the front. The back read *Pony in a Million* and *Stable Star of the Year*. I looked up and saw the real Buzby's head appear over a stable door with his bridle slipped over one ear where he'd obviously been rubbing. He gave Emma a delighted squeal and started kicking wildly at the door. I tried to cover up an angry purple bruise on my arm where he had sunk his teeth in just minutes earlier, all because I didn't have a titbit for him.

"I overslept." Emma ran straight towards him, her cheeks pink with excitement. "I couldn't sleep, I've got so many ideas. Oh, Buz—" She stopped suddenly and her face fell. "I've forgotten your liquorice allsorts!"

The lesson got off to a shaky start, mainly because Buzby, in a really bad mood, kept bull-dozing into Monty's behind. As a result Monty bucked Steph off.

"Keep your distance!" Janice screeched. Steph was nearly in tears because she thought she'd broken a tooth. Emma was trotting round and round with her reins like washing lines, completely out of control.

"OK, that's it, everyone turn in." Janice sounded murderous. "How many times do I have to tell you to keep a horse a good distance from the ride ahead. You should be able to see the hocks of the pony in front."

Steph glared at Emma who was quivering like a jelly because Buzby had decided it was the ideal moment for a good shake.

"Has anybody got any questions?" Janice asked. Emma stuck up her hand but the instructor had already turned her back. "Prepare to walk and walk on."

They all set off around the school with Kate leading file on Archie who was a palomino with a really cheeky expression. According to Emma, he and Buzby were inseparable and sure enough, Buzby wouldn't settle until he was following Archie nose to tail.

Kate was definitely the better rider but then she was the oldest at thirteen. She concentrated hard and had a nice seat and rhythm. Archie could be really good if he'd stop acting the fool and pay attention.

Sophie had a natural advantage with really long legs which wrapped around the pony's sides, but she tended to lean too far back and have her reins too long.

"OK, circle to the rear of the ride in turn." Janice made no secret of the fact she was bored rigid.

When it came to Rachel's turn, Rusty was a bit slow and had to trot to catch up with the rest of the ride. Janice singled her out and made her do it again which caused Rachel to turn bright red and lose her stirrups.

"Give him a kick, Rachel, for goodness' sake." Janice nagged constantly which only made her go to pieces and ride worse than ever.

"Rachel always holds us back," Steph muttered to Sophie as she rode past giving Monty a boot in the ribs with her outside leg.

But Rachel finally got the gist of what Janice was saying and got Rusty moving forward. Only I noticed that she was close to tears and utterly mortified.

Emma didn't stop talking for the whole lesson which made me want to gag her. I'd already decided that Janice was a terrible instructor lacking any kind of discipline, enthusiasm or encouragement. By the time they got on to jumping, it was complete chaos with everyone shooting off in different directions. I decided to sneak off before Janice collared me into helping with the poles and found something else to criticize.

We were having a meeting in the saloon straight after the lesson but that still gave me fifteen minutes to have a good look around the school. Up until now I'd only seen the yard and the manege. I wanted to familiarize myself with all the different horses and ponies and with the facilities. At that moment I had no idea of the shock that was in store for me. I had no idea that my life was about to change for ever.

There were eight horses and thirteen ponies at Brook House, all varying in size from a Shetland to a Shire, and all different types, which was a good thing. It was quite obvious though that the ones who'd been schooled had clearly forgotten it, and the others had just blasted through life, eating, sleeping and behaving badly.

The two New Forest ponies, Elvis and Faldo, were in a four acre field with the rest of the ponies and were having a tussle with a little Shetland who was quite clearly the boss. They were dark brown with tiny white stars on their foreheads and long unpulled manes which I was itching to get my hands into. They had no idea about basic good manners and grabbed at my arm, eager for horse nuts.

I took out my notebook and jotted down various details, then moved on to the horse paddock where big Frank was dozing under a horse chestnut tree. Ebony Jane, the ex-racehorse, was standing next to him and the other horses were clustered around the water trough.

Sophie had already told me that it was the children rather than the adults who had defected to Horseworld Centre. In the week they still had quite a good turnover of office workers and housewives, keen to take up a glamorous hobby, but at weekends and in the holidays, the ponies were standing idle, and that's where Brook House had made most of its money before.

There was a corrugated barn at the back of a row of stables half full of hay and straw. A couple of fields had been cut for hay but it obviously wasn't enough to last the winter. I noted down that some cross-country fences had become overgrown and it would be a good idea to clear the weeds and get them back in use.

I was just thinking about going back to the saloon and waiting for the girls when a flicker of movement on the other side of a thick thorn hedge caught my eye. I knew it was a horse but I couldn't work out why it was separated from the others. A bright red chestnut body flickered through the foliage and I heard a loud impatient snort. My heart skipped a beat and I dropped my notebook.

If I could just push through a gap I'd be into the field. The horse started trotting towards me. I dropped down onto my hands and knees and shuffled and scraped under the barbed wire. I had to push blind through some creeper which was blocking the view. My shoulders squeezed through a foot-wide gap in the hedge. I could hear the horse pawing and snorting, obviously hearing me too. I grabbed at a handful of sticky creeper and that was it – I was through.

"Whoa boy, whoa, steady there." My heart beat wildly with excitement. I was staring at the most beautiful chestnut Arab I'd ever seen.

He was exactly the same as the picture above my bed. His lovely dished face tapered down to soft black flared nostrils showing pink inside. Every nerve in his body was tensed ready to spring away. I could barely breathe with emotion. He was incredible. He was a vision.

I scrabbled onto my feet far too fast and he shied away, the long, fiery-red tail splaying out over his back. Despite his fear he was overcome with curiosity, and after a few minutes took a tentative step forward to sniff at my outstretched hand. His breath was hot and wary, but unable to resist, he snatched at the horse nuts in my hand and then backed off.

"Whoa boy, whoa now, I'm not going to hurt you." I had a job keeping my voice steady as I was trembling all over. He pawed the ground and I offered him another handful, his whiskers tickling my palm as his lips fumbled velvet soft and he took the food. I knew he was checking me out as much as anything else but he stayed put and that had to count for something.

My brain reeled with possible explanations. A riding school would never have an Arab like this as one of the school horses. He'd be far too lively. I didn't even know if this was Mrs Brentford's field. He could belong to somebody else, anyone in the surrounding area.

At a rough guess I'd say he was about 14.2 hands. Tenderly I reached out and ran my hand down the impressive long silky mane which trailed the top of his shoulder. Then, with a jolt I realized – that thick crested neck, the sheer power and energy – he wasn't just an ordinary horse, he was a stallion!

"Jodie!" Kate's voice sliced through my whirring thoughts. It brought me crashing down to earth. The meeting! They must have finished ages ago. "Jodie, is that you?"

I scrabbled back through the hedge, snagging my sweatshirt on the wire. "Just one second," I croaked, getting entwined in creeper.

Kate was waiting on the other side, her arms crossed in front of her, feigning boredom, her hair still flattened and sweaty from the riding hat.

"You've got to tell me," I blurted out, brushing down my jeans, still in a state of excitement. "Who does that horse belong to?"

Kate's face registered surprise. "You mean she hasn't told you?"

"Who? What?" I didn't follow her.

"Well, well." The smugness flooding into Kate's face was unmistakeable. I could see her choosing her words carefully for maximum impact. "The horse is called Minstrel." She hesitated, drawing breath, scrutinizing my face for every movement. "And as you are obviously completely unaware," she continued, a triumphant smile playing on her lips, "he belongs to Sophie."

Chapter Three

"Treasure hunt, picnics, Own a Pony Week, Western riding, barbecue, quiz nights . . ." Emma reeled off the ideas from her list, gesticulating wildly with her free hand to emphasize each point. Kate and I barged in through the louvred doors, red-faced and out of breath.

"Why not just bring in the Household Cavalry and be done with it?" Steph pretended to yawn and flicked through *Smash Hits* focusing all her attention on a picture of Peter Andre.

"We've only got the summer holidays," Kate butted in, "and whatever plans we come up with have got to be cleared with Mrs Brentford."

"Oh come on." Steph looked up, all superior. "She's more interested in her bridge parties and playing golf than Brook House. We could paint all the stables pink and she wouldn't notice."

"That's not true." Emma leapt to her defence. "She's just lost all her fight – she doesn't know what to do."

"Oh yeah, let's see if you still say that next time

she gives you a mouthful for leaving baling string all over the place."

Sophie sat in the corner, doodling on an old newspaper. All I could think of was Minstrel. How could she turn her back on such a fabulous horse? I felt sick. Last night I'd been so excited, bursting with ideas and determination. Now I just felt let down and a complete fool. How could she be a friend if she kept something from me that was so important? Yesterday afternoon we'd talked for hours about our favourite horses and not a word about Minstrel.

"There's the annual Brook House Show and Gymkhana." Kate immediately took over. "That's always a success, and it's a good opportunity to recruit new riders—"

"Excuse me," Sophie interrupted, sticking up her hand, "but last year Archie bucked off three novices and Buzby wouldn't move in the gymkhana races. They're hardly a good advertisement for well-behaved ponies, are they?"

"I think the first thing we've got to do is clean up the place." I stood up and spoke for the first time. The silence seemed to go on for ever. Rachel, who hadn't said a word so far, coughed nervously.

"Look, I know you're just trying to help," said Kate in her condescending voice, "but I think it's going to take a lot more than knocking down a few cobwebs to save the school." Steph giggled and

28

Emma and Sophie stared out of the window, refusing to give me any support.

"Well, um, actually, I agree." Rachel's voice wobbled with nerves. Everyone turned round and stared as if it had been the chair that had spoken and not Rachel. Kate glared, her eyebrows shooting up. "Well, nobody likes riding somewhere shabby, do they?" Rachel was starting to blush and squirmed uneasily under the laser rays coming from Kate.

Steph tossed back her bouncy dark blond hair and made a kind of deep guttural snort. The girl was obviously obnoxious but I still wasn't prepared for her cutting, spiteful remark. "Well, we'll buy you two a bottle of bleach and a bucket but if you don't mind we'll concentrate on more important issues like finding new riders."

I winced as if physically stung.

"Hey, that's a bit rough." Sophie finally leapt to my defence, but it was too late.

"Well, you do that." My voice trembled and I tried to fight the urge to run out of the saloon. "Because this five pack, six pack thing you've got going is a load of rubbish. You're not interested in the horses, you just want to score points off each other. And every moment you squabble, every hour you spend fighting means there's less and less chance of the horses having a roof over their heads. You say you care about Buzby, about Archie, Rocket,

Rusty, but all you really care about is yourselves, about who's the best. Well, it makes me sick. And when Brook House closes down I hope you'll be really proud of yourselves."

Kate gaped and Steph sat speechless. Emma started smirking and immediately stuck up her hand. "When do we begin?" She beamed, delighted that I'd put Kate in her place.

"The long-term plan is to be voted Riding School of the Year." I was going to pull out my notebook but decided against it.

"We could be in a photo story for *In the Saddle*," Sophie suggested, trying to be supportive, but I couldn't even look her in the eye.

"We could form our own pony club!" said Emma.

"And who says Brook House is closing down?" The deep authoritative voice from the doorway made everyone jump. I turned round to see a tiny sparrow-like woman with grey wispy hair.

"I'd like to see Jodie Williams in the house, right now," she boomed, her beady eyes darting round the room.

"That's Mrs Brentford," Emma mouthed, as soon as she'd turned on her heel and clipped off towards the house.

"Oh great," I groaned, feeling weary with dread. "I thought you said she was nice?"

"You've blown it now." Kate pushed past me,

looking as if she wanted to cheer. "She'll eat you for breakfast."

"Good luck." Rachel smiled warmly, oozing sympathy. Sophie hung back, pretending to rearrange some plastic chairs. Emma linked arms and frog-marched me out of the saloon and towards the house. I felt like Mary, Queen of Scots going off to be beheaded.

"Just stay calm." Emma fluttered around nervously. "You'll be fine. It's quite an honour to be invited into the house, you know." She desperately tried to fish for good points but failed miserably.

"What, even though I'm probably going to be banned from ever coming here again and given a bill for a new saddle?"

"Look on the bright side of life, why don't you?" Emma clutched my hand and dragged me along the side of a privet hedge to a small gate. "Just smile sweetly and agree with everything she says."

"And what if I don't?"

"Then you still smile sweetly and agree with everything she says?"

I braced myself and opened the little gate which was covered in delicate pink roses. The whole framework shuddered and creaked on its hinges and a flurry of petals cascaded to the ground.

"Wish me luck." I half turned back.

"Break a leg." Emma stuck up her thumb and I had to smile at the irony.

31

I walked up the cottage path and knocked on the faded green door, shocked at just how much I wanted to keep coming here. I was hooked whether I liked it or not.

"That was quite a speech you gave in there." Mrs Brentford bustled me into the kitchen down some stone steps, telling me to mind my head as I went. She had to be less then five feet tall but carried herself with a grace and a poise which made her seem much taller. Entering the kitchen was like stepping back in time. There was an old stone sink and an Aga and a big wooden table in the middle with a rocking chair pulled up at one end.

"So Riding School of the Year, eh? That's some task you've set yourself." She put on a pair of glasses hanging round her neck on a string which looked uncannily like an old bootlace, and examined me from top to bottom. "So do you always get so passionate about your beliefs?"

"Only when it concerns horses." I tried to keep my voice level.

"And other people's business by the sound of it."

I squirmed painfully and watched an insect zigzag across the floor. "We didn't know you were there." I murmured so low she almost had to lip-read.

"How old are you?"

"Twelve."

"Sixty-nine." She tapped at her head. "Getting

ready for the scrap heap according to my daughter. So what makes you think you can save this riding school when I obviously can't?"

I dragged in my breath, taken aback by her directness. "Well, um, to be honest . . ." I was scrabbling wildly for something to say, but my mind was a total blank.

"I don't bite, at least not after lunch," Mrs Brentford prompted.

"Well, there are six of us and it's the summer holidays. We're enthusiastic and hard-working and we're determined and dedicated. And we owe it to the horses. They've taught so many people to ride, it's not right that they should be split up. They're happy here."

"You could always go to Horseworld Centre." Mrs Brentford sat down heavily in the rocking chair, not taking her eyes off me for a second.

"But all we'd be is a number," I whipped back at her. "We wouldn't be able to groom and hang out and do all the horsy things everybody dreams about. We'd be in and out on a conveyor belt and all we'd have is one measly hour a week. We love horses, Mrs Brentford. All we want is to be around them. Brook House is the only place in the whole area which gives us that chance. And we'll do anything to help. Anything." I broke off, blushing, my breath rattling from nerves. I knew I sounded desperate but I didn't know what else to do. It was how I felt.

For a second Mrs Brentford seemed impressed but then she narrowed her eyes, cloaking her real feelings.

"You didn't sound very united in the saloon," she said finally, running the tips of her fingers over her lined forehead. "And then there's the small matter of Frank's saddle . . ."

"I can get a job, I can pay that off," I gulped, digging my fingernails into the sweaty palms of my hands. "I can get a paper round. It wouldn't take many weeks. And as for the girls, we all get on really well, you just caught us at a bad moment." I'd now resorted to telling lies to keep coming to Brook House. "No, that's not exactly true." I took it back. "We don't all get on well, but we still care about the riding school."

A small, thin smile played on Mrs Brentford's lips. "Thank you for being honest, that means a lot." She stood up, scraping back the chair, and brushing down her jumper. "How about I give you one week to clean up the stables, the tack room, feed room and all the ponies. That should pay off the debt, don't you think? You can rope in those other girls and that uppity little Miss Kate and her pal with no manners. I'm sure you can sort them out."

A huge wave of delirious joy rose up inside me. I felt like kissing her on both cheeks.

"And you might as well know," she continued,

34

waving her hand dismissively, "Janice handed her notice in a few days ago. There won't be any lessons until the end of the week when the new instructor arrives. So, as long as it's OK with Sandra, if you want to ride the ponies every day . . ."

It got better and better.

"The girls will be thrilled." I was on cloud nine.

Mrs Brentford leaned forward, cocking her head slightly and sucking in her cheeks. It was as if she was trying to make a decision.

"Jodie." Her voice softened, her face crinkling like a crumpled-up paper bag. "Your mum rang and told me about the accident."

I felt the euphoria drain out of me as if someone had pulled a plug. "You won't say anything?" I pleaded. "She had no right." I couldn't believe my mother had interfered like that. It was none of her business.

"She was just worried, that's all. It's inevitable."

"But it's my secret, I'm the one who has to live with it. She had no right." I stared blindly towards a corner of the tiled kitchen floor, the old familiar resentment boiling up.

"I'm sorry you feel like that, Jodie, because while you keep it all bottled up inside you like this you'll never get over it and on with your life."

Any confidence I had was engulfed by embarrassment. I stared out of the window struggling like crazy to stop my jaw from shaking.

"You don't know what it's like," I murmured. "In and out of hospital like a yo-yo, this treatment, that treatment, never being able to wear a skirt or shorts, being called a freak at the swimming baths, people staring – you can't even imagine."

I felt hollow inside. A tear slipped down my cheek and into my mouth. It was as if I had a huge wound inside me and Mrs Brentford had just pulled off the scab. "You feel sorry for me." I knew I was being irrational but the words and the hurt came tumbling out. "That's why you're being so nice. I don't want pity. I don't want sympathy. I can't handle it."

"Now you listen to me." Mrs Brentford grabbed my arm. "I don't feel sorry for you, you've had a rough two years but you've still got two legs, two arms, you're healthy and luckier than most. So you've got a metal plate in your leg and the scars to prove it. So what? It's what's in your heart that matters most, in your character." She stepped back, her eyes as hard as bullets. "If anyone's feeling sorry for you, Jodie, it's yourself. You're wallowing in self-pity and if I'm trying to do anything it's make you snap out of it."

I was speechless. Nobody had ever spoken to me like that before, they'd always tiptoed around the subject. I felt raw with outrage but deep down I knew she was close to the truth. "Now I've said all I want to say, the rest is up to you." She turned her back, brushing me off, indicating the conversation was over. Numbly, I fumbled for the door, my shoulders sagging, a thousand thoughts scurrying through my mind.

"Oh and Jodie?"

I jerked upright.

"If you've got anything about you you'll be riding at the Brook House Show in two weeks' time. Don't let a natural talent go to waste."

And not for the first time I wondered just how much my mother had actually told her.

"I can't believe it! Did she really say all that?" Emma was trying to put hoof oil on Buzby but he kept lifting up each foot as soon as she got anywhere near.

"Just think, one whole week of riding." She gave up and sat on the outside tap which Steph said would break under her weight. "We've got to cherish every moment. This is going to be the best week of my entire life."

"Well, I can ride Monty whenever I want," Steph boasted and nearly got a hoof-oil brush in her face.

"I think we ought to start with the tack room," I suggested, already plotting and planning. "It's a pigsty in there."

"Yeah, I agree." Steph wrinkled up her nose. "Emma's been leaving banana skins behind the rug baskets."

"I have not!"

"I wonder what the new instructor's going to be like?" said Steph dreamily, no doubt conjuring up pictures of Carl Hester.

"Strict, mean, frumpy, and resembling the back end of a bus," Kate threw in, leading Archie onto a patch of grass. "And has anybody seen my new green lead rope?"

"I also think," I struggled on, "that as the Brook House Show is definitely going ahead, we ought to school the ponies this week for their best events. At least then, they'll stand a chance against the other ponies."

Kate's face blackened and she deliberately ignored me. Steph muttered something under her breath. Even Archie glared at me, a daisy hanging from his mouth. Emma rabbited on about a "pamper day" for Buzby and a mint-flavoured equine football which she was saving up for. Any positive thoughts I was still clinging on to quickly evaporated.

"Has anyone, by any chance," I asked, shooting Kate a withering glance, "heard of the words Troop Motivation?"

"Why didn't you tell me?"

Sophie was in Rocket's stable, keeping a low profile. All the horses were being turned out in the fields for the week but Rocket suffered from sweet itch so he stayed in to avoid the midges. Sweet itch is an allergy to midge bites which causes horses to rub their manes and tails, often until they are raw. Sophie was putting some soothing benzyl benzoate lotion on Rocket but there was more on the door frame and her T-shirt than on his neck.

"You own the next best thing to Milton and you didn't tell me." I still felt hurt and shut out and it came across in my voice.

"Oh." Sophie stiffened visibly, concentrating on picking out bits of straw from an old dandy brush. Her blond hair fell forwards so I couldn't read the expression on her face. It was ages before she spoke. When she did her voice was stilted and shaky. "Let me guess." She finally looked up, meeting my eyes with a mixture of guilt and sadness. "Kate couldn't wait to tell you."

Chapter Four

"He was a birthday present. I've had him for three months." Sophie sat on the village green bench staring vaguely at a bag of chips.

We'd sneaked off into the village while the other girls weren't looking. There was a Post Office, a fish and chip shop, a mini-supermarket, a newsagent's and a pub. I'd bought a copy of *In the Saddle* which had a picture of the famous event riders Ash Burgess and Alex Johnson on the front cover. According to Emma they lived close by, at a really smart event yard.

Awkwardly, Sophie told me how she'd asked the girls to keep Minstrel a secret because she couldn't stand the million and one questions when people found out.

"I haven't been near Minstrel since the day I got him and that's the way I want it to stay." Her lips tightened and she clenched her hands together. "It's a personal thing between me and my dad, OK?"

I couldn't believe that such a fantastic horse had been turned out in a field for the whole summer. No wonder he was so wild, he was never handled.

Sophie explained how when Minstrel first arrived, everyone thought they could ride him. "Steph was the worst, she put me down all the time, but when I thrust the saddle at her she was terrified. Janice and Sandra both managed to get on him but were bucked off almost immediately."

I listened in grim fascination. "But what on earth made your dad buy you an Arab and a stallion of all things? It's like buying a Ferrari for someone who's just passed their test."

"Because he's stupid and thinks he knows everything, and whoever sold Minstrel to my dad must have seen him coming a hundred miles off." Sophie's voice was full of bitterness.

I leaned back, trying to absorb all the facts, completely blown away by it all. To be overfaced by the wrong horse was the worst thing in the world but I couldn't help feeling sorry for Minstrel. He was a victim too. And he must be so bored and lonely.

A mother and two children walked past to feed the ducks, the kids staring at our jodhpurs and boots with envy. Sophie's hand was gripping on to the armrest of the bench so hard that the knuckles had turned white. "If I still haven't ridden him after six months, Dad said he'd sell him, that's the deal."

"And you've got no intentions of trying?" I asked tentatively.

"The day a horsebox comes to fetch Minstrel will

41

be the best day of my life. I've just got three months to go."

"You hate Minstrel that much?" I said, incredulous.

"I don't hate *him* at all." Sophie pushed her hair behind her ears. "But I hate everything he stands for." She sat staring ahead, biting down on her bottom lip, her eyes screwed up against the sun.

"You know, I mean, I don't want to pry, but sometimes it helps to talk about things."

Sophie forced a smile and shrugged her shoulders, still staring ahead. "Every time I look at Minstrel I see my dad, pushing me to be the best all the time. It's not good enough to just have fun with a riding school pony, I've got to showjump, become a winner. I can't just be me, I've got to be competitive. I've got to be as good as my sister." Sophie hurled a chip towards a group of starlings and threw the rest in the rubbish bin. "It's quite sad really, I even wrote in to an agony aunt column once but they didn't print the letter. I think they thought I was too pathetic."

"So your sister rides?" I prompted, driven by curiosity to find out more.

"No, that's why I took it up, because she didn't want to. Life would be unbearable if she rode. You see, my sister excels at everything. You name it, tennis, hockey, netball, she's on all the teams. Next to Natalie, I'm a complete failure." Sophie sat hunched forward, her shoulders shaking, her long legs awkwardly splayed out. I knew she wanted to cry but was biting it back because I was there. Now she'd started talking it seemed she couldn't stop.

"I've never been sporty before so when I asked to go to riding school Dad was over the moon. Even Mum thought it was great being able to have a riding hat in the back of the car and gymkhana stickers in the window. And then Dad came to watch me and that was it, I went to pieces, and he said I was useless and couldn't possibly ride a donkey like Rocket. He went out and bought Minstrel and started interfering in my life like he always does. He wanted me to go to Horseworld Centre but I like it here. At Brook House nobody is particularly good at anything, everybody is just ordinary and loves horses, warts and all, for what they are. I belong here more than I do in my own home. You see, Jodie, my dad doesn't love me, he never has done. But it doesn't bother me any more, because I've learnt to live with it. And now I've got Rocket."

A huge lump formed in my throat. I hardly knew what to say. My parents had always been so brilliant and supportive. I couldn't imagine what it must be like to feel as isolated as Sophie. I reached out and held her hand, squeezing reassuringly. The tears had started to spill down her cheeks.

"You know," I started in a whisper, "at my old riding school we had a special pact that everybody had to help each other, so that nobody ever felt alone or unsure. It really helped me when I had to go through some bad things." I hesitated and then went on, "I think the Six Pack should have a rule that we're always there for each other. No matter what."

"I think that's a very good idea." Sophie's fingers clasped mine, gripping tight. "I'm so pleased you came to Brook House, Jodie, because somehow now I think everything's going to be all right." She shuddered slightly and a crooked smile tugged at the corners of her mouth.

And for the first time in two years I realized I wasn't the only twelve-year-old girl to have problems. A huge chunk of bitterness melted into nothing.

"Bending, ride and run, mug, potato, sack, musical sticks . . ."

"Well you'd better cross out Archie for the potato race," said Kate, glancing over Emma's list. "Last year he ate all the potatoes and that's before the races even started."

Sophie and I slipped into the saloon looking sheepish.

"Where've you been?" Emma immediately rounded on us, as if we'd deliberately left her out. "Oh I nearly forgot," she cried, nudging Kate so hard her biro flipped off the page, "put Buz down for the flag race – he's utterly, incredibly ace at it."

"Don't tell me, you've trained him to pick up the flags with his teeth?" Steph teased as she walked in carrying her lunch box and a Wagon Wheel.

"Ha ha, not quite." Emma stuck out her tongue.

"Well, nobody can beat Monty at bending," Steph boasted. "He's a whirlwind."

"Um, I thought we were going to clean out the tack room?" Everybody ignored me and carried on with their gymkhana-mania. "If we don't do the cleaning up, Mrs Brentford won't let us ride the ponies." I tried to load my voice with warning.

"Oh lighten up, Jodie, we'll only be an hour. Then we can start your precious cleaning operation."

"Rachel's gone to tack up Rusty for you," said Kate, giving me a sly glance and watching my expression like a hawk. "If you can't ride at all we can always put you on the lead rein."

"She doesn't have to do anything she doesn't want to do." Sophie immediately leapt to my side.

"Oh for heaven's sake, she doesn't need a nanny," Kate snapped, pressing down her riding hat. "Now are we going to get started or wait until Christmas?"

This was the second time the ponies had been out that day which was nothing for riding school ponies, but they were all bad-tempered and lethargic, swishing at flies and trying to drag their heads down to tug at grass.

Rachel led out Blossom who was blowing herself out so her girth wouldn't meet – a common trick with ponies. Rachel was very pale; she was breathing heavily and looked frightened. I knew for a fact that she'd only ever ridden Rusty, and Blossom's rolling, wickedly naughty eyes were scaring her to death.

"It's OK," I said, taking Blossom's reins and turning her back round. "I'm not riding, so you can have Rusty."

Kate, who was just about to mount Archie, did a quick double take and flipped her foot out of the near stirrup. Archie, taking advantage of the situation, sidled into Buzby who, knocked off balance, stood on Emma's toe.

"What do you mean, you're not riding?"

"In case you'd forgotten," I said, glaring back at her with equal venom, "it was only yesterday that I hurt my ankle. You wouldn't want me to drop any more saddles now, would you?"

Kate's eyes swooped down to my jodphur boot as if looking for evidence of swelling. "Well, it's funny," she grunted, tugging Archie's head away from a flower basket, "you've not had a hint of a limp all day."

Chapter Five

"Three, two, one . . . *Go!*"

Monty did a half rear and shot off and Buzby stared blankly, then crashed into the first bending pole.

"Kick him on!" Kate shouted to Emma who was making futile attempts to neck-rein with her hands sticking out to the side.

Monty whizzed down the line of poles weaving in and out, but completely failed to stop, sailing on for two laps of the field before finally pulling up with Steph perched painfully on the pommel of the saddle, her riding hat slammed down over her nose.

"Wonderful control," Kate sneered, then gave Steph a lecture about flapping her legs even though her own arms were poking about like knitting needles.

"I don't think I can do this," Rachel whispered, leading Rusty across, who was neighing frantically to Ebony Jane in the adjoining field. Her hands were shaking so much she couldn't pull on her special pimple gloves.

"If you knock a pole down you're eliminated,"

Steph shouted to Emma who had jumped off and was readjusting Buzby's noseband.

Rachel stared ahead, overwhelmed with black despair.

"Just take your time," I whispered, trying to instil her with confidence. "As you approach the last pole on your way up the course, go slightly wide so you can make a tight turn. Sit up and use your seat to drive him round."

Kate flew down the course, racing Steph, leaning catlike over Archie's stubby neck and brushing the last pole with hardly an inch to spare.

"Don't let her get to you," I urged, giving Rachel a leg-up. "You can't be expected to ride like that. You're just a novice." Rachel smiled weakly and gathered up the reins.

"I'll give you a head start," Kate shouted to Rachel.

Rusty walked slowly down to the poles, not batting an eyelid.

"Do you think she's all right?" Emma whispered. "I mean, she's only had a few lessons." Rusty's ears cocked back and forth taking in the line of poles. Steph did the start. "Get ready, get set . . . Go!"

Archie bounded forward, his eyes rolling gleefully as he whipped round the first pole.

Rusty broke into a steady trot, lifting his head up to tip Rachel back in the saddle when she fell forward.

"Isn't he a sweetheart?" Sophie clasped her hands together and started cheering.

Unfortunately Rusty came to a grinding halt at the last pole, unsure exactly what Rachel wanted. Keeping her cool she gently patted him on the neck and opened her right rein.

"Good boy, Rusty!" Emma shouted hoarsely. Archie, on hearing the shouting, set off in a volley of bucks, imitating a wild bronco, crashed chest first through the last pea cane and galloped three times round a horse chestnut tree before depositing Kate near a clump of thistles.

"Oh dear," Emma giggled, burying her head in Buzby's mane. Kate blushed scarlet and dragged a delighted Archie back to the other ponies. Sophie stuggled to control her facial muscles but began to giggle when a huge rip in Kate's jods came into view, exposing sky-blue knickers.

"Well done, Rachel," I patted Rusty's neck, keen to take the spotlight off Kate.

"What about the mug race?" Sophie piped up, patiently holding Rocket who hadn't had a go yet.

"I'll take you on," Kate snarled, practically grinding her teeth together. Archie was still blowing so Steph suggested she rode Monty.

"Well, it takes two mugs to make a race," teased Sophie, flicking back her long hair into a pink scrunchy. We all knew Kate was determined to win.

The mug race was more complicated and

demanded a lot of skill. Three mugs are placed on the centre three poles in a line of five. Riders race to the furthest mug, grab it and place it on the next pole up. They then return to the middle pole, grabbing the mug and moving it one pole up. Finally they transfer the first mug to the middle pole before racing home.

Emma picked up the plastic cups taken from thermos flasks and placed them on the poles. It was important not to use anything that could smash and hurt the horses.

The air was prickly with tension. Monty side-stepped and fidgeted as Kate lengthened the stirrups. Rocket stood waiting for the slightest leg aid from Sophie. He always wore a leather neck-strap which riders could grab hold of if they lost their balance.

"When you're ready . . ." Steph moved into position for the countdown, still holding Archie. Monty stepped up, sniffing the air excitedly, sweat trickling down his grey neck. Emma and Rachel moved closer to me; Buzby and Rusty were more interested in cramming their mouths with grass.

Kate stared at the line of poles.

"On your marks. Get set. *Go!*"

They shot off, burning down the lines, necks outstretched, one chestnut, one grey, nose to nose. Both girls grabbed the furthest mug and turned neck and neck.

"Come on, Sophie!" Emma yelled, both her hands round her mouth. Rocket was doing everything she asked of him and moved slightly ahead. Sophie grabbed the next mug first. The ground rattled with hollow hoof beats.

"The middle pole!" Emma bawled, even though she wasn't supposed to offer help. Sophie snatched the mug and kicked Rocket on from a standstill into a gallop. Monty was in full flight, bursting up to the first pole, taking advantage of Sophie's few moments of hesitation.

"There's nothing in it," I murmured, gripped with the excitement despite myself. Rachel was clinging on to my arm, squeezing tighter and tighter. "Come on, Sophie – go for it!"

Kate grabbed the last mug at lightning speed. One minute her hand was round it, next minute it flipped up into the air, spinning and then hurtling towards Monty's feet, skimming softly through the long grass. Monty was spooked and ran backwards, threatening to rear. His running martingale tightened but didn't deter him.

"You've got to get off and pick it up!" Emma shrieked, knowing the rules off by heart.

Kate leapt off and ran towards the mug, dragging Monty behind her. But he was having none of it. As soon as she tried to get back on, he went crazy. Kate couldn't even get within three feet of the stirrup. He swirled round and round in tight circles and the harder she pulled on the reins the faster he went.

Sophie flew past the finish line, punching the air with her right arm. Rachel started jumping up and down and ran across to kiss Rocket on the nose.

"You stupid, useless pony." Kate, boiling mad, flung Monty's reins at Steph. "You try and control the idiot," she yelled, "he's your pony." Bright pink spots of humiliation glowed on her cheeks. "These gymkhana games are a complete waste of time."

"Try telling that to Mary King," said Emma, "she's now a champion eventer."

Kate glared at us and then flounced off back to the stables, the rip in her jods getting larger with every stride.

"There goes the Incredible Sulk," said Emma as soon as Kate was out of earshot.

"Well, now we've got rid of the big bad wolf," Rachel said, perking up and shedding some of her shyness, "does anyone fancy taking me on at the flag race?"

I spent an hour in Minstrel's field trying to get him to accept me. All he did was pace relentlessly up and down the side of the thorn hedge, his hind hooves clicking into his front ones as his energy bubbled over. He didn't want anything to do with me. Despite my offerings of carrots, mints and horse nuts, he stuck his head in the air and trotted off, his expression distant and aloof. It was almost as if he'd decided he didn't want anything to do with human beings.

It didn't take me long to realize that he'd probably been watching the gymkhana games from a gap in the hedge. The ground was kicked up to dust and fresh droppings were trodden into the bare earth. Horses are just like people, and my guess was that Minstrel was jealous and felt snubbed and left out. I could hardly blame him. All he'd seen for three months was the four sides of his boring field.

Poor, poor Minstrel. "Come on, boy, you've got to snap out of it. If you don't learn to trust someone soon, heaven knows where you'll end up." I sprawled aimlessly on the grass, sprinkling the horse nuts I'd used to tempt him onto a patch of soil. Defeated.

Minstrel stood at a safe distance, suspicious, his ears flicking back and forth, but interested enough to keep watching. His mane was so long the breeze lifted it up. He had the classic Arab dished head and flared nostrils and his tail fanned out over his back, highlights bleached in from the sun. He was perfect. Outstanding. But I still couldn't ride him. There was a raging war going on in my head. One voice egged me on, and I felt the thrill of sitting on that broad chestnut back. The other filled me with panic. What if the same thing happened again? What if I couldn't do it? What if my leg wasn't strong enough? Raw fear washed over me.

Minstrel snorted, and went hurtling off towards the far corner, revelling in his own power and speed. "Show off," I said, picking up the horse nuts and hurling them towards a clump of grass.

A crazy horse and a girl with a smashed leg and no courage. What a winning pair. The only thing Minstrel and I had in common was our hang-ups. And that wasn't nearly enough to win at the Brook House Annual Open Show. Even if Sophie did give me permission to ride him.

Chapter Six

"You're late!" Emma shouted, bounding down the drive the next morning with a streak of white emulsion drying on her cheek, clutching a paintbrush. "We've got tons done already, you wouldn't believe it." She bustled me into the yard where Steph was plunging Ebony Jane's black tail into a bucket of hot water. Half the contents of the tack room was sprawled out on the concrete, including all the saddles and a pile of numnahs a foot high.

"Hey, watch out," shrieked Emma, as Steph swirled Ebony's tail round and round to shake off excess water.

Archie was tied up by the next stable with strange pink rollers in his mane and Tinky, the little black Shetland, was wandering loose, treading on various items of tack and raiding someone's lunch box. "We're having a pamper day, you know, brush and go," she giggled, "and we're determined to have the tack room decorated and spick and span by tonight."

Sophie came out of the saloon carrying a dustpan and brush and a pair of rubber gloves. Kate was knocking dust out of some old horse blankets and disturbing all sorts of creepy crawlies.

"Next!" Steph shouted. Emma quickly led Ebony Jane into her stable and Rachel appeared with Blossom, tying her up to the metal ring with a quick release knot. It was just like a conveyor belt. They were even using proper horse shampoo.

"This is amazing," I said, still slightly suspicious. "Is this really the same group of girls who were clawing each other's eyes out yesterday?"

"No, we've been replaced by alien androids." Emma hooted at her own joke.

"Come on, Emma, we need some more hot water." Steph threw a dripping wet sponge at Emma and caught her on the back of the neck.

Just as Emma turned on the outside tap, Kate happened to be walking across the yard and got caught in the line of fire. Unfortunately the jet of water from the hosepipe drenched her expensive new suede boots.

"You pig!" she screeched in an alarmingly extra-terrestrial voice. The scene that followed was complete mayhem. Kate ran forward and grabbed the hosepipe, flicking it up and hitting Emma with a jet straight in her face. Emma screamed and Blossom pulled back on her head collar, snapping the strap, and hurtled off in the direction of the main gate. Steph and Sophie were after her in a shot which left Emma, Rachel, Kate and me to face a furious Mrs Brentford.

It wouldn't have been so bad if the yard hadn't been an absolute tip.

"This isn't good enough, girls!" She walked stiffly across to the tap and turned off the gushing water, still flooding out of the hosepipe. "I want all this cleared up by the time I get back from golf this afternoon. Lift your game, girls, otherwise you'll all be out on your ear. Is that clear?" There was no doubt she meant it. I knew she felt I'd let her down.

"She is such a hypocrite!" Kate let rip as soon as we were alone. "She sticks her head in the sand and refuses to acknowledge that the riding school is in trouble. At least we're trying to do something about it. All she's doing is running away." I had to admit that, for the first time since I'd met her, Kate did have a point.

"So where's Blossom?" Emma asked in a deadpan voice.

"That's the million dollar question," said Rachel staring down the drive. "So where exactly do we start looking?"

Blossom was in her element, haring round the next door neighbour's vegetable patch, her fat little belly brushing the rows of sweet peas. Sophie and Steph were scarlet and out of breath. Every time they got close she slipped out of range. Eventually we got her cornered and she shot under the runner beans and hid under the foliage, trying to look innocent.

"At least we know what class to enter her for at the show," panted Emma, resting her hands on her knees. Blossom pulled at a runner bean. "Most Appealing Pony."

"She'll have to appeal to somebody's better nature when this lot gets discovered," said Sophie as she dragged her out like a tugboat, "otherwise we're well and truly done for."

"God, it's hot," Sophie lay on the grass, running an ice cube over her forehead and cheeks. The tack room was like a furnace and we were taking it in turns to do the painting. Everybody was in shorts and crop tops – I was the only one sweltering in stretch jeans and a baggy T-shirt. The dull, thrumming ache had started up in my leg. Any extremes of temperature always set it off, and stupidly, I'd left my painkillers at home on the kitchen sink.

I'd caught the early bus that morning and sneaked round to the back fields before anyone arrived to spend an hour with Minstrel, trying to coax him to come to me. I sat in the middle of the field pretending to read a book and he'd eventually come over and started sniffing my hair, curious to see what I was doing. It had felt like a real breakthrough. Minstrel loved being the centre of attention and ignoring him seemed the best way of getting him to do what I wanted. After endless patience I had managed to slip on a head collar and lead him up and down. He was even more brilliant than I had imagined. He just seemed to float through the air.

"Jodie?" Sophie's voice brought me back to reality. She was staring at my legs. "Why don't you put some shorts on?"

"I'm OK, I don't wear shorts," I replied.

Emma sat up, fanning herself with a dock leaf, her face bright pink from the sun. Sophie rummaged in her rucksack, spilling out deodorant, hoof pick, mane comb and fly repellent. "Don't be daft," she said, "everybody wears shorts. Here – I knew I'd brought a spare pair." To my horror she whipped out a pair of crumpled Union Jack knee-length shorts and tossed them over so they half-fell in my lap. I was frozen rigid with panic.

"I don't want them." I brushed them off, suddenly feeling cold and sick. Sophie flinched, obviously hurt. For a moment no one said anything, no one moved. "Just leave it, all right? You don't understand, nobody does." I leapt up, too fast, twanging my leg, emotions rioting inside me. I was making a complete fool of myself but I didn't know what else to do. I couldn't handle it. I couldn't handle my life.

"Jodie?"

I stumbled off towards the stables, tripping over

the hosepipe, cannoning into Rusty's stable door. Why did I overreact like this? Why couldn't I just tell people the truth and be done with it?

I headed towards the saloon wanting a few minutes to myself before I went back to apologize to Sophie. I could hear raised voices before I even got to the louvred doors. I paused, rocking on my heels, unsure what to do next. The voices belonged to Kate and Rachel, I was sure of it. I thought about sneaking past but Kate's voice was so clear I couldn't help overhearing. I hovered uncertainly, feeling compelled to listen, and peered through the crack in the door.

Kate was going for the jugular. "Don't you ever humiliate me like that again," she hissed. "I'm the one who runs things round here, not Jodie. And next time we do gymkhana races, don't make me look a fool."

Rachel said something which I couldn't quite hear.

"Just remember what I know," said Kate. "One word from me and you'll never see Brook House again. And then what will happen to your precious little Rusty?"

Rachel blanched and recoiled, stepping back against the table. My breath caught in my throat. Kate was not only bossy and a bad loser she was something far worse – a bully. And whatever dark secret she knew about Rachel was having a devastating effect. Poor Rachel looked utterly terrified.

I didn't have time to think. Suddenly Kate was walking towards the door. I pressed up against the wall, my heart beating furiously. She marched out, stomping across to the tack room without even a backward glance. I'd escaped from being caught by the skin of my teeth. But I had to act quickly – before my luck ran out. If Kate looked back now she'd know I'd been listening. I dived into the saloon because it was the only place available. Rachel was gasping for breath.

"Rachel!" Fear rose up inside me. I'd never seen anybody like this. "Rachel, what is it? What can I do?" I held her shoulders. Frantically she pointed towards a blue sports bag slung in the corner.

"Look Jodie, I'm really sorry if I upset . . ." Sophie crashed through the louvred doors, head down, intent on getting out what she had to say. As soon as she saw Rachel she stopped dead in her tracks. "Oh no!" She belted across to the blue bag, turned it upside down and rummaged around.

"Here!" Sophie thrust something into Rachel's hand. An inhaler. Rachel sucked in deep hungry breaths, her eyes relaxing as the colour slowly trickled back into her cheeks. Relief surged through me. She was going to be all right. Sophie kept a comforting arm round her shoulders as her breathing gradually righted itself, the wheezing subsiding.

Rachel gave me a lopsided, guilty grin and sat down on one of the plastic chairs. Even now she looked pale and exhausted.

"She has asthma." Sophie tried to be matter of fact. "Something usually sets it off." She cocked an eyebrow at Rachel, speculative, thoughtful. "I wonder what it could have been?"

Chapter Seven

"Paint fumes, definitely," said Rachel nodding, trying to convince herself as we both tacked up Rusty. I decided not to mention what I'd overheard to anyone, not until I'd had time to sleep on it. I didn't want to cause more trouble for Rachel.

Rusty gently nudged my back insisting that I carry on brushing his face. He was quite bony round the eyes so I used a soft water brush and dabbed it under his forelock. Not many ponies liked their faces being brushed, but Rusty loved it. He was a strawberry roan which meant that his coat was a mixture of white, red and black hairs. He wore a simple snaffle bridle which was one of the mildest types of bit, unlike Archie and Buzby who wore kimblewicks because the bars or gums of their mouths had gone hard from too much rough handling. Most riding school ponies were dead to the hand and leg, because of novice riders. In some ways they were a real challenge but usually responded to a good rider. Rusty was just an angel and tried to please everybody.

"True or false?" Emma appeared over the stable

door, holding the latest edition of *In the Saddle*. "A family of greater crested newts lives in the water jump at Hickstead and have to be moved every year before the Derby."

"That's not fair," I said. "It's supposed to be off the top of your head, not from a magazine." Emma and I were having a true or false competition and up to now Emma hadn't got a single point.

Rachel and I carried on brushing Rusty.

"Sandra says the diary's nearly full for next week and guess what?" Emma pouted her lips, desperate to tell. "The new instructor's going to be starting too." We were suddenly interested. "That's all I know," she added, putting an end to the suspense. "I hope she's like Zoe Ball."

"Oh no, Mary King," said Rachel, "She's so nice."

"Just as long as she's not a replica of Janice," I added, "otherwise there'll be no riding school left to worry about."

"Oh, and about the newts, it was true," called Emma as she ran off. "One point to me."

The tack room was finished by three o'clock so we had the rest of the afternoon to school the ponies. It looked a million times better by anyone's standards. We'd even pinned up posters of different breeds of ponies over the cracks in the walls.

We led the ponies into the manege, Archie, Buzby

and Rusty. The air was humid and full of midges, and Rocket tried to rub his tail on one of the fence posts. Rachel clambered onto Rusty, seemingly OK, although Sophie and I were watching over her like hawks.

The manege was a rectangle filled with sand, with a jumping lane down one side. There was a line of three jumps already at a height of two foot six, the last one being a spread with a little red and white filler at the front. Buzby eyed it dubiously and skitted across the arena, pulling at the reins which slid through Emma's hands.

Kate was already on Archie, circling him at the far end and trying to get him to do a square halt. That is when all four hooves halt together. To do this you have to squeeze with your hands, sit up and keep your legs on. In any downward transition such as trot to walk or walk to halt, it is really important to hold the horse together with your legs every stride.

Sophie mounted Rocket, making sure she hopped round and didn't jab him in the ribs with her toe. Rachel suggested doing some exercises and started touching her toes and doing half scissors.

"That's baby stuff," taunted Steph as she marched in, clutching a can of Coke and dragging Monty who wasn't looking very cooperative.

"In case you've forgotten, Rachel's a beginner." Sophie rolled her eyes in annoyance.

65

"Oh crikey, Kate's already started." Steph, not hearing, dumped the Coke and her sweatshirt in my arms and frantically tightened the girth. "Kate's invited me to her farm in Cornwall for two weeks," she couldn't help boasting. "We're going to ride proper thoroughbred horses."

"Oh, bully for you," Emma mocked, "Nice to know that Kate's got a new lapdog at last."

"I'll ignore that comment," Steph bristled, pursing her lips. "Jealousy doesn't become you, Emma, you should know better." She stuck her nose in the air and rode off with her elbows flapping.

"Well, she's got as much chance of going to Cornwall as I have of going to planet Mars." Emma wrinkled her nose.

"How do you know that?" I looked up.

"Because," said Emma, wagging a finger, "we've all been invited to precious Cornwall at some stage over the last year, haven't we, Soph? And never mind thoroughbred horses, we haven't even seen as much as a Cornish pasty."

"It's a schooling programme!" I explained in exasperation. I handed round the detailed printouts which I'd done on my brother's computer. "It's designed to show up each pony's strengths and weaknesses."

I'd spent all last night programming in each horse and pony's age, temperament and ability, to

66

produce individual worksheets. I'd even done horsy graphics in the corner which looked really cool. I was quite proud of what I'd come up with.

"But according to this we don't have any strengths at all." Emma was referring to Buzby.

"And what exactly is a figure-of-eight-and-a-half halt?" Rachel was nonplussed.

"You're a funny girl, Jodie." Sophie flipped through the pages. "Only you could come up with something as organized as this."

We'd just been practising jumping which Rocket was surprisingly good at. Buzby took off in a kind of helicopter-style and landed on the other side, all four feet clumped together, his head bashing Emma on the nose. Rachel wisely decided to stick to flat-work and I helped her with rising trot and changing diagonals. Kate, so far, had ignored us which was fine by me. Steph decided to jump Monty and promptly demolished the whole jumping lane.

"What about you, Kate?" Sophie shouted across, a slight challenge rising in her voice.

"Archie doesn't jump," Kate shouted back, her voice flat and dismissive.

"But every pony jumps," Emma argued. "Even Buzby. Don't tell me you're scared."

It wasn't meant to be a criticism. I think it just popped out as a joke. But even so, it struck a raw nerve. Kate rode across looking black with rage.

Suddenly the air hung heavy with tension.

Nobody spoke. Kate's mouth disappeared into a tight line. "I really don't think I'm the one you should be accusing of being scared." She glared straight at me with bullet-hard eyes. "As Jodie obviously knows so much about riding I think she should be the one to jump Archie, don't you?"

Steph's face lit up as she sensed trouble. Sophie's mouth dropped open in panic. It was almost as if I knew this was going to happen. As if I wanted someone to put me on the spot, push me into a corner. Make the decision for me.

"I'll ride," I blurted out, my heart hammering. "But not Archie." It was now or never. I could hardly hold my voice steady. I glanced at Sophie for support, resolve strengthening inside me. "If it's all right with you, Soph," I stammered, turning my gaze to Kate, adrenalin pumping through my body, "I'll ride Minstrel."

"He'll kill you!" Sophie ran after me, white with fear, as I headed for Minstrel's field. "This is crazy, you can't ride."

For once Emma didn't have anything to say. Kate immediately backed off, arguing that I was taking the dare too far. There was no sign of Mrs Brentford at the house.

"*Jodie, stop it!*" Sophie refused to let me pass, so I ducked under her arm.

"She's bluffing," Steph said, not at all sure.

I'd never felt more certain of anything in my whole life.

"What if Rocket's saddle doesn't fit?" Sophie tried a new angle.

"Then I'll fetch another one that does." I marched on, determined, concentrating on taking level strides, making each leg work as if nothing had ever happened.

Minstrel charged up to the gate, snorting. On guard as six girls headed towards him.

"I don't want anyone else to go in the field." My voice shook.

"Fine," Steph snapped. "It's your funeral." Rachel, Sophie and Emma glared at her with maximum venom.

"You don't have to do this," Kate said, crumbling slightly.

Minstrel tore up the field at a gallop, then came trotting back, tossing his beautiful copper-red head and showing off with a few extended strides.

"Crikey," Rachel gulped. "He's enormous."

"Whoa boy, steady now, there's my little beauty," I coaxed and tried to hide the frantic pelting of my heart as I ran a hand over the massive crested neck which could only belong to a stallion. Minstrel stamped at some flies, each vein on his chest and flanks pulsing under the surface with barely contained energy. I stood stock-still and let him sniff over the saddle, squealing and thrashing about as he picked up the scent of another horse.

"Please God, let him be safe," I said to myself, crossing my fingers for a second, then easing the saddle and numnah onto the broad, powerful back. Minstrel quivered but didn't move. He only tensed as I tightened the girth, gently pulling on the buckle. It was almost as if he was eager to get on with the job. I moved round to the right-hand side, readjusting Sophie's riding hat and easing down the stirrup. Minstrel was a good hand bigger than anything I'd ever ridden before. His withers seemed to be stuck up in another galaxy.

"I don't believe this," Kate cut in, breaking my concentration, "She's getting on on the wrong side." Minstrel sidestepped away from my foot, his trust in me suddenly subsiding. Rachel's eyes grew like saucers, shocked at my lack of basic knowledge.

For a second I felt like giving in. Then Kate's cold sneer lodged in my brain like an irritating wasp. I had something to prove.

"I'll give you a leg-up." Sophie hopped over the fence. My left leg would never have stood the strain of getting on from the correct side. My physiotherapist had already informed me of that. Minstrel allowed Sophie to approach, watching warily as she bent down to support my leg.

"After three," she mumbled.

I gathered up the reins, relishing the feel of soft leather between my fingers.

"Three, two, one – up."

I eased my leg over Minstrel's back, settling into the saddle. I could barely breathe for nerves. Minstrel immediately hunched and flattened his ears.

"It's all right, boy, I'm not going to hurt you."

The heat coming through his burning skin reminded me that it was all new for him too. We were both feeling our way. I closed my eyes and pushed him forward. The strength and power were unbelievable. He just seemed to devour the ground with massive long strides.

"Hold steady, hold steady," I murmured to myself, trying to keep my hands as light as possible and mould my left leg round his side. Minstrel snorted and launched forward like no other horse I'd ever been on. He just seemed to float through the air, his hooves not touching the ground. Every other pony I'd ridden had a definite thud. Minstrel was in a class of his own. I probably relaxed too early. I released the pressure on the reins just a little, so he could stretch forward and shift into canter. I was going through a mental checklist – shoulders back, hands still, elbows in, chin up, but my heart was soaring. Hot, emotional tears trickled down my cheeks and into the chin guard of Sophie's riding hat. It was really happening. I was back in the saddle.

Minstrel bounded forward, swishing through the thick grass, leaning into the bridle. His canter was so smooth I hardly moved in the saddle. We were gelling completely when suddenly Frank's huge head poked through the hedge taking us both by surprise. Minstrel slammed on the brakes. Frank's enormous ears wafted back and forth as he pushed harder against the fence. I tilted forwards and lost my left stirrup.

We would have been all right if, in an effort to keep on top, I hadn't accidentally jabbed Minstrel in the mouth. It was only a tweak but it sent him absolutely berserk. Throwing back his head, he lunged forward, hurling the reins loose and bunching up for an almighty buck. I clamped my knees tight on the saddle flaps and shut my eyes.

"Jodie!" Sophie's stricken voice rent the air.

The bucks came fast and varied, Minstrel contorting himself into every position possible. I'd never felt anything like it. He set off on a diagonal across the field, arching his back and lifting all four feet off the ground at once like a bronco. The secret was to get his head up and push him out of it, but I didn't dare put any pressure on the reins in case he flipped completely.

My eyes were a blur of tears. A branch switched across my cheek as we hurtled under some low lying trees. It was like being stuck on the worst ride at Alton Towers. "I don't know what to do," I mumbled, flinging my arms round Minstrel's neck. "Oh please stop, *please*!"

For a few seconds Minstrel galloped even faster, still trying to shake me off like an annoying fly. He was all bucked out now and the fun seemed to have gone out of his game. I caught a glimpse of the five girls, staring with wild panic, horror-stricken. I grinned and tried to look as if I knew what I was doing.

Suddenly, with no warning, Minstrel dropped into trot and then into walk, his ears back, ready to listen to me. The tension just seemed to flood out of his body and he moved forward as if in a dressage test. The whirlwind had passed. I patted his neck, laughing and crying at the same time. "Good boy, clever boy." I buried my face in his silky red mane and patted his shoulder. Gently I neck-reined him back to the gate, trembling like crazy, but mostly with elation.

"How on earth did you manage to stay on?" Emma was looking at me with new respect. Even Steph didn't have any snide remark.

Sophie turned away quickly, trying to hide the hurt that was written all over her face. "You never told us that you could ride."

I slithered down from Minstrel who was relishing all the attention, rubbing his nose on my arm, not letting me move a centimetre away from him.

It was now or never. Bending down, I slowly

rolled up the bottom of my jean jods, tugging the material higher and higher until it exposed the mangled left calf with its criss-crosses of purple-blue scars and a dent the size of a fifty pence piece.

"I had a riding accident." My voice faltered. "I was fooling around on the roads and my pony slipped and rolled on top of me. It was all my fault. I broke my leg in seven places and severed some nerves. I didn't tell you because I was ashamed and angry, and, well, I was scared. It was easier just to let you believe I couldn't ride."

For a moment, all the girls were lost for words.

"We didn't know," Steph ventured at last.

"How could you?" I gulped back a wave of emotion. "This is the first time I've told anyone."

Kate suddenly turned and walked off without saying a word.

"What's eating her?" Emma stared after her.

"That must have taken so much courage," Sophie said in a half whisper.

And then my face crumpled with relief and emotion and I hugged Minstrel's neck, burying my face in his mane, thanking him over and over again for giving me back something so special – my confidence.

Chapter Eight

The next few days at Brook House were fantastic. It was as if by riding Minstrel I'd passed some sort of special initiation ceremony. All the girls worked like slaves to get the stables, feed room and saloon looking immaculate. Every horse and pony received a make-over, a bath, a mane and tail pull and a feathers and ears trim. We didn't touch their whiskers because horses use them as feelers and it isn't right to cut them off.

Kate was unusually quiet and poured all her energies into launching the Brook House Young Riders Club and producing the first newsletter which Sophie promised to copy on her dad's photocopier. There were profiles on three of the riding school ponies, Buzby, Rocket and Rusty, their likes, dislikes, personalities, breeds, and tips on how best to ride them and also on grooming and stable management. Kate asked me to produce a special helpline page which I secretly thought was a brilliant idea, and I concentrated on articles with headlines like, "Too Scared to Jump" and "I Can't Stop!", offering riding tips, quotes and personal experiences from various riders at the school. Kate did a star profile on the new riding instructor, getting all the information from Mrs Brentford but refusing to show it to anyone.

"That girl is so annoying." Sophie threw herself onto the new settee in the saloon which had been donated by Emma's parents. "Why does she always have to be queen bee?"

Apart from bragging about her horsy uncle in Hong Kong and pretending she knew everything about Arabs, Kate hadn't caused any more trouble. Rachel refused to open up to me about the argument they'd had and just stayed out of her way. In fact, since I'd ridden Minstrel, Rachel had elevated me to hero worship status. Nobody mentioned the accident, which was just as well because I didn't want to go on and on about it. Everybody was really understanding though and even Kate showed a grudging admiration.

I spent every spare minute with Minstrel, talking to him, handling him and schooling him on the manege in between lessons. Sophie was thrilled to bits that he was going so well but showed no inclination to try him out herself. On the inside of the saloon door Steph had pinned up a list of some of the ponies with the events they should be entered for at the Brook House Show next to their names.

*ROCKET: Novice jumping – 14.2hh and under.
Best ridden.
BUZBY: Most appealing pony? Flag race, potato,
minimus, fancy dress.
RUSTY: Best turned out. Veteran pony. Bending,
mug, minimus.
ARCHIE: Best ridden. Definitely no jumping.
BLOSSOM: Best riding school pony. Most
appealing pony. (Someone apologize to next-door
neighbour for garden.)
MONTY: Everything.*

I was itching to add Minstrel's name for the open jumping in the 14.2hh and under category. Yesterday, I'd secretly tried him over an upright and a spread and he'd been nothing short of brilliant.

"He's fantastic!" Emma blasted into the saloon, dark blond hair flopping round her face. She was slightly out of breath, her lips parted. "Carl Hester eat your heart out, they'll be flocking here in droves. We'll be the biggest riding school in the country. Buzby could become a cult figure."

Steph and Rachel were too busy playing with a Cyberpet to take much notice. Kate was applying some denim-coloured nail varnish which was supposed to be the latest craze and didn't even look up.

"Excuse me?" I interrupted Emma in mid-flow. "What exactly are you talking about?"

Kate stood up, trying to look as bored as possible.

"I think she's referring to the new temporary riding instructor," she said dismissively. "His name's Guy Marshall and he's a showjumper. He's on the arena right now. Oh, and he's invited me round to see his horses which I thought was rather sweet."

"I just can't take it in." Sophie stuck her feet forward on Rocket and fiddled with the stirrups. "Pinch me hard someone, quick! Two years at riding school and we've finally got a good instructor!"

Guy was absolutely drop-dead gorgeous with soft brown eyes and unruly blond hair. He couldn't have been more than twenty-seven years old and, even better, he was a superb instructor. The riding school had never been so busy. Within a week Mrs Brentford had to start doing evening lessons to fit everyone in. Ebony Jane and Frank were brought out of semi-retirement and Guy even started breaking in Elvis and Faldo who thought it was great to be part of the team. The whole place was buzzing. Even pupils who had just been walking and trotting for months progressed to canter and jumping.

Guy insisted on discipline and told Steph off twice for getting too close to Rachel in our group lesson, telling her that next time she'd have to leave the arena. Emma didn't gossip once and even Buzby decided to behave and kept giving Guy respectful glances, especially after he'd been chased down the long side with the lunge whip.

Within no time Guy had Rachel doing rising trot properly. He started her off by showing her how to roll out of the saddle in walk. Novices tended to shoot up too high in the saddle when really all you have to do is follow the horse's movement. After half an hour doing sitting trot she could rise out of the saddle in rhythm.

Minstrel hated being in a group lesson so I'd had twenty minutes on my own with Guy earlier. He'd said that Minstrel could go right to the very top and was really impressed with my jumping position. However I had to learn not to fold my upper body before take-off and to leave Minstrel alone in the last three strides. Guy said the rider's job was to keep the horse balanced, in rhythm at the right speed, and going straight. I'd never learnt so much in so short a time. The secret to jumping a course was to think and look ahead, choosing exactly the right line to each fence. Minstrel tended to buck after each jump and I had to sit up and drive him forward. Guy showed me how to use my left seat bone and thigh to compensate for the weakness in my calf.

Buzby was rapidly running out of tricks when Guy showed Emma how to stop him squashing her leg against the surrounding fence. All she had to do was use more outside leg and inside rein to push him away and if that didn't work she had to give him a short sharp smack down the outside shoulder with the riding crop. Buzby immediately mended his ways.

"He's utterly brilliant," Sophie gushed after Rocket had jumped a fence of two foot nine without any hesitation. Once Sophie had learnt to keep her legs wrapped around Rocket's sides on the approach to the jump, she grew and grew in confidence. It was all about technique.

Kate was skulking around the stables with a migraine so Guy suggested I ride Archie in her place. I would never have dreamed of riding him but Guy was really persuasive and Kate was nowhere in sight.

Archie was quite stubby in his neck and shoulder which made his stride short but he had a natural rhythm so he was good at flatwork. Guy asked me to form the rear of the ride and then told us all to ride down the centre line in single file before splitting off in opposite directions when we reached a certain point. The ponies wanted to follow each other, so we had to use lots of leg and ride a straight line to the outside track.

Guy was altering the jumping lane to a small fence with a filler and a pole three strides in front to guide the pony in. "OK," he said, shooting me a sizzling, megawatt smile, "let's see Archie in action."

80

"But he can't jump," I protested. Archie, immediately sensing something different, latched onto Buzby like a magnet.

"I'll decide that," said Guy, raising the pole on the jump a notch higher. "Emma can give you a lead – just keep your legs on and wait for the jump to come to you."

Buzby set off in a stuffy trot, furious that he had to go in the lead. Guy had put some red tape on Emma's reins so she knew exactly where to hold them. She still flapped her elbows but her riding had improved enormously. Archie followed on, swishing his tail and rolling his eyes.

"Think positive, think positive," I said to myself as I turned him into the jumping lane just as Buzby cleared the fence with a flourish. "Come on, Archie, you can do it." I lined him up straight, aiming for the middle of the fence.

"Come on, Archie!" Rachel shouted out from on top of Rusty, not knowing that you had to be quiet.

My whole concentration was focused on the jump. Archie tensed, bracing himself, his eyes wide with shock. I squeezed my legs round his sides and thought hard about clearing the jump. For a few seconds Archie paddled, unsure, his palomino head flicking up. Then he seemed to make up his mind and bounded forward, flying into the air, his forelegs tucked up. He cleared the pole by a foot. I was

81

so taken aback I lost both stirrups and collapsed on his neck.

"Whoopee!" Emma shrieked, insistent that Archie had his eyes closed going over the fence. "He was mega!" I patted him ecstatically and Archie swanked past Buzby, practically grinning with delight. Buzby scowled and tried to nip his shoulder to bring him back down to earth.

"Who said this pony couldn't jump?" Guy cocked an eyebrow at me and tutted under his breath. Sophie caught my gaze; our confusion was mutual. Kate was a really good rider. Why on earth, after two years at Brook House, had she convinced everybody that Archie couldn't jump?

We dismounted and ran up the stirrups ready to go back to the stables. Guy gave us all a rundown of our good and bad points and where we'd improved. Rachel was glowing with happiness and hugging Rusty to death. Guy was the best instructor ever. He inspired everyone with confidence. Back in the yard, the next ride were waiting in the office with Sandra. Sophie reluctantly handed over Rocket to a girl in a bright pink body protector.

I put Archie in his stable with the reins under his stirrups just in case he was being used on the next ride which was a one hour hack. That's when I spotted Kate in Minstrel's stable, beaming from ear to ear. Suddenly, without any real reason, my blood ran cold.

I crossed the yard instinctively knowing that something was wrong. As Kate swivelled round, I saw the Magic Mane Puller clasped in her right hand. She'd been showing off with it all morning – it was a revolutionary trimmer which left manes neatly pulled but in a fraction of the time. Everybody was buying them. The worst thought possible crossed my mind. Surely she wouldn't, couldn't . . . *Oh no, please.*

"There you are!" She opened the stable door wearing her smug, "everything's left to me" smile. "Somebody had to tidy him up, he looked a right mess."

By the water bucket was a huge pile of fine chestnut hair swept into a neat pile. Minstrel whickered and barged for the door, delighted to see me.

"Oh no," I whimpered. His gorgeous long mane was hacked back to five centimetres in length and stuck up on the crest of his neck where it was too short to lie down. Kate waited for praise, oblivious to the harm she'd done.

"Oh dear." Sophie came up behind me.

It was only then that I realized my shoulders were shaking. "You stupid girl." My voice came out as a hoarse whisper. Minstrel backed up a step, his ears twitching. "Everybody knows that Arabs have long manes. Only an idiot would do this." I waved a hand at the cropped hair lying on the floor. "You're the one who's supposed to know everything about Arabs."

Kate rocked back on her heels, flinching at the white-hot anger in my voice. But I didn't care. "Even Rachel wouldn't have made a gaffe like this," I continued, my voice rising.

Somewhere in the back of my mind cogs started rolling, pieces of the jigsaw clicking into place. "But you don't really know anything do you?" I was speaking slowly now, fumbling through the fog to get at the truth. "The uncle in Hong Kong, a farm in Cornwall, an Arab for your fifteenth birthday – it's all lies, nothing but lies. You're just an ordinary girl like me trying to make yourself sound important. You're a cheat, a con."

Kate went pale, tears springing into her eyes. Emma, Rachel and Steph joined Sophie at the door, open-mouthed with shock.

"You even lied about Archie not being able to jump. Don't tell me you're too scared to jump after you've made fun of everybody else?" A crimson flush of embarrassment flooded up Kate's neck.

"God, I'm right, aren't I? You can't help yourself, you're a compulsive liar" Kate pushed past me, scuffing my shoulder. She tore off towards the saloon, stifling a sob, head bowed down.

"All the rubbish we took from her," said Sophie, slowly shaking her head in disbelief. "Why would anyone want to make up stories like that?"

We headed off to the local shop, all five of us, trying to absorb what we'd found out, just needing to get away from the stables. By the time we came back up the drive an hour later, Kate had gone. All that was left of her was a cardboard certificate verifying her as a member of the Six Pack, which had been ripped in half, and the file on the Young Riders Club. The Six Pack had effectively become the Five Pack.

"Good riddance." Emma picked up the torn card and hurled it in the bin.

I helped Guy with evening stables, rubbing down the horses and filling hay nets, lugging water buckets across the yard until my legs were soaked. Minstrel was in particularly high spirits and refused to let me put on his summer rug or pick out his feet. He looked ridiculous with a short mane but there was nothing anybody could do apart from wait until it grew back.

"Neither of us is perfect now." I scratched the top of his withers which he loved and he carefully balanced his chin on my shoulder. All my dreams were tied up with Minstrel. It was almost as if fate had given me a second chance. Somebody had looked down and put a beautiful, talented stallion in my path which nobody wanted. I didn't dream about the accident any more, I dreamt about Minstrel and what we could achieve together.

I saw Sophie heading straight for Minstrel's stable. I could tell immediately that something was wrong. Rocket was waiting impatiently for his food but Sophie didn't even look across when he banged at his door. She was totally absorbed in something else.

"Um, can I have a word?" She bit down on her lip, twiddling nervously with a toggle on her fleece sweatshirt. "I talked to my dad last night," she said, looking away, searching for the right words. I knew Sophie well enough to notice she was faintly embarrassed. "He's offered to finance the riding school as a silent partner if I enter Minstrel for the Brook House Show." I stared at her, uncomprehending. "He wants me to ride," she added and stroked Minstrel's cheek, tracing the outline of his jawbone.

I felt as if someone had chucked ice water all over me. "But you can't." I dropped the body brush which made Minstrel run to the back of the stable. "That's emotional blackmail, it's not fair. He's manipulating you. Anyway, the riding school's doing really well."

Something in Sophie's eyes made me break off and a lump formed in my throat. It wasn't just Sophie's dad. Sophie wanted to ride Minstrel. It showed in the sparkle of excitement, the dilated pupils dancing with anxiety and adrenalin. "I think I can do it," she murmured. "I've got so much more confidence now. It's a chance to finally impress

Dad." She raced on, her mind made up. "I can't do it without you, though. You will help me, won't you?" She fixed me with an intense gaze.

I forced back bitter, burning tears and pulled my mouth into a smile. "Of course I will," I whispered. "After all, Minstrel is your horse."

Chapter Nine

"Are you sure this is legal?" I was crouched behind a Vauxhall Estate, glancing round, terrified that we might be seen. Emma was darting round the car park, flicking photocopied sheets of Kate's profile on Guy under everyone's windscreens. We'd talked Emma's mum into dropping us off at Horseworld Centre on the pretext of visiting their saddlery shop. She didn't suspect a thing.

"Hurry up, can't you?" I hissed, convinced I'd heard footsteps approaching. My heart was hammering.

Emma had come up with the bright idea of poaching Horseworld's customers by sticking Guy's picture on everyone's windscreens. I'd only gone along with it out of sheer curiosity to see the riding school and now my nerves were stretched to breaking point. I'd been irritable and depressed all morning about Sophie riding Minstrel and the last thing I wanted was to get caught red-handed, crouched next to a car wheel. Eventually, after what seemed like hours but must only have been a couple of minutes, I stood up and decided to rescue a stray sheet of paper which had got trapped under a pitchfork. Emma had completely disappeared from sight.

Horseworld Centre wasn't half as smart as I'd imagined. I couldn't help noticing the loose straw in the grates and corners and the scruffy stable doors streaked with dirt. Brook House was now a hundred times better. The only thing that Horseworld Centre had which we didn't, was an indoor school.

"Can I help you?"

I leapt round, twisting my foot in my haste. A tallish man was standing directly behind me, smiling at my discomfort, dressed in jeans and an Iron Maiden T-shirt.

"Um, I, well . . ." I began, and quickly stuffed the crumpled sheet of paper in my pocket. "I was interested in some lessons." It was the only thing I could think of to say. Any minute now, he'd spot the fliers or Emma would come bolting round the corner.

"Oh well, you've come to the right person." A cheery smile was fixed on his face. "I'm the chief instructor." My eyebrows rose with shock. Mrs Brentford always insisted on a shirt and tie and jodhpurs and jacket for instructors. He looked too scruffy to be a qualified teacher.

"Of course it depends what you're interested in.

We do one or two hour hacks, group lessons, or private."

He led me towards the first row of stables where a chestnut pony was staggering about in a stupor. It was obviously in a bad way.

"If you'd just excuse me." The instructor shot off to answer a telephone which was ringing in a nearby office. Relief surged through me in waves. *But where was Emma?*

Suddenly the sliding door of the school scraped back and ponies filed out, automatically heading for their own stables despite having riders on their backs, just like at Brook House. A cluster of mothers chatted while heading for the car park area so I couldn't get across without being noticed.

I was running now, my breath rasping, just wanting to escape. At each stable door I stopped and looked in, desperate to find Emma, but just seeing gorgeous ponies munching at hay nets. They were all so eye-catching and good-looking – not the usual riding school types at all. It was as if they'd been hand-picked for their beauty and nothing else.

A cold prickle of fear ran down my back. Most beginners wanted to ride beautiful highly-bred ponies but it was usually a recipe for disaster. I was shocked when I pushed open the mouth of a bay 13.2. From what I could tell by looking at her teeth, she was only three years old!

"Finally!" Emma's voice hissed behind me.

"Where've you been? Can't you stay in one spot for two minutes?"

"*Me* stay in one spot, what about *you*?" I broke off when I saw the strain in her face. Emma was always so jolly and joking, but this time she looked really worried.

"Take a look at this." She pulled a red and black poster out of her jeans pocket and opened it out. The words leapt out with sickening clarity: Horse-world Show and Gymkhana. Open Jumping and Ridden Classes. Sunday 14th August. Prompt Start.

The same day as the Brook House Show.

"We're really in trouble now." Emma voiced my own whirring thoughts. "This is a cheap trick and they've done it on purpose."

Even worse, the poster advertised local celebrity eventers, Ash Burgess and Alex Johnson as guests of honour. I leaned back against the wooden stable partition feeling sick with disappointment. All the work we'd put in over the last two weeks . . . Who'd want to come to Brook House now?

"We already know." Sophie raised her head out of her hands, her eyes red-rimmed and swollen. She was slumped in the saloon looking thoroughly depressed. "And it gets a whole lot worse, believe me."

"Mrs Brentford's closing down the riding school." Steph walked in behind us, blurting out the

91

devastating news before Sophie had a chance to finish.

"She's selling out to a builder." Sophie's voice caught in her throat. "Rocket's stable is likely to become a retirement bungalow! All the horses are going up for sale. They'll be split up and sent goodness knows where. Dear, sweet ponies like Rusty who's done nothing but try to please all his life. Frank and Ebony Jane, what's going to happen to them? It makes me sick. We can't let it happen."

I moved across to her, putting my arms round her shoulders as she let the tears fall freely.

Emma stood stock-still, unable to speak. Steph raked a hand through her hair and pressed her forehead against the cool glass pane of the window. "Dad will sell Monty for sure now. He's just been trying to find an excuse."

"Could someone find Rachel?" Sophie mopped at her eyes with a crumpled tissue. "She ran off when we told her. I'm worried about her asthma. You know how she feels about Rusty – he's her life, she worships him."

"And what about Buzby?" Emma spoke for the first time in an unnatural voice. "I'd rather kidnap him than let him go to some grotty kid who doesn't understand his special ways. Without Buz there's no point to anything."

"We won't let it happen," I surprised myself with my own determination.

"I appreciate what you're saying, Jodie," Sophie half-smiled, struggling to find strength. "But at the end of the day we're just a bunch of kids. And who's going to listen to us?"

Dear Rusty,
I'll miss you heaps. I'll never forget you and the brill times we had together.
Rachel

The note fluttered against Rusty's door, stuck down with a piece of sellotape.

"I'll go and find her." Emma shot off, brushing away fresh tears.

Brook House mattered. The people. The horses. There was character here. Real love and concern.

"I respected you." I couldn't hold it in any longer. It didn't matter if I got banned now. There was nothing to get banned from.

Mrs Brentford swivelled round, achingly slowly, every trace of spirit drained from her face. I paused, momentarily taken aback, and then remembered the horses. "How could you? How could you sell out to a builder?"

The words hung in the air. An accusation. A betrayal. I needed an answer. An explanation. "I could understand it if there were no bookings, but

Guy's turned all that around, every lesson is full. The ponies are loving it, they've got a new lease of life, a sense of purpose."

I broke off, clenching my hands into tight fists, frustration making it difficult to speak. "H-how can you take that away from everyone? How could you let us build up our hopes?"

It was ages before she answered. For one moment I thought she was going to throw me out. Then her eyes softened and she flopped down into an armchair. "I'm sixty-nine years old. I've got arthritis and a bad hip. We might be busy at the moment, but come the winter it'll be the same old story. Horseworld has us beat, they've got the facilities. All I've got is a pile of debts and a tumbling down yard full of geriatric animals. I shouldn't even be telling you this. I don't have to answer to a twelve-year-old girl. I've been here for thirty years – don't you think it's a hard enough wrench?"

I swallowed hard, my turn to listen, knowing there was another side to the story but refusing to hear. "When I was all ready for quitting you told me I was feeling sorry for myself. You made me pull myself together when everybody else was just being nice. Well now it's my turn." I gulped, desperately unsure but deciding to take the bull by the horns. "Don't give up on Brook House, Mrs Brentford, not now, when it's really got a chance. We need you, the horses need you, and you wouldn't be happy living

94

anywhere else. Because if you stop fighting, what else is there left?"

Sophie was waiting anxiously as I came out of the house. I shook my head but she already knew from my face that it hadn't done any good.

"They exchange contracts next week," I gulped. "I should think they'll want to pull down the stables straight away. They've been after Brook House for years."

Sophie stood tall, shaking like a leaf and clutching a skull cap covered with blue velvet. "Well, then I've got to take Minstrel to the Horse-world Show. It's our only chance." Her hands trembled as she slammed down the cap, pushing her hair behind her ears. "If I keep my part of the deal, Dad might just buy Brook House. There's still time – we've got a few days."

"It's a long shot." I held back, not wanting her to build up her hopes.

"Jodie, I've got to try. I've got to do everything I can to save Rocket and the others. Now, please will you teach me to ride my horse?"

Minstrel powered round the arena, flicking out his toes, ignoring Sophie's leg aids, but keeping one eye firmly fixed on me, standing in the centre. Sophie clung to the reins, her body rigid, telling Minstrel to go forward with her leg but confusing him by pulling on his mouth.

"You've got to let him flow," I shouted. "Drop the inside rein and push him forward with your inside leg."

Sophie collapsed through her shoulder and had to grab hold of the pommel to keep her balance. Her face was white and tight with fear but she kept on trying, determined to succeed.

"One, two, three, four. One, two, one, two." I counted out the rhythm to walk and trot, trying to get her to relax and loosen up. If you tense in the saddle the horse immediately picks it up and it sets him on edge. It was Sophie's nerves which made it so difficult for her to ride Minstrel. She didn't trust him like she trusted Rocket.

"Come on, Soph, don't give up." Emma led Buzby on to the arena. He was staring goggle-eyed at Minstrel, now trotting on the spot, which is called "piaffe" in dressage terms. Sophie completely lost her concentration and shot up his neck.

Rachel followed leading Rusty, dry-eyed but her face still red and puffy. Emma had found her crying her eyes out in the hayloft.

Now Minstrel had an audience he really started showing off, arching his neck and extending his trot, turning in his quarters and trying to pirouette round. Stallions are always more powerful and lively than geldings but Minstrel seemed to have rockets under his hooves. It made my heart thump just watching him.

Buzby was in total awe, obviously convinced that Minstrel had oodles of street cred.

"Come on, Minstrel," I murmured. "If only you knew how important this is."

Rachel circled Rusty and did a perfect rein-back. Suddenly I had an idea.

"Take Minstrel behind Rusty," I yelled, crossing my fingers behind my back. Rusty was an old schoolmaster and he might just be the steadying influence that Minstrel needed. Within seconds Minstrel dropped to walk and followed Rusty's lead, copying his every move.

"It's working!" Sophie was ecstatic. "I can ride him!"

And at exactly the same moment another idea formulated in my mind. Brook House might be closing down but the ponies deserved one last chance, they'd all worked so hard at their re-schooling.

"Let's take them all to Horseworld," I blurted out, excitement brimming up as my thoughts gathered speed. "Let's show everyone that it's not about breeding and bloodlines, it's personality that counts and good riding."

Emma's mouth dropped open and then snapped shut again.

"We can hire the ponies for the day and hack there," I babbled.

"But what about the roads?" said Rachel despondently. "You haven't been out since your accident."

"We can help each other," I enthused. "That's what the Five Pack is all about, isn't it? We can do it. I know we can. Let's show everybody. Let's go out on a high note."

"We'll be like a posse." Emma started to look dreamy.

I held out my hand and Rachel put hers on top. Then Sophie. Then Emma. Finally Rusty nuzzled his chin on Emma's hand as if he approved.

"That's settled then. We're going to the Horseworld Show!"

Chapter Ten

"Dad might just keep Monty." A flicker of hope glimmered in Steph's eyes when we told her our plan. "I've never won a rosette before." Emma was determined that every Brook House pony was going to pick up a rosette, even if it was just for clear round jumping.

It was Guy's morning off so we'd agreed to help Sandra out by doing all the mucking out and hay nets. He was as upset as we were about the ponies being sold.

"It's growing back." Sophie came out of Minstrel's stable, convinced his mane had grown a third of a centimetre.

Emma was studying an article in *In the Saddle* on how to ride a showjumping course and still couldn't grasp how to turn direction in mid-air.

"I'd just concentrate on clearing the jumps." Steph laughed, ruffling her hair and making a face like Buzby.

We were all trying to think positive but it wasn't easy. Steph had driven us mad all morning taking photographs of the horses with her dad's camera but at least it had taken our minds off what was happening. And for the first time ever she didn't boast about it. I couldn't imagine Steph becoming a close friend but without Kate's influence she seemed to be turning into a nicer person.

"I hope Rachel's all right." Sophie glanced at her watch, her eyes narrowing. Rachel had become so quiet and withdrawn and she was spending every second with Rusty. "She should be back from the field by now."

"Hello, is anyone there?" A high-pitched, tinkly voice came from outside. Then we heard a car door bang. A customer.

Two women with a baby in a pushchair were glancing round the stable yard, uncertain. "We're looking for an instructor called Guy Marshall?" The one with the baby hesitated and then pulled something out of her handbag. "Someone put this on our windscreen and we'd really like to book some lessons – there are ten of us."

Emma nearly choked on her sandwich, then grinned at me as if to say I told you so. The photo-copied sheet on Guy and Brook House fluttered in the woman's hand, slightly torn where it had been caught by the windscreen wiper.

"Also," the other woman prompted, "we've all got children who'd love to join the Young Riders Club. Where do we get an application form and how much does it cost? We think it's a brilliant idea."

We all stared at her in amazement, and then Sophie started to explain that it was Guy's morning off but that Mrs Brentford should be somewhere in the house.

"You're wasting your time," Steph snapped suddenly, ignoring Sophie's dig in the ribs. "The riding school's closing down. All the horses are homeless and they're going to pull down the stables and build bungalows. It couldn't get any worse, we'll never be able to ride again." She turned away, her eyes filling with tears and her jaw trembling. I'd never seen Steph get emotional before.

"But that's terrible." Both women looked horrified.

"What was that?" Emma stiffened suddenly.

We could definitely hear shouting.

"It's coming from the back field," muttered Sophie, moving forward. I immediately imagined trespassers, hooligans frightening the horses.

"We saw two men in suits with measuring sticks if that's any help," announced one of the women. The voices were getting louder. Definitely men's voices. And someone else. Someone familiar. Rachel!

We charged across the yard. Buzby, Archie and Rocket were huddled by the gate, tails held high, staring across the field towards the trees. Suddenly, between two old oaks we saw Rachel riding Rusty bareback with just a head collar and lead rein. There were two men close by, stumbling away from her through a patch of nettles. Rachel urged Rusty on – she was riding straight at them!

"Rachel!" Sophie screamed.

My brain whirred with panic. She'd completely lost it. Sophie was the fastest runner and streaked ahead of the rest of us.

"Get out of here, go on, get out! Get out!" Rachel blazed, her voice husky and cracked with emotion. Rusty shied to one side, skewing his head upwards, and spinning round, confused and frightened.

"No wonder this place has gone belly up," said one of the men. "The quicker these nags and interfering kids disappear, the better."

"Leave her alone," shouted Emma, fiercely protective of Rachel.

"They were measuring out the field," Rachel spluttered, finally coming to a halt.

"They were frightening the horses and they shouldn't be here."

"I could report her for assault," threatened the man. "I could have you all done. I'm sure Mrs Brentford would want to know about this."

"Leave it, Greg," said his colleague. "We'll come back another day. They're just kids after all. Come on, we're due back at the office."

"Good riddance," Emma yelled, undaunted.

"We've got to stop them!" said Rachel, tears starting down her cheeks. But this was the hard, cold reality. The riding school was going to close down. It was inevitable. I saw Sophie's face crumple under the pressure. Our only chance was her dad.

"Did they give their names?" Steph asked abruptly, her eyes flashing with excitement. It seemed a really insensitive thing to say.

"Oh get real, Steph," Emma snapped. "It was hardly a polite conversation."

"I was just curious," she said pouting, but her mind was quite clearly buzzing a hundred miles away.

"You are a seriously weird girl," Emma threw back at her, but for once Steph didn't retaliate. She was too busy fiddling with the lens on her camera which was still slung round her neck.

"There is something we could do." She dropped her voice almost to a whisper.

"What?" Emma sneered, ready with a cutting reply.

"Nothing." Steph clammed up, her face going blank. "It was a stupid idea anyway."

Guy and Sandra helped us with all the preparations for the show and Mrs Brentford decided to spend a few days with her daughter, at least until the stables were sold.

In an effort to cheer us up, Guy told us endless

stories about life on the showjumping circuit and all the famous riders. Guy was just starting out with two novice horses which were Danish warmbloods, and he had to make as much money from teaching as he could.

He showed Rachel how to do deep-breathing exercises in case her chest tightened when she got nervous and gave me some warm-up exercises to keep my leg loose and relaxed. It was very similar to what my physio had suggested. With the regular daily exercise I'd only suffered with cramp once since my first day and that had been in the middle of the night.

"Where's Rachel?" Emma munched on some crisps while cleaning Buzby's bridle. The show was the day after tomorrow and we'd all started to get really nervous.

This was the first day of the holidays that Rachel hadn't turned up. And for that matter neither had Steph. It was ten o'clock on Friday morning and Guy was in the arena doing a group lesson. Sophie was parading around in a hacking jacket which she'd bought in a second hand shop for five pounds. She had an allowance from her dad which meant she could buy whatever she fancied, but she hardly ever used it. If Sophie wanted she could be really big-headed but she never was which was probably why she was so popular.

"This is weird." I came back out of the office after

answering the telephone three times in succession. All three people had been offering homes for the ponies and saying how horrified they were to read about it in the paper.

"What's going on?" asked Emma.

The phone rang again, and at the same time a car turned into the drive. Steph leapt out of the passenger door clutching a newspaper and waving at us like crazy through the window.

"I have a distinct feeling we're about to find out."

"That was someone wanting to take Rusty." Sophie came back from the office nonplussed. "She seemed to think he was about to be put down."

"Steph, what have you done?" My voice sounded cold and strained.

Oblivious to any problem, Steph, grinning like a Chesire cat, slapped the newspaper down on the saloon table and swivelled it round so we could all read the front page.

RIDING HAVEN TO BE RIPPED UP FOR HOUSES. FIVE GIRLS FIGHT TO SAVE THEIR FOUR-LEGGED FRIENDS.

Underneath was a picture of Rachel and Rusty chasing off the two men.

"Oh my goodness!" Emma slapped a hand across her mouth. "You took this picture."

"And I went to the newspaper." Steph proudly

pointed at the text. "They've quoted me almost word for word."

We all sat and stared. Sophie went to answer the phone which rang and rang.

"Don't you see?" Steph thrummed her finger against the article. "This is going to save the stables."

"It's Mrs Brentford." Sophie slid back into her seat looking white. "She's read the Weekly Gazette and she wants to speak to you."

Steph jolted slightly, her excitement slipping away.

"I'm not joking, Steph, there's fireworks coming down the phone. I think she mentioned something about skinning you alive."

"Jodie, there's someone to see you," Mum shouted up the stairs.

I was in the middle of dusting my model horse collection and after that I planned to try and make a hay net out of some baling twine I'd brought from the stables. I glanced through the net curtain but didn't recognize the red car outside. I knew all the cars belonging to the girls' parents, apart from Rachel's, as she always arrived alone.

"It's Rachel!" Mum shouted even louder. I could tell by the edge in her voice that something wasn't quite right. I came out to the edge of the stairs and Rachel was already halfway up, her eyes red and swollen.

"I'll take Mrs Whitehead into the sitting room while you have a little chat," Mum said in her "stepping on eggshells" voice.

My brother opened his bedroom door, took one look and shut it again, turning up Oasis on his annoying new CD player.

"Take no notice," I grunted. "He's going through the change – into an alien."

Rachel collapsed on the edge of the bed, turning her hands over and over in her lap. "I should have t-told you," she stammered. "You're going to hate me."

"I don't think so." I sat back, somewhat startled.

"I've lied to everybody and now I'll never be able to s-see Rusty again." Tears were flooding down her face, and she struggled to hold her voice steady. "Nobody knew I was going riding. I told Mum I was going to Grandad's. And Grandad I was staying at a friend's. Mum saw the newspaper and went mad."

"Oh." I sat silent for a few moments, lost for words.

"Mum won't let me go near the stables again. She wraps me up in cotton wool, she won't let me do anything. It's not fair. If she let me live my life for once I wouldn't have to sneak behind her back."

"And did Kate know all this?" I asked.

107

"How did you guess that?" Rachel glanced up.

"Just a hunch. I remember when I first met you, you looked terrified when I suggested we come to the stables together, and it was obvious Kate had got some hold over you."

"Yeah, she knew. Like a fool I told her. That was before I realized she was such a toad. Here." She pulled something out of a carrier bag she had brought with her. "I bought this for Rusty. I was going to give it to him just before the show." It was a bright red head collar with a matching lead rope.

"But you are still coming? I mean, you've got to talk your mum round."

"That's mission impossible." Rachel managed a half smile. "Mum's convinced horses are dangerous and they'll give me an asthma attack. She won't change her mind. I'd better go. It was all I could do to get her to bring me here."

"But you can't just leave." I started to panic.

"I'll stay in touch, I promise."

"Rachel!"

She was down the stairs and out of the door before I even had chance to get her phone number. I was left holding Rusty's head collar which must have cost an arm and a leg. Poor, poor Rachel. And poor Rusty. I couldn't quite take it in. Surely the last thing Rachel needed was to be cut off from horses. Even if she had deceived her mum?

*

"There's someone to see you." Guy came straight up to me as soon as I arrived at the stables the next morning. "She's round by the field gate. Oh and Jodie, go easy on her, eh?"

I truly expected to see Mrs Brentford, or possibly Rachel. I was amazed when I saw who it really was.

She had her arms wrapped around Archie's neck. He was gently nuzzling her shoulder in delight.

It was Kate.

I felt myself stiffen visibly.

"I know I'm the last person you want to see," she said, hesitating, "but I've got to speak to someone."

Archie moved away and Kate dropped her eyes, overcome with embarrassment. "It's about Horse-world Centre – I've been having some riding lessons there."

I flinched in surprise, although on second thoughts, it wasn't really much of a shock.

"Jodie," she began, fidgeting nervously and fighting for the right words. "You'll never believe what's happening there . . ."

Chapter Eleven

"She's making it up," Emma said flatly. We were huddled in the saloon trying to absorb what Kate had told us. "It's so over the top it can't possibly be true."

Kate was waiting in the tack room until we'd reached a decision.

"After the pack of lies she's told us, how can we believe a word she says?" Steph said what we were all thinking.

"It adds up though," I said thoughtfully. A niggling hunch wouldn't leave me alone.

Kate had told us that at Horseworld they were buying young unbroken ponies cheap from the sales and banging them straight into the riding school where they quickly picked up what to do from the older ponies and were worked so hard that they were too tired to play up. They were then sold after a few months for huge sums of money as potential show ponies.

"That's why they were all so good-looking and well-bred," I burst out. "They didn't look like riding school ponies because they weren't. And that's why

110

one was only three years old. I think it's true, for once in her life I think Kate's telling the truth."

Sophie pursed her lips. "But what about the rest? If that was really happening . . ."

Kate had told us that if they had particular trouble with a pony they resorted to doping it. Amazingly, there hadn't been an accident yet, but the show was coming up. Kate had overheard a conversation between the owner and the head instructor and hadn't dared go back since. But then she read about Brook House in the paper and knew she had to speak out.

"Anyone can fall into the trap of telling lies," I said, thinking of Rachel. "She deserves another chance."

Steph and Emma scowled.

"If we can expose them," I whispered, hardly daring to believe it, "the council will close them down. It's a lifeline for Brook House."

"We'll, tell Guy," Sophie said decisively. "He'll know what to do."

"We're not letting her back into the Five Pack until she's proved herself." Emma was adamant.

"Well, what are we waiting for?" I jumped up, feeling suddenly that everything was going to come right. "We haven't got a moment to lose!"

"I thought I knew what sheer terror was when I failed my maths assignment." Emma came out of

Buzby's stable looking pea-green. "But this is far worse."

I didn't tell anyone that I'd already been sick three times, and it wasn't the show that was scaring me to death but the ride there on the roads.

I was to take Rusty in Rachel's place because he was foolproof and the one I trusted the most. It didn't seem right without Rachel but we were all careful not to say so. I tacked up Rusty and fitted his new red head collar under his bridle so we could tie him up if necessary.

Guy was taking Minstrel in his horsebox because we didn't have a clue how he would behave on the roads. Sophie was riding Rocket who I was going to enter for the jumping when we got there.

I stared in front of the mirror in the outside cloakroom after redoing my white show tie for the sixth time. "You can do it, you can do it, you know you can, you can," I chanted away to the mirror like I used to when I was younger.

"How did it happen?" Kate appeared behind me, leaning against the doorframe, interested but not mocking.

"I became friends with a girl who thought horses were for showing off with. We were out riding one day and she dared me to ride down the middle white line on a quiet road. Anyway, I did, a car came, and my pony reared and then fell on my leg. The car swerved. Nobody else was hurt, but from the knee down my leg was a mess."

"I'm sorry." She really did seem to mean it.

"Listen," she said awkwardly, "if you help me get Archie round the clear round jumping, I'll help you get down the road. Deal?"

"A problem shared is a problem halved." I managed a smile, suddenly feeling quite tearful. I stuck out my hand and she gave it a stilted shake.

"Jodie, before, when I was a pig . . ." She paused. "Well, the truth was I was jealous. You seemed to have everything – you could ride really well, you were popular and you didn't seem scared of anything."

"Well, I was." I grinned, feeling my cheeks tighten. "I still am."

"I know." Kate smiled warmly and it made her look so much nicer. "I was horrible to everyone because I hated myself. I made up those stories because I didn't want to be ordinary. But you know, now that I am, it's quite nice. Because you don't have to pretend. And it's a lot easier to keep friends."

"Yeah, I know." I thought of Rachel, isolated.

"And I can honestly say, if there's a gate or a treble in the clear round I shall curl up and die."

"You can do it, you can do it," I repeated under my breath. Rusty steadily put one hoof in front of the other as cars whizzed past. Most drivers were fantastic and slowed right down but the odd one hardly seemed to notice us at all. Kate was on my outside riding Archie who had to keep waiting for Rusty who was smaller and had a shorter stride. Sophie was ahead on Rocket, and Steph and Emma behind on Monty and Buzby.

I was doing it. I was facing up to my fear and overcoming it. Just. Beads of sweat trickled down the inside of my white shirt and my hands shook as I clasped the reins.

Sophie waved her right arm up and down to slow a lorry and I wanted to close my eyes as it crunched past. Rusty didn't bat an eyelid.

"Just another mile or so." Kate registered my lifeless face. "You're doing really well."

I decided at that moment to take the BHS Road Safety Test and learn how to be totally responsible on the roads.

Cars and trailers streamed into the showground. There were far more people here than we ever imagined.

"He's there!" Emma yelled her head off as she spotted Ash Burgess, the celebrity guest chatting to Guy by the horsebox. "What a babe!"

I practically had to stuff a riding glove in her mouth to stop her wolf whistling. Buzby who was wearing a bright red browband with matching numnah and bandages decided to set off after a pretty bay mare who had just deposited her rider by the secretary's tent. Archie was more interested in someone dressed up as a chicken carrying a huge chocolate egg than in romance.

"That's my fancy dress costume!" Emma was hoarse with outrage. "What am I going to do now there's another chicken? I'll be eliminated!"

"Oh, I don't know." Sophie smothered a smile. "It could be the start of a beautiful friendship."

Guy had all the extra equipment we needed so we made our way over to the horsebox where Minstrel was kicking pieces out of the sides. Ash Burgess disappeared which was hardly surprising with six eager girls riding towards him.

We had told Guy everything about Horseworld Centre and he had listened and formulated a plan. We trusted him completely and he hadn't once doubted us. Everything was in place. In the meantime, our job was to show everyone how brilliant the Brook House ponies really were.

"Look at them," exclaimed Emma. A posse of riding school riders came from the stables, all the ponies wearing matching numnahs embossed with the Horseworld logo. "How on earth are we going to beat them?"

The clear round jumping had already started in ring one and the lead rein class had just finished. "It will be me next," gulped Steph as the tannoy announced the best ridden 13.2hh and under. Guy had entered us all for our various classes.

"I can't do it," Sophie moaned, wilting against Rocket's shoulder. "I can't ride Minstrel, I can't. I must have been crazy to even think it."

Right on cue Minstrel half-reared, lashing out with one of his hind legs against the horsebox side. Sophie squirmed with fear. Emma shuffled awkwardly and toyed with Buzby's reins. Two girls strolling past giggled behind their hands. We just caught a few snatched words . . . "Wouldn't be seen dead on any of them . . . The grey one looks like my grandad's wolfhound."

Emma went bright red in the face and took a step forward.

"Take no notice." I grasped her arm.

Kate and Steph's confidence shattered like broken glass.

"Come on, girls, don't let them get to you." It was so obvious they were crumbling. "We're better than any of them."

"Oh yeah." Emma rolled her eyes. "Says who?"

I was losing them.

"We'll be a laughing stock," Steph mumbled.

Rusty yawned, resting a hind leg, looking tired out before he even started.

"Don't give up now," I pleaded, "not now we've come this far."

Emma's eyes hooked onto something by the

entrance gates. A wave of excitement ran right through her.

"What is it?" We all followed her gaze.

"It's Rachel!" Steph finally croaked in disbelief. "And she's wearing her jodhpurs!"

Rachel was hurtling across the grass field, arms flailing and a huge grin plastered across her face.

Rusty perked up, jerking his head towards her voice.

"I can ride!" she yelled out, catching her hairnet which was slipping down her neck. Rusty started whinnying and wouldn't rest until he'd licked her face, devoured six polos and happily sucked her hair, his chin resting on top of her head.

Emma gave Rachel a hug and then we all did, apart from Kate who shuffled awkwardly with embarrassment. "I don't know what your mum said to mine," Rachel ran on, chattering non-stop, "but it did the trick. As long as I have my inhaler I can ride whenever I want." She gave Rusty a kiss on the nose for good measure and pulled down the stirrups.

"Shouldn't you be getting ready?" She glanced at Rocket and Buzby and Archie grazing with their saddles propped by the horsebox. "It might be my imagination but I thought we were going to wipe the board?"

"She's a different girl," said Sophie hopping

nervously from foot to foot, clutching her arms to her chest, even though it was a warm day.

Rachel was in a corner of the field with her mum, warming up for the best ridden. Rusty was putting every ounce of concentration into helping her as much as possible. Guy was giving Kate a few words of encouragement, especially after Archie tried to roll in a cowpat and she lost her stirrups.

"Come on, Mrs Brentford, where are you?" I scanned the showground for her birdlike figure. She had to come, she just had to!

"Oh no." Sophie went as white as her show shirt and her eyes filled with panic. "It's my dad!"

"A clear round for Brook House Buzby!" the tannoy bawled out as Buzby hauled Emma out of the arena before she could even collect her rosette. Steph shot forward and grabbed the orange ribbon before a pretty Welsh Mountain pony devoured it in one gulp.

"We did it!" Emma dangled round Buzby's neck, patting him non-stop, her riding hat slipping off in the process. "Our first rosette!"

Buzby had hurled himself round the clear round course giving everything a wide berth and nearly unseating Emma at the spread. It was only a fluke that he had taken the right fence at the end because Emma's hat had tipped over her eyes and she couldn't see a thing.

"It's Mum and Dad!" Emma suddenly pointed to two people striding towards us waving a thermos flask and a camera. Emma slid off Buzby and overcome with emotion promptly burst into tears.

"I'm not riding Minstrel." Sophie threw back her head and openly defied her dad. He was a big man with an intense gaze, huge bushy eyebrows and a shock of black hair. Just looking at him intimidated me.

Sophie stuck out her chin, her cheeks flushed. "All you think about is winning, being the best, but it's taking part that counts. Rocket might be common and ordinary to you but I love him and I'm going to ride him – and I don't care if we come last because I'm going to enjoy every minute of it. He's ordinary-looking and with no great breeding but has a heart of gold and that's the most important thing. And I know you don't love me and you think I'm useless but it's my life and I've got to do my own thing. All I ever wanted was for you to be proud of me but more than anything else I want to be proud of myself." Sophie broke off, gasping, her eyes shining.

I ducked down to put some hoof oil on Rocket, feeling as awkward as a fish out of water but neither of them seemed to notice.

"Oh you daft little sugar," Her dad's voice cracked as he opened his arms and Sophie flew into them. "You're the kindest, sweetest person I've ever known. How could you possibly think I don't love you?"

Chapter Twelve

"You're riding Minstrel!" Steph charged up from the secretary's tent, her fair hair hanging over one eye. "Sophie had your name down all along – she's taking Rocket in the novice."

A rush of adrenalin scorched through my veins and I had to stop myself screaming out loud. I was riding Minstrel. I was riding Minstrel! It was a miracle!

"Come quick!" Emma tore up on Buzby who now had the orange rosette pinned to his bridle and was walking three hands taller. "It's Rachel, she's been pulled in first in the best ridden."

"Keep calm, Rachel." Steph clasped her hands together as the first four ponies showed off their skills in reverse order. After the initial parade around the judge the competitors had to do a display in walk, trot and canter, usually with a figure-of-eight and rein-back and sometimes an extended trot. Archie wasn't even in the running in the back row.

"Kate's going to be livid," cried Steph, her eyes dancing at the thought of trouble. "I'll bet a bumper burger with triple onions that she'll go mad when she comes out."

"Done." I shook hands, hoping that Kate really had changed.

Rachel moved off on Rusty, keeping her shoulders back and her hands really still.

"She's concentrating like crazy." Emma latched on to my arm.

The secret was to blank out the fact that you were at a show with people watching, and pretend you were schooling in the field back at home. Rachel visibly relaxed as if she'd just remembered. Rusty strode out and did the best show of his life. It didn't matter that he was old with grey hairs and a stringy body. He was trying every second, straining to help Rachel, and flexing his neck like a dressage horse.

"He's beautiful," Emma croaked, who always welled up at anything emotional. Even Buzby behaved and stared at his stable mate as if to pick up tips.

Rachel was awarded the first rosette which was such an achievement for someone who had just started riding. Kate got nothing and Archie sidled out of the ring in disgrace.

"Here goes." Steph winked, but Kate proved everybody wrong and went straight across to Rachel who was still gawping at the rosette in a daze.

"Well done." She held out her hand. "You did brilliantly and you deserved to win."

Rachel looked stunned but soon started grinning.

"I was hoping, well, maybe we could start again as friends?"

"It's that pony!" I seized Emma's wrist, my eyes trailing a familiar pony with a white blaze. It was a chestnut, the one I'd seen at Horseworld staggering about.

Now it was plodding along in first gear behind two other ponies with a novice rider on its back who didn't seem to know anything. It didn't take much working out. Rachel and Steph read our thoughts instantly. Kate wheeled Archie round, her face set in a grim line. "That's the one," she said angrily, "that's the pony that's being doped."

"Where's Guy?" Emma nibbled on her thumbnail, scouring the showground for the slightest glimpse. Any plan we'd had was disintegrating before our eyes. He should have been here by now.

"We can't do anything yet." Kate's voice was loaded with warning. "You heard what Guy said."

The novice jumping was well under way with a fat cob exploding out of the ring after sixteen faults. I had to focus on Minstrel. This was my big chance to prove to myself once and for all. I couldn't blow it.

"I've got to go!" I swallowed hard with nerves.

Kate read my thoughts immediately and volunteered to help. "Are you sure this is what you want?" She touched my arm with real concern.

A group of people had crowded round the horsebox where Minstrel was snorting and stamping, looking about to burst out of his skin. His neck was arched and he was straining on the lead rope. He'd never looked more beautiful.

"I'm perfectly positive," I told her, striding purposefully up the ramp. After all, how many people got to ride a pure-bred Arabian stallion?

"He's nuts." Two girls jolted back against the ropes as I rode into the collecting ring with Minstrel swinging his quarters first one way and then the other, and then moving sideways in the perfect half pass.

"Whoa boy, steady now." I was shaking with nerves.

"Jodie!" Sophie yelled, and rode Rocket towards us. "It's all sorted out," she gasped, "Dad's finally listened, he's even talking about buying Rocket. Isn't that fantastic?"

She didn't mention anything about the riding school.

"That's brilliant," I said and really meant it.

Suddenly a gasp went up from the ringside viewers and Minstrel leapt in the air as if he'd been touched with electricity.

"It's Steph," cried Sophie, standing up in her stirrups. "She's fallen off."

I had no idea she was even in the ring.

Emma ran up, dragging Buzby. "Steph's bombed out," she shouted.

Steph rode out of the ring, grass-stained and close to tears, with Monty looking bewildered and slightly shaken. "I know I've let everyone down," she gulped, obviously overhearing Emma's remark. "Why don't you all have a good laugh, eh? Stupid old Steph who falls at the second fence. Well go on, I know I'm useless." Her face crumpled and she kicked Monty forward towards the horsebox, desperate to get away.

"Leave her." I stopped Emma following. "Just give her a few minutes, she'll be OK."

"Poor Steph," said Rachel as she appeared on Rusty, "she was trying so hard."

"It's you!" Kate rushed up, checking Sophie's show number. "They're calling you, you're in next!"

"Oh crikey." Sophie dropped her whip and went white. "Where's Dad?"

"Whoa boy, steady boy." Minstrel froze, I could feel each muscle grow taut like drawn elastic.

"She's over the planks," Emma commentated, balancing on a cavaletti jump to see, while Buzby tore at some juicy grass.

I forced a smile onto my rigid face and tightened

the reins. Minstrel was about to explode. And then I saw why. The chestnut we'd spotted earlier was sidling up to Rusty with a vicious expression on its bland face, one hind leg poised ready to lash out. Minstrel erupted in rage. I clung on as best I could as he flew forward with his teeth bared, and cannoned straight into the chestnut's quarters.

"What the hell?" A man wearing a Horseworld sweatshirt dived forward. The girl on the chestnut burst into tears. Rachel stared stunned as Rusty escaped injury by the skin of his teeth. And it was all thanks to Minstrel.

"You fantastic, gorgeous horse," I cried, flinging myself forward, patting Minstrel's thick, crested neck and praising him until I went hoarse.

"It's dangerous, that horse," someone yelled out. "It's a stallion!" Then there was pandemonium.

"There's nothing in the rules to say that a stallion can't enter," Kate yelled back at the man in the sweatshirt.

"I run the show, sweetheart, so I should know."

I got off Minstrel and tried to calm him but all the shouting was driving him wild. Rachel brought Rusty alongside, which seemed to quieten him a little.

"Where's Guy?" Emma was on the verge of tears. A woman with an unstable hairdo was threatening to throw out all the Brook House riders.

"That's because we're beating them hands

down." Steph pushed forward with Monty, her eyes red-rimmed but set with determination. "You can't throw us out," she cried, and glanced round, almost manic, "because there's something you all ought to know—"

"Guy's coming," Sophie interrupted as she pushed Rocket through the crowds, her eyes blazing with triumph. We'd completely forgotten about her showjumping round. "That's the pony," she yelled, pointing wildly at the chestnut.

A look of horror darkened the face of the man in the Horseworld sweatshirt.

"Hallelujah!" Emma punched the air with her fist as Guy and Mrs Brentford appeared behind Rocket. Mrs Brentford pulled herself up to her full height, a smirk playing on her lips. "Graham Harris, we have reason to believe that you have been illegally doping riding school horses."

"You interfering old bag, how dare you?" He sprang forward. "I'll sue you for slander."

"I wouldn't try it." Sophie's dad stepped up, twice the size and doubly fierce. "You see, we have a vet here and a council official. It seems you have a record for breaching your licence more times than most people have had hot dinners."

"We're saved!" Emma leapt round Rachel's neck, clinging on like a monkey. We all fell together in a scrum, clutching each others' hands, our cries of delight mingling with Emma's screechy laughter. I had a dreamy grin on my face and Sophie was happier than I'd ever seen her.

"The Brook House Six Pack for ever!" Emma yelled, scaring Buzby who was tied up to the horsebox, trying to peel the varnish off with his teeth.

"Does this mean I'm reinstated?" Kate asked, trying to disguise her anxiety.

"Of course." Sophie smiled warmly. "There's no need for secrets, or pretence any more – we all know each other, warts and all. From now on, we'll be there for each other – like real friends."

Kate put an arm round Rachel's shoulder. Then we all put our hands together and swore agreement.

Brook House Riding School was saved. So were Rocket, Buzby, Archie, dear old Rusty, Ebony Jane, Frank and all the other gorgeous horses I'd grown to love. They wouldn't have to be split up, not ever.

Mrs Brentford wasn't selling out to the building company. Neither was she retiring. Sophie's dad had agreed to fund the school as a silent partner. Horseworld Centre would lose its licence for sure and three people had already come up to us and asked about the Young Riders Club. We referred them to Kate as reigning president.

Archie had attracted quite a fan club already and desperately tried to look shamefaced when he stole a little girl's ice cream. All the ponies were thoroughly enjoying the show and even Buzby was being well-behaved, with an over-docile expression on his face, which no doubt meant he was plotting his next trick.

Guy had raced back to the school to fetch Frank so that Mrs Brentford could enter the veteran in hand class. The show was carrying on because there were too many people there demanding that it should.

The only hiccup was that Minstrel had been relegated to the open class because a complaint had been lodged that he was over 14.2 hands. After being measured by the vet it turned out that he was fifteen hands with shoes. There was no rule to say that a stallion couldn't enter but the course for the taller ponies was far too big for us to manage.

I was sick with disappointment but elated for Sophie who with no pressure from her dad sailed round the novice to get fourth place and a green rosette and grooming bag.

Kate plucked up courage to enter the pairs clear round jumping with Emma and we pushed her into the ring with Archie who gawked at the tiny double as if it were a fire-breathing dragon. Kate set off tight-lipped and wooden with terror, but by the final fence she was jumping her socks off and loving every minute. Archie played to the spectators as only he could.

"You were brilliant." Emma shook her hand as

they rode out and then threw herself round Buzby's neck.

"Did I really say I was too scared to jump?" Kate grinned wildly, pushing back her riding hat and buzzing with the thrill. "From now on, Archie, we're going to have a jumping lesson every week, even if it means cancelling *Teen Dreams*, cleaning Dad's car and mowing the lawn."

"Jodie!" Guy strode up, catching admiring glances from all surrounding females but barely noticing. It made me feel important and temporarily deadened the sting of disappointment.

"Mrs Brentford says if you don't ride Minstrel in the open, she's going to ban you from Brook House and Sophie's dad is backing her up."

"You're joking." I almost gagged. "You are joking, aren't you?"

"You can do it!" Sophie squeezed my arm, followed by Emma and Rachel in a state of hyper-excitement.

"I'll talk you through the course," promised Guy, narrowing his eyes, gauging my reaction. "It's not that big, honestly. Minstrel can do it with his eyes closed and so can you."

Fear knocked me sideways and then suddenly gave way to a new feeling of recklessness. What if I didn't try? How would I feel riding home knowing that I hadn't given it a go? Minstrel deserved a chance – we both did.

"I'll meet you at the main ring in two minutes." Guy shot off, striding up to the secretary's tent.

"Remember how you first rode Minstrel when nobody else dared?" Kate looked at me with such intensity.

"Yeah, and remember how I dropped Frank's saddle when my leg seized up?"

"That won't happen." Kate practically grabbed hold of my shoulders and shook me. "It's mind over matter."

Steph was already brandishing my riding hat and gloves.

"You lot are nothing but a pack of overbearing bullies, do you know that?"

"Yep." Emma and Sophie frogmarched me forward. "It's all part of the Six Pack service."

"Two more to go and then you're in." Guy re-designed the practice jump to make a spread.

I'd never felt more sick in my life. My insides were churning up until I had to bend over the pommel of the saddle and clutch my stomach. Guy pretended not to notice. If I was sick now I'd never live it down.

"They're falling like flies," Emma reported back, filling me with confidence – not! Sophie altered my stirrups and Kate read out quotations from her diary which was supposed to make me feel better but didn't.

By now a wave of anxiety was crashing around inside me. I desperately wanted Mum to turn up but there was no sign. She'd promised to be here an hour ago.

A seventeen-hand, lanky thoroughbred with a giraffe neck, loped out of the ring with four faults. Amazingly there hadn't been a clear round yet. Guy said the standard of riding was appalling and the course was so flimsy, a fly could knock a pole down. I didn't care. At least when I blitzed every jump it woudn't be quite so embarassing.

Minstrel floated round the practice ring, delighted to be finally taking part and quivering with excitement. Even worse, every person in a hundred yards radius was staring at us.

"The greatest form of defence is attack." Mrs Brentford appeared from nowhere, beaming from ear to ear and reminding me of a little leprechaun or maybe a fairy, only she'd look ridiculous in a tutu. "Forget about your leg and it will forget about you," she whispered.

"Two minutes and then you're on." Guy cast an anxious glance at Minstrel. My teeth were chattering. "Hold him off the road jump and get a straight approach."

"Guy," I whispered, suddenly cracking altogether, "I don't think I can do it." I was convinced my left leg would be useless and Minstrel would take off in the ring. I just couldn't go through with it.

I was struggling to dismount when Mum's voice pierced across from the other side of the ring. I blinked in surprise when I saw who was there beside her. It was Dad. They were both waving frantically. I tried to wave back but was suspended half on, half off, as Minstrel danced on the spot and I desperately tried to scrabble back into the seat.

But everything was OK now. A lovely exhilarating warmth was flooding through me. Mum and Dad were here. They were still smiling as the loudspeaker crackled and spluttered and then called in number 37. That was my number.

"Ladies and gentlemen, we have with us a very special young lady who has overcome a terrible riding accident and debilitating injuries. This is her first time back in the ring and I'd like you to put your hands together and give a very warm welcome to Jodie and her young horse Minstrel."

I nearly died. Clapping broke out all round the ring, someone cheered and whistled and I saw Guy clapping with his hands above his head and Mum sticking up her thumbs. She wasn't freaking out, even though I was on horseback.

So this was facing up to my problem? Somebody had done this deliberately and I could bet all my post office savings it was Mrs Brentford. But somehow it wasn't too bad. I wasn't dying with embarrassment. It was no longer a huge secret. I didn't feel resentful or angry. I'd come to terms with my accident and moved on: I wasn't feeling sorry for myself any more, I was living my life.

"In you go, love, be quick." The steward guided us into the ring.

Minstrel seemed to sense my new peace of mind and walked quietly towards the start. I heard a group of girls gasp and admire Minstrel's beauty. But then I was sitting on every girl's dream – a chestnut Arabian stallion, and only I could ride him.

The first fence loomed up. Then the second. My leg didn't seize up. Minstrel listened to every aid I gave him and apart from missing out a stride at the double he did a perfect round. Nothing came down because he gave everything a foot to spare. Minstrel proved that he wasn't crazy or uncontrollable but a first-class showjumper who just needed some understanding. We both proved something in those few minutes which would stay with us for ever.

"You were brilliant!" The whole of the Six Pack went crazy as soon as I rode out of the ring. People were still clapping as I dismounted. All I could think of was Mum and Dad. And then suddenly they were there, wrapping their arms round me and kissing my hair. We clung to each other for what seemed like ages and I really couldn't speak. Minstrel was furious at being ignored and clonked me on the head with his chin.

I won a small silver trophy, a rosette and a red

cooler sheet for Minstrel which clashed with his chestnut coat.

Mrs Brentford came and congratulated me and then dashed off to the veteran class which she won with Frank who knocked spots off everybody at the grand old age of 22. Nobody was quite sure whether the veteran award was for Frank or Mrs Brentford!

Emma came last in the fancy dress mainly because Buzby had eaten all her tail feathers and she had fallen off trying to flap her arms like a chicken. Steph did incredibly well in the gymkhana races, picking up a fourth, a third and a second in the flag race. Altogether we'd collected thirteen rosettes, two trophies and countless horsy items between us. Not bad for a bunch of ponies everybody had written off.

I surprised even myself by linking arms with Dad and strolling round in Sophie's Union Jack shorts without feeling the slightest bit self-conscious. It turned out to be Kate who had tipped off the commentator. She eventually admitted it after chasing Archie round the beer tent for half an hour.

"Jodie!" Sophie charged up just as I had finally found a few moments to thank Minstrel for the best day of my life. "Something incredible's happened," she gasped. "Are you listening? This is so important."

"You have my undivided attention." I tried to keep a straight face and failed.

"Dad wants you to have Minstrel on loan. He'll pay all the expenses. You can have him as your very own horse – we won't have to sell him." She gave me a hug and then Minstrel, and searched my face for a reaction.

I could feel the emotion building up like a tidal wave about to sweep through my body, but for the moment I was numb.

"Jodie?" Sophie's jaw went slack and she narrowed her eyes in panic. "Don't you want him?"

And then it came. Dizzy, heady euphoria that had me dancing round the horsebox, clutching Sophie's hands, tears of happiness and relief springing up in my eyes.

"It's j-just the best," I stuttered, my mouth collapsing so that I sounded unintelligible. I mumbled another sentence and Sophie's face clouded over in confusion. Minstrel half-heartedly kicked his partition for attention.

I blew my nose and took a deep breath but all that came out was a whimper. "I said . . ." I paused, struggling to find composure.

Sophie's nose twitched as she tried not to laugh.

"I was going to say . . ." I paused again, and then deliberately raising my voice to mega-decibels, I shouted, "Brook House is the best riding school in the world!"

Emma

Chapter One

"I heard him on the phone," insisted Steph, wringing her hands in despair. "He was telling his mother that she was the most fantastic girl he'd ever clapped eyes on, with a brilliant personality and just what he'd been looking for all his life."

"Are you sure he was talking about a woman?" said Kate.

"Well who do you think he was talking about, the prime minister?" Steph paced up and down, getting more and more irate. "Anyway, he's been wearing a new aftershave lately, that says it all."

"Oh big deal." Kate folded her arms. "Good detective work, Sherlock."

"Just because he's our riding instructor, doesn't mean he has to be a monk," Rachel pointed out.

I was sitting at the table writing out pony care fact sheets in an effort to swot up for the riding school stable management certificate.

We'd officially formed what we called the "Six Pack" at the start of the summer holidays. Six horse-mad girls all dedicated to Brook House

Riding School which had very nearly closed down. Sophie's dad had stepped in at the last moment as a silent partner and saved the school and the horses. Since then Brook House had gone from strength to strength and we all dedicated our weekends and every spare moment to helping out with the ponies and improving our riding. Sophie was really nice, Jodie quite serious, Rachel shy, Kate bossy and Steph moody, but we all had one thing in common – Horses!

"You don't get it, do you?" Steph raised her arms in alarm. "If Guy falls in love there'll be no special evening lessons or picnics or quizzes or pony weeks. He'll be too busy going out on dates – he won't have time for us!"

Real concern flickered over everyone's faces. All the Six Pack helped out at weekends and holidays and in return were often given a free lesson from Guy. We'd all got used to hogging his time; we'd had him all to ourselves for five weeks and our riding had come on in leaps and bounds. Without Guy's energy and enthusiasm, Brook House would revert back to being just an ordinary riding school instead of something dynamic and special.

"We've got to do something," Sophie muttered.

"It's for his own good," nodded Kate.

"And for Brook House, and for his showjumping career," said Rachel.

"And for the horses," I added, thinking as always of our four-legged friends.

"We don't have a choice." Sophie chased away any doubts. We all nodded.

"Only nineteen hours to go!" Rachel burst into the horsy saloon where we hung out between lessons and chores, looking as if she was about to explode with excitement.

Own a Pony Week had been Guy's idea and had proved a sell-out success. Basically each person had a pony to look after for the whole week which involved grooming, feeding, mucking out and riding. There were loads of activities planned such as group lessons, hacks, a treasure hunt, cross country, polo and even ice skating one evening. It was just the most happening event ever. I'd got my name down first and booked Buzby, my favourite riding school pony. Owning him for a week was going to be incredible. And it all started at nine tomorrow morning.

I slipped into Buzby's stable where he was tacked up waiting for the next ride. He was a gorgeous dapple grey. He was cheeky and mischievous but I loved him to bits and spent all my spare time looking after him and pretending he was mine. Now it was really going to happen, at least for one week.

I rummaged through my new grooming box which had taken me ages to save up for and pulled out the "cactus cloth" which was supposed to make stable stains miraculously disappear. Buzby scowled, knotting his woolly brows together in disapproval.

Guy wasn't just an ordinary riding instructor. He was a showjumper with two Dutch warmblood horses and his ambition was to ride for England one day. Even Kate, who was scared of jumping, had improved beyond all recognition.

It was our ambition for Brook House to be voted Riding School of the Year but we all knew we had heaps of improving to do before then. I bent down and brushed out Buzby's fetlocks which seemed to act as magnets for bits of dried mud.

"Where's Steph?" Sophie popped her head over the door, looking harassed. "She's wanted pronto in the arena."

I shrugged. Steph was really good at disappearing when there was work to be done.

"OK," I groaned, "I'll try and find her." There was no way I was going to do Steph's chores for her, especially the lead rein class. I checked the saloon and then went to see if she was with her grey pony, Monty.

I eventually tracked her down in the office where she was bent over the desk.

144

"You creep," I howled, after peering over her right shoulder.

"Get lost, Emma." She spun round, eyes blazing, and stuffed the half wrapped present inside her jacket pocket. "It's nothing to do with you."

It was Guy's birthday today and I'd bought him a pencil with a horsy rubber and made a carrot and mint cake for his horses, although Buzby had already devoured half of it. We all knew that Steph had a crush on Guy but now it stood out a mile – she'd bought him a pair of leather riding gloves which must have cost a bomb.

I danced around the office tormenting her until she turned bright red.

"Ouch." She came up behind me and yanked at my hair.

"That'll teach you to grow up." She could be so spiteful. "You can be such a baby, Emma. At least I don't play with model horses and pretend to ride broomsticks. At least boys like me. You'll never get a boyfriend the way you behave."

"You snake!" I squeaked, really stung. I reeled back and desperately tried to think of something to say. I knew I'd regret it as soon as the words tumbled out.

"Well that's where you're wrong," I croaked, "because boys do like me. In fact, as a matter of fact . . ." I floundered but couldn't stop myself. " . . . I've got a boyfriend."

Steph gaped and then opened and shut her mouth in shock. A wave of triumph swept over me when I saw her lost for words.

"You're kidding."

"I am not! His name's Craig and he's horse-mad and he thinks Buzby's the best pony in the world."

"Well then he must be a fool." Steph raised an eyebrow, unsure what to think.

I really did have a pen pal called Craig who was coming to Brook House for Own a Pony Week but I'd never met him face to face before.

"Well you'll be able to judge for yourself," I snapped back, digging myself a ten foot hole, "because he's coming here tomorrow – and he's staying the whole week!"

Chapter Two

"Emma, breakfast!" Mum bellowed up through the floorboards.

I always believe that if you blank something out of your mind then somehow it will go away or at least not turn out half as bad. So on the morning of Own a Pony Week I leapt out of bed, revelling in the thrill of looking after Buzby for a whole week and not giving Craig or Guy a second thought.

Mickey, my pet hamster, irritated that I'd been up for two minutes without noticing him, raced frantically on his wheel for thirty seconds, leapt off and flipped over the lego jumps I'd set up in his cage. I gave him his Happy Hamster treat which had become a morning ritual and pulled on my best jods and yellow riding shirt. Grabbing my riding hat, I ran onto the landing, and clinging to the banister, pretended the stairs were a cross-country complex at Badminton.

Dad was in his special chair, not reading his paper for once. Mum was wearing her anxious look which said, "I've got to support your dad so please understand." Something was definitely up.

"Now, Emma, about this pony week." Dad's glasses always steamed up when he drank his tea. I tried not to smile. "We've spent a lot of money at that riding school this year and it seems to us all you've learnt is how to have your head in the clouds. You're still in the same riding group that you were in at the start of the year."

"Yes, but Dad—"

"I don't want to hear your excuses, Emma. I'm not paying out for special riding courses if all you're going to do is muck about with your friends."

"But I don't," I protested, a lump of panic rising in my throat.

"Your mum and I, well we've decided, that if you don't pass the certificate for this pony week, well . . . we're going to have to reconsider your weekly lessons."

"What?" I fell forward on my chair which I'd been rocking back. "But you can't." I looked at Mum pleadingly but she buried her head in the fridge.

"Anyway, it'd be a good thing if you took up another sport – it's not as if we'll ever be able to buy you a pony. What about netball or gymnastics – there are other things apart from riding."

"There are *not*!" I yelled, knowing I shouldn't really answer back, but unable to stop myself. "Riding is everything. Without ponies I'd shrivel up and die."

"Now, Emma, you're being dramatic." Dad shuffled awkwardly.

"*I am not*." I could feel my face going crimson. "If you take me away from Brook House, I'll never speak to you again. Not ever. And I'll stop eating. I'll go on a fast."

Dad smiled as if that was funny and I burst into tears, huge racking sobs that startled even me. As a baby I'd been able to sob for England and I obviously hadn't lost the knack.

"I hate you." I drew back, gasping from the shock of what I'd just said, feeling as if someone had slapped me across the face. Then I grabbed my bag and bolted for the door, unable to look at their wounded faces.

Mum and Dad had adopted me when I was three years old and had been fantastic parents ever since. I knew they tried to afford as much as they could and it wasn't always easy. I felt terrible about what I'd said. The bus was five minutes late so I dived into the newsagent's and bought two Mars Bars, a Bounty and some Chocolate Buttons.

The car had to beep three times before I registered

Sophie hanging out of the window. I usually had a lift with Rachel but she was at the dentist.

"Why didn't you tell me you needed a lift?" Sophie homed in on my face and the chocolate bulging out of my pockets. Mr Green eased the expensive Jaguar out of the bus lane and pretended not to notice that I'd been crying. Sophie immediately squeezed my hand. We had a rule in the Six Pack that we would all be there for each other, through thick and thin, and although we had our squabbles, when it really counted we didn't let each other down.

"We'll talk about it at the stables," Sophie whispered and I felt the frantic beating in my chest beginning to ease. Sophie was the nicest person I'd ever met and even though her dad was rich she was normal and down to earth and never once showed off. All her thoughts were always for other people.

"There's only one thing you can do," said Sophie. We were sitting on a straw bale in the barn. It was the only private place we could find – the yard was buzzing. "You've got to pass the stable management certificate."

"You don't understand," I hissed at Sophie, trying to keep the tremble out of my voice. "You're talking to the person who only got three per cent in her last school exam."

"But this is different – it's assessed on the whole week, and it's about horses."

"Sophie, you're not listening. You're a brain, I never remember anything. I'm thick."

"You are not, you just panic. Now have faith. You can do it, I'll help you." Sophie put an arm round my shoulder but I still felt completely hopeless.

"Emma Parker?" Guy called out my name and I went up to get my special badge and schedule for the week. The saloon was milling with people and the Six Pack had resorted to sitting on top of the table we usually reserved for cleaning tack.

There was no sign of Craig. I remembered seeing his picture in *In the Saddle* and it was his carrot-red hair that had first drawn me to him. I thought he looked interesting and good fun.

"Rachel Banks? Jessica Friar?" Every pony at the riding school had been booked apart from Elvis and Faldo, two New Forest ponies who had only just been broken in. Rachel came back with her badge marked Rusty – her favourite pony. Guy explained that today we were going to ride in the school so that everybody could get used to their ponies.

A whoop went up from the front when Guy confirmed that the last day was cross-country with a professional photographer coming in to take pictures of everyone jumping, free of charge. Despite everything, a flame of excitement was lighting up in my stomach. This was it! We'd all thought of nothing else for weeks. Various instructions followed, for example no running round the stables, keeping the muck heap tidy, no leaving gates open and everybody being responsible for their own belongings.

I was just beginning to breathe a sigh of relief that I'd got off scot-free, when the western-style louvred doors flew back on their hinges and Craig stumbled in, mumbling some apology about getting up late, his red face matching his hair.

I was so embarrassed, I couldn't look up. Craig pushed forward and grabbed the only available chair, which was Guy's, then winked at me and mouthed hello. I smiled back woodenly and cursed Steph who was thumping her chest, imitating a beating heart. I barely heard the rest of Guy's instructions and suddenly decided this was the worst day of my life. And it wasn't going to get any better.

"He's awful!" Kate rode up on Archie. "What on earth do you see in him?"

You could always rely on friends to be honest.

There were three other boys on pony week but they were all quiet and normal. In Craig's letters he said he could ride but there was no evidence of it in the school. His reins were up round his chin and his feet rammed back in the stirrups. Guy was trying to instruct us but Craig was keeping a one-way conversation going with Sophie.

After half an hour he had fallen off twice but the worst thing was that he was doing it deliberately to show off in front of Sophie. Guy seemed to be getting really annoyed and I felt he was blaming me. The more worried I got the more nervous I became and my riding deteriorated. I lost all my coordination and Buzby ploughed into a holly bush which scratched me all down the side of my face.

"You OK?" Rachel kicked forward on Rusty. "There are too many riders on the arena," she whispered. "Guy should have separated us into two groups."

"As nearly everybody seems to have bonded with their ponies, I'd like to move on to canter." Guy paced up and down in front of a pair of jump wings.

"Oh cripes." Rachel snuck back into her position, two rides behind.

"If he carries on riding this badly, he'll kill

himself." Steph trotted past on Monty looking bemused. "Do something, Emma, he's your boyfriend." Softening just a little, I remembered how I used to talk non-stop in riding lessons because I was so nervous. Craig was probably acting the fool for the same reason.

"If you just sit back and push your heel down you'll find it a lot easier to stay on," I said, riding up to him and putting on my friendliest smile.

He wrinkled up his freckled face as if he was going to crack a joke. Then, like a viper, he spat out, "Shut up, fatso, I don't need your help."

Two girls in the line tittered but Guy was up at the other end and didn't hear, thank goodness. I felt mortified, as if this awful boy had just viciously squeezed my heart and wrung the life out of it. Nobody had ever referred to my weight before, at least not to my face. I could feel hot colour sweeping up my neck. My chest felt tight. I had to get away. Out of the arena. I couldn't stem the tears that were welling up.

"Emma Parker, where are you going?" Guy was always really strict on his lessons and we respected him for it.

"Buz, walk on!" I thumped my heels into Buzby's sides but he wouldn't budge. I felt as if my cheeks were going to burst into flame. Gradually the whole ride were pulling up and staring.

"Get on!" I flapped the reins in vain and then in desperation raised my crop and tapped Buz down the shoulder. Squealing with indignation he flattened his ears and arched his back in a stilted buck. I could feel Craig's mocking eyes boring into me and everybody else's too.

"Emma, what's the matter?" Sophie was suddenly there on Rocket, the picture of concern.

I couldn't stand it any more. I was whirring with humiliation.

"Just leave it," I mumbled and jumped off Buz. I fled to the saloon, racking sobs breaking loose as soon as I was through the doors. At that moment it wasn't Craig I hated, or the girls who had giggled, it was me – for being so thick and stupid. I stared down at my round, fleshy arms and angrily pinched the loose skin until a vivid red mark flared up.

"Emma?"

My head jerked up in alarm. "Jodie!" I couldn't believe she was sitting there, as large as life. "But you're supposed to be in India!" A lovely warm surge of comfort ran through me. Good, solid, practical Jodie who had a solution for everything. She was at my side in seconds, hugging me and passing me endless tissues.

"Mum and I came home early because Dad had

to work all the time and I was missing Minstrel so much I felt ill."

She'd had her hair cut which made her look more grown-up and she was in new clothes which showed off her skinny figure. "You look wonderful," I croaked, tears still streaming down my face. "I'm s-so glad you're back."

"Me too." She grasped my hands and stared pointedly into my swollen eyes. "But Em, you've got to tell me, what's happened to get you into this state?"

Chapter Three

"These are nags, not quality horses," snapped the girl, turning on her heel and clipping past Frank's stable. "Where's the owner? I'm not going to be ripped off."

She'd appeared from nowhere in a flashy sports car without an appointment and had demanded to be shown the horses. She was every riding school's worst nightmare. She had big loop earrings and high heels and thought she knew everything. We weren't supposed to be rude to customers, but she wasn't a horse lover – it stood out a mile.

Guy was having a meeting in the house with the owner, Mrs Brentford, the full-time groom, Sandra, and Sophie's dad. Everyone else was having lunch in the saloon and playing charades. I'd sneaked out to give Buzby a coconut slice and check his water.

"This is Ebony Jane." I introduced the gorgeous bay horse in the next stable. She was an ex-race-horse with a sweet nature, and was one of the most popular horses at the riding school. She was old now, with weak hocks which prevented her from jumping, but she was safe and trustworthy and had taught hundreds of people to ride.

"Ebby won a race once, a handicap. There's a picture of her in the tack room." I kissed her soft nose and then stood on the hinge of the door to undo her head collar.

"OK, I don't want the dinosaur's history." The girl's face crumpled as if she'd just eaten something distasteful. "Have you got anything better?"

"But Ebby's lovely," I protested. "She's kind and gentle and wouldn't hurt a fly." The words poured out but she wasn't even listening. She'd moved on to the next stable where her critical eyes were greedily devouring Minstrel.

"Now this looks more like it," she said. The stunning chestnut Arab glanced across from his hay net, snorted, then went back to the more serious matter of eating.

"He's not in the riding school," I informed her, with great pleasure.

"This is the one I'm riding," she claimed, completely ignoring me and rushing forward to draw back the bolt on the stable door.

"He's not on offer." Jodie's voice was hard and brittle behind me.

The girl stopped in her tracks and swivelled round, her lips parted.

"As Emma's just told you, he's not a riding school horse."

She glanced sideways as if noticing me for the first time. Then she weighed up Jodie. After a brief silence she seemed to accept the situation.

"Fair enough," she said, her interest in Minstrel fizzling out in a flash. For a second I felt envious of Jodie for the way she could handle grown-ups at the age of twelve – only a year older than me.

"Perhaps you could tell me where I could find Guy Marshall?"

"Right here." Jodie pointed to where Guy was striding out of the house, looking intently at the girl, his face splitting into a wide grin. It was so unlike Guy because usually he hated undesirable clients. I tried to knot my brows together to warn him that she was trouble.

"I thought you'd got lost," he almost gasped, holding out a sun-browned hand and clasping hers. Jodie and I exchanged looks of confusion. Guy never behaved like this.

"It seems your little pupils don't follow the celebrities like they used to." The girl stepped nearer to Guy as if she was sharing a private joke with him. Then she looked pointedly at us, her tawny, oval eyes glittering with amusement. "You see, girls," she said flicking back her oat-blond hair, "I'm Cindy Morell. And if you've read any pony

159

magazines lately you'll know that I'm a famous eventer."

"Cindy Morell was here and you didn't recognize her?" Steph's voice was stony with shock. She was pressed up against the saloon window with Kate and Sophie, in the vain hope that Cindy might return that afternoon and they could get her autograph.

"Well, she kind of looked different without her riding gear," I mumbled, feeling quite important since I'd been the first to meet her. Not only was she a famous eventer, but she was romantically linked with a vet from the fab TV series *Animal Kingdom* which I watched religiously every week.

"So why does somebody like that want to hire a riding school horse?" Rachel was sitting at the table showing the least enthusiasm.

"Because she's up here staying with relatives and she wants a horse to ride." Kate rolled her eyes as if Rachel was stupid.

"There's got to be more to it than that," said Rachel screwing up her elflike face. "Haven't any of you considered for one second that she might be the mystery girlfriend?"

Steph's jaw dropped. Kate let out a low groan. Jodie, who had been writing her diary, looked up with total indifference. "I don't know why you're all so star-struck," she grumbled. "And you, Emma, know as well as I do that Cindy Morell is ambitious and mean. And if Guy does get involved with her she'll eat him for breakfast."

I blushed uncomfortably, knowing full well that I'd turned a blind eye to Cindy's behaviour since I'd found out that she was famous.

"Oh no!" Steph turned from the window, a hand flying up to her mouth. "It's Guy, he's seen us, and he's coming across – he looks furious."

"Well, for once we haven't done anything wrong," Jodie said and carried on writing.

Steph and Kate looked at each other, the colour draining from their faces. "W-we kind of left a load of magazines open in the office about how relationships can ruin your life."

"Oh great, girls, full marks for subtlety," said Jodie, wincing.

We could hear Guy's footsteps approaching. "Quick!" whispered Kate, and we all dived for the horsy manuals on the table and started reading, regardless of the fact that every book was upside down.

"Look, I'm sorry, OK? I didn't realize you'd get that upset." Craig hovered in the doorway of Buzby's stable, awkwardly shuffling his feet. "At my riding school we're always calling each other names, but it doesn't mean anything."

In the half-light of the stable he almost looked genuine. He swallowed hard, rubbing his hand up his neck nervously, and again repeated, "I – I didn't mean it."

Buzby stepped backwards so I couldn't hide behind his shoulder any longer. Feeling exposed, I fixed my eyes on the far manger, humiliation colouring my cheeks for the second time. I'd never forget those girls tittering.

"Look, I can't be that bad – Buzby likes me." Craig shot me a look of appeal as Buzby started licking his outstretched hand. Trust Buz to betray me.

"Can't we be friends?" He deliberately softened his voice. "For Buzby's sake at least." I had to admit, when Craig was being nice he did have a certain charm.

"Look! Up there!" He pointed sharply at the rafters. I'd looked up before I even realized. "Got you!" He had his head cocked to one side and a smile playing on his lips. Before I could stop myself I was smiling back.

"That's better," he said, patting Buzby's nose.

"If you like I could show you all the horses in the yard and we could pair up for the treasure hunt tomorrow," I offered.

The smile slipped from Craig's face. "Listen," he said changing the subject, "if that Marshall bloke asks, we're the best of friends, OK?"

I nodded mutely as he backed out of the stable. "If you need any help . . ." I shouted, but he didn't answer.

"My, my." Steph popped her head round the door, grinning triumphantly and clutching the big yard brush in front of her. She made no secret of the fact that she'd been listening behind the door. "We're getting very pally, aren't we? I thought you hated his guts?"

"That was this morning," I said, pulling a face. "Anyway, it was a misunderstanding."

"Puh. I've never seen you so upset."

"Steph, can't you go back to your sweeping or something? Or better still, go trample on the muck heap."

"What's the matter?" Sophie came over, weighed down with two saddles and countless bridles that she was carting back to the tack room.

"Craig's apologized and now Emma's in love again."

"No I am not!" I snapped, all uptight.

"Oh Em." Sophie dropped her load and looked at me as if I were weak in the head. "Don't forgive too easily. You always see everyone through rose-coloured spectacles."

"Excuse me?" I raised my voice indignantly.

A blue car swung into the drive and pulled up on the grass verge near the barn. It was Mum and Dad. My heart somersaulted and landed somewhere near my knees. "If anyone's got some apologizing to do, it's me," I groaned. And leaving them to it, I walked across the yard rehearsing what I was going to say for the hundredth time that day.

"I'm sorry," I said. Guy was absolutely livid. My eyes filled with tears and I wanted to put my hands over my mouth to stop myself from sobbing.

I had arrived at the stable the next morning to find that someone had left the pitchfork in Buzby's stable and the lid off the feed bin full of the coarse mix that was kept especially for him.

"Have you any idea what could have happened if he'd stood on that pitchfork?" Guy asked.

I nodded, hardly able to breathe for the knot of fear in my chest. It was too unbearable to even think about it.

"The whole idea of pony week is that you are responsible for your own pony. You were the last in his stable." Guy was speaking extra-slowly as if to emphasize each word.

I remembered quite clearly bedding Buz down and filling up his water. I *couldn't* have left the

164

fork in the stable – I'd never done anything like that in my life. I was always so careful. But no matter how much I tried, I couldn't actually remember putting the pitchfork back in the feed room. I'd been thrown first by Craig, and then by Mum and Dad arriving.

"And then there's the feed bins." Guy sank back in the swivel chair, looking tired and drawn. "How many times have I told you girls to replace the lids?"

"L-lots," I stammered, feeling worse than I'd ever felt in my life.

"If vermin get to the food, they can spread infection. I expected better of you, Emma. I know how much you love that pony."

My eyes welled up and the floor became a blur.

"Had it been anybody else, I'd have sent them packing." said Guy. "Anyway, let this be the end of it. But I don't want to have to call you back in here." There was more than a hint of warning in his voice. "If you want a certificate at the end of the week it's got to be flying colours from now on. I can't give you preferential treatment."

"No. Thanks." I stumbled out of the door in a daze.

"It could have happened to anybody." Rachel was trying her best to make me feel better. All the Six

165

Pack were being ultra-supportive but I still felt like the most useless person in the world. At least I wasn't the only person to get told off that morning. Someone had left a dismantled bridle on the radiator to dry.

Rachel got two star points for the tidiest stable and the cleanest grooming kit. I tried not to feel too jealous. At least Buzby had done well in the showjumping. Guy had set up a "Chase me Charlie" where the jump gradually gets higher and riders are knocked out if they have a refusal or four faults. Although Buzby was one-paced and tended to jump in slow motion, he was really careful and snapped up his front legs.

When the jump was at two foot nine with a spread there was just Steph, Craig and myself left in. Craig, as if by magic, had suddenly started riding properly.

"As you seem to have miraculously discovered the art of riding, perhaps you could go first?" Guy smiled tightly at Craig, well aware that up to now he'd just been larking about.

"Good luck." I grinned at him as Foxy sidled towards the jump, swishing her tail. Craig was riding on a really short rein, kicking her forward with grim determination. She flew over the jump like a gazelle, but clipped the left wing. The top pole rolled, wavered and then tipped off, flopping on to the soft sand.

"You should have used more left leg," Guy called. "And slower, much slower, it's not a race."

A few minutes later Steph turned bright red when Monty ground to a halt in front of the red and white poles.

"OK, Emma, you're next."

I wheeled Buzby round and kicked extra-hard to get him away from the other ponies. Remembering everything that Guy had taught us I clamped my legs round his sides and kept them there all the way to the jump. Buzby saw a good stride and lengthened, grunting with the effort. All the other ponies, including Minstrel, had got over-excited at repeating the same jump and made mistakes, but Buz only ever got excited about food.

"Come on, boy." This was his chance to shine. I forgot how scared I was and squeezed harder, snapping my eyes shut as he launched himself upwards. "Go on! Go on!"

Kate dropped her reins and started clapping like mad. Buz shot off round the arena, as startled as everyone else. The poles were still in their cups. He'd given it a good, wide berth.

"You brilliant, gorgeous, wonderful pony." I collapsed on his neck, hugging him to death, kissing his spiky mane.

"Well done." Steph rode up, a forced smile on her face. "You'd think your boyfriend would at least have congratulated you," she taunted in a thin voice.

"And I suppose you aren't peeved in the slightest?" Kate rode past, arching her eyebrows at Steph, who we all knew liked to be the best at everything.

"Oh Steph, lay off. You've just got the hump because you lost." Sophie flicked a bread roll at Steph and got a reprimanding look from Guy across the room. The saloon had been turned into a dinner hall with long trestle-tables and wooden chairs, and Mrs Brentford and Sandra were serving up hot chicken curry, jacket potatoes or vegetarian chilli.

Steph was laying into me relentlessly about Craig sitting at another table.

"Well can you blame him? The Six Pack are pretty formidable." Rachel grabbed her glass of water after testing the chicken curry. "What's in that?" she gasped.

"Kangaroo meat," Steph answered, peering at the other table over her shoulder. There were four boys and eleven girls on pony week and everyone seemed to have split off into groups.

"The girl with the long plait fancies Craig,"

Steph whispered dramatically, covering her mouth with her hand. "Watch out, Em."

It was as if she knew I was hiding something. I shuffled uneasily, my conscience pricking me more and more. I was just about to change the subject to the treasure hunt which was starting at two o'clock when Guy came across with two orange rosettes, handing one to Rachel and the other to me. In the middle was printed Brook House Riding School: Special Achievement. It was fantastic. It was a life-saver. When my parents saw this they'd have to let me carry on riding.

"Well done, Em," said Sophie, obviously sensing the relief I felt.

"Well aren't you going to show your boyfriend?" Steph's voice grated, oozing resentment.

"There's something I've got to tell you," I blurted out, my conscience finally winning. "Craig's not my boyfriend. I lied. He's my pen pal and until yesterday. I'd only seen his photograph. We hardly know each other."

Silence. Steph glowed with smugness. "I knew it, I just knew it."

Kate looked thunderous. There was a rule in the Six Pack about being totally honest with one another.

"It's all right, Em, don't worry," Sophie reassured me, but even she sounded wounded.

"No it's not!" Kate leapt up, scraping back her chair. "I got chucked out of the Six Pack for telling lies – you can't just ignore it."

"Your case was very different," Jodie mumbled.

"No it wasn't. A lie is a lie. And I think it stinks." She stalked off causing everyone to glance across with casual interest.

"She'll come round." Sophie grimaced, pursing her lips.

"Yeah," said Rachel trying to ease the awkwardness.

Gradually, one by one, they all got up and left, leaving me sitting there on my own, staring at a huge plate of chilli. I looked up at Craig's table. He had his back to me, but the girl with the long plait stared back. She was one of the girls who had tittered the first day in the arena. My face flushed and I was about to look away when she puffed out her cheeks, making fun of my weight. I jerked my head away. And for the first time in my life, I skipped lunch and left the table.

Chapter Four

"A feather, a fir cone, a hoof pick, a ball of lambswool? Is this for real?" Sophie screwed up her nose as she scanned the list.

> A pair of odd socks
> A lead rope
> A chocolate egg
> A strand of horse hair
> A rubber band

"They're easy." Kate snatched the list from Sophie, running her finger impatiently down the page. "Oh cripes, these are the difficult ones." She read aloud, slowly for emphasis: "A golf ball, a round white stone, a four-leaf clover!"

"Look, there are clues," said Jodie, trying to read upside down. "They must have hidden things deliberately."

"Not a four-leaf clover," Kate scoffed. "I've never even seen one."

"They could be plastic," Sophie suggested sensibly.

"Now listen up everybody," said Guy walking round with a clipboard. "I want you all to split up into groups of three and you'll be started off at ten-minute intervals. You've got three hours to find as many treasures as you can. There are twenty items altogether, some more difficult than others. The route is all mapped out for you and you are not to stray from the designated trail. Is that clear?"

"Yes, Mr Marshall."

"There'll be refreshments back at the stables for when you finish, which must be within three hours or you'll be eliminated. Each team must work together and stay together. There's a set of saddle-bags for one member of each team which can be used for carrying the treasure and soft drinks and snacks, but remember, no glass bottles or containers. Are there any questions?"

Kate shot up her hand. "Can we pick our own teams?"

"I don't see why not, providing there's no squabbling."

"I bag Steph and Sophie." Kate glared at me, making her feelings quite plain.

"That leaves Rachel, Jodie and Emma." Sophie stated the obvious.

"There'll be special achievement rosettes for the

team which collects the most treasures as well as a horsy prize for each member."

My heart gave a little jump. If I could win two rosettes in one day Mum and Dad would be mega-impressed.

"Are there any more questions?" Guy waited, seeming anxious to get on.

"Just one." Craig waved his arm. I looked away quickly. Ever since the Chase me Charlie he'd treated me as if I was invisible. I couldn't help feeling a sting of rejection.

"Yes, Craig?" Even Guy bristled with dislike.

"I was just wondering, Mr Marshall," he said, loitering by the window having hardly listened to a word about the treasure hunt, "Could this possibly be Cindy Morell coming up the drive in the black and gold horsebox?"

Hysteria swept through the saloon. Within seconds, everybody had forgotten the treasure hunt and dashed outside. Cindy was driving the lorry herself and we could vaguely see a horse's head through one of the six windows.

"It's mega." Sophie grabbed my arm in excitement.

Steph rushed out of the saloon with a pen and notepad. "I've got to get her autograph!"

"What's going on?" Jodie appeared at my elbow, refusing to get caught up in the euphoria.

Cindy hopped down from the cab, wearing a pair of mauve jodhpurs and leather boots with spurs. Her sunglasses covered most of her face but her mouth curled up in a smug smile. Something seemed to be amusing her.

"What's wrong with you two?" Steph came back a minute later, triumphantly waving a piece of paper with Cindy's autograph. "She's really nice." She narrowed her eyes at Jodie. "You made her out to be awful."

Suddenly a loud, piercing neigh and a clattering of hoofs made everyone flinch in alarm. Guy strode up the horsebox ramp. All the riding school horses barged against their doors, Buzby with a thatch of hay between his ears. Minstrel started rearing and snorting and Jodie had to dash over to shut his top door. As a stallion he always became more excitable than the others.

Sophie rushed over after talking to Sandra. "I've found out what's going on," she said, her face glowing with excitement. "Guy's buying a horse from Cindy and having it here on a week's trial. It's an intermediate eventer—"

Before she could finish, a huge dun horse of about seventeen hands scrabbled down the ramp, hauling Guy for a few strides before it felt the jerk of the lead rein and came back to a halt. Cindy quietly observed everything from near the house where she was talking to Mrs Brentford.

The horse was fantastic. Its coat gleamed like golden syrup. It had a black mane and tail and black points which was normal for a dun horse, but around its eyes were unusual shadowy black rings. Cindy must have read everybody's thoughts because she shouted across, "Her stable name's Panda, for obvious reasons."

Guy was besotted. He couldn't stop patting or stroking her even when she gave him several friendly nips. Frank was the biggest riding school horse but he was half-Shire. Panda was big but athletic with it and really beautiful.

Annoyed that she had to stand still, she nudged Guy's shoulder, and managed to knock him slightly off balance in spite of his strength.

"So what do you think?" Guy was chuckling as he spotted us edging closer, dying to give Panda a stroke. Steph stared at him as if he'd gone crazy. Guy's brown eyes which were his best feature had softened to putty. He was hooked. "Isn't she the most fantastic girl in the world?"

"Well how was I to know he was talking about a horse?" Steph's face throbbed with annoyance at making such a gaffe. "Anybody else could have made the same mistake. I mean, the most fantastic girl in the world – it *had* to be a woman."

Rachel and Sophie howled with laughter and we clunked our crops together as we always did before the start of a lesson or a hack for good luck. I tightened Buzby's girth and felt the first drops of rain slither down my neck. Oh please let it stay fine, I thought. We all looked up at the leaden sky. The last thing we needed was to spend three hours digging up chocolate eggs and various other weird objects in the pouring rain.

Steph, Sophie and Kate were called up to the start which was at the end of the drive where Guy and Sandra were standing holding red armbands.

"Leave some treasure for us," Jodie shouted.

Minstrel whirled round in tight circles, his powerful red neck glistening like an oil slick as he lathered up in excitement. A couple of riders from the other teams shot admiring looks at Jodie as she coaxed him forward without the slightest show of nerves. Jodie had taken over the stallion when nobody else dared ride him. He belonged to Sophie but Jodie now had him on permanent loan. Sophie wasn't competitive and Rocket, who belonged to the riding school, suited her down to the ground.

Buzby shuffled forward, sulking because he had to carry the saddlebags. I dropped in line behind

Rachel and Rusty and was just about to shout to Jodie when a weird sensation shuddered right through me. It felt as if someone was staring straight through my back. Unable to stop myself, I glanced round.

And there was Craig. He was right behind me on Foxy and his eyes were like stones. He didn't smile or even move a muscle, but just stared back at me as if I didn't exist.

"What shall we do now?" Jodie cantered back up the grassy track on Minstrel who thought the last two hours had been one big hoot and was still bursting with energy. Buzby came to a dead stop as he heard me undoing the velcro fastening on my pocket. He wouldn't move forward until I'd given him three wine gums which he slurped for ages.

"We've got sixteen." Rachel crossed off the feather and the dock leaf which we'd found by the stream along with a stone which would have to pass as round and white. For the last half hour we hadn't found anything and had just ridden round and round in endless circles. Kate, Steph and Sophie were just ahead and had turned off the track in the direction of the stables. Heavy black clouds were looming.

"I think we ought to call it quits," said Rachel,

propping her knees up over the saddle flaps and resting her elbows.

Rachel and Jodie were my two closest friends, except for Sophie who was more like a big sister really. Rachel was the quietest and had only been riding for a few months. She suffered from asthma and was only allowed to ride if she had someone with her. She was already a better rider than Steph who'd been going to Brook House for three years. Rusty was her favourite pony and since she'd been at the stables he'd had a new lease of life. At twenty years old he could hold his own with any of the other ponies.

Jodie was the most practical and the best rider by far. Guy said she could be a professional if she stuck at it and Minstrel was already winning at shows. Everybody paid attention to Jodie, even Kate. Mrs Brentford said Jodie had an old head on young shoulders.

"We can't go back," I gulped, suddenly aware of what Rachel was saying. "We can't, we've got four more treasures to find."

"Emma, what is the matter with you?" Jodie looked bemused. "And why have you suddenly turned ultra-competitive – you're usually the first to give in."

"Just because winning this treasure hunt is

important to me, OK? I – I can't explain." And I couldn't – not about my parents.

"I don't want Minstrel out in a storm." Jodie was trying her best to keep the stallion calm, but he hated standing still for more than five seconds and he seemed to sense a storm was brewing.

"You go on," I said, trying to sound matter of fact. "I'll catch up – there's just one more place I want to check."

"But Guy said we weren't to split up." Rachel fiddled with her reins, concerned.

"We're not," I replied lightly. "I'll be fifteen minutes, if that, and who's going to know?"

Minstrel started pawing at the stony track and jerking his head up and down to show he was bored. "We'll come with you," said Jodie, but she sounded reluctant.

"Look, guys, will you just give me some space, please?"

Buzby strode down the narrow bridleway, convinced we must be taking a short cut, for why else would we be leaving the others? I shortened my reins to cross a wooden bridge over a dyke, then let him stretch into canter down a grassy track which ran alongside Rhododendron Wood. Mrs Brentford owned part of the wood where we had cross-country fences and where we'd be competing on the last day of pony week.

It was exhilarating to be alone for once with no instructor barking instructions and no other riders getting in the way. Buzby seemed to enjoy the freedom and I didn't have to squeeze him half as hard to keep him in canter.

On the edge of Mrs Brentford's boundary was a wooden shed which must have been used by the gamekeeper years ago. We called it Rhododendron Shed and were always dreaming of converting it into a secret headquarters for the Six Pack. I was positive I'd seen some toadstools growing round the back last Sunday when Sophie and I had come on a group hack. If we could just take back one more treasure, it might be the difference between winning and losing. I was desperate for another special achievement rosette. I could think of nothing else.

Buz slowed down abruptly and I had to grasp the martingale strap to keep my balance. A rabbit scuttled across the track, followed by a pheasant which disappeared into the undergrowth. Silence hung in the air. We entered the wood down a narrow track. The soft ground deadened the hoof beats and all we could hear was the gentle rustle of leaves as the breeze seemed to change direction and grow stronger. Buz became tense and I had to tap him down the shoulder to keep him moving forward.

There was the shed. It was just ahead, surrounded by wild rhododendron bushes which had been an expanse of dense colour earlier in the year. Mrs Brentford had been in the local paper asking people to preserve our national heritage and not to leave litter on footpaths.

I jumped off and dragged Buzby forward. He groaned until he spotted some thick, luxuriant grass. There was no way I'd get him to go behind the shed so I took off the lead rope wrapped round my waist and attached it to the head collar under his bridle. Then I unfastened the reins so he wouldn't stand on them and tied him to a branch in a quick release knot but with enough rope to allow him to carry on eating.

The toadstools were in a cluster, half out of sight, and I snapped off the largest and wrapped it carefully in a tissue. Seventeen out of twenty. Surely we had to win. Then I noticed that another one of the pale peach stalks had been broken off near the base and as I stood up, I caught sight of the hoof marks stamped into the grass. Somebody had already been here.

I suddenly became aware of the black, rain-laden sky. A nervous shiver rippled up my back. The practical voice in my head told me to stop being so stupid, and that there was nothing to be afraid of. But even so, I shrank back in a sudden wave of fear.

I yelled Buzby's name to break the heavy silence and it echoed through the trees as if the wood was whispering back to me. Buz shot up his head and looked at me like a naughty schoolboy and I felt all right again. Of course I wasn't all alone – I had Buz, and he was mean enough to scare anybody off. A smile forced its way onto my lips as I thought about how much he'd improved. When I first rode him he used to go down on one knee to throw riders off. He cow-kicked and bucked and deliberately trod on people's toes. For a lovely moment, I really felt, more than ever before, that he was my very own pony.

A wild thrashing from the shed cut through the silence making us both jump with terror. My heart pounded beneath my ribs. Something was banging against the window in a frenzy and I knew instinctively that it was alive. Buzby's huge brown eyes were glued to the shed, his body alert and his jaw half open, trailing uneaten grass. If it was something really bad he'd have pulled backwards by now. I forced myself to turn round and look, swallowing deeply, my stomach muscles clenching at the thought of what I might see . . .

It was a bird. A sparrow. It was flying into the window and stunning itself over and over again, desperate to escape. It must have got in through the roof.

I breathed a long sigh of relief. I'd have to open the door and free it. And quickly. Before the poor thing knocked itself out. The shed was very low, but with a sturdy bolt which seemed much too big for the door.

I hauled it back and peered into the musty dimness. There was an old chair in the corner and some kind of stove. A roll of netting was propped up in the far corner together with some wooden crates. The sparrow was perched on one of them, its beady eyes darting to the open door. Its needle-thin legs quivered and it fluttered its left wing which had a feather hanging loose.

"Poor little thing," I whispered, ducking my head as I stepped inside with the intention of shooing it out. It blinked at me once and then seeing an escape route, it launched itself upwards and hovered in the air for a few seconds, panic-stricken. I clapped my hands and it swerved through the doorway and out into the fresh air and freedom. I'd saved its life.

Suddenly a deafening crack of thunder ripped through the dark sky. I swung my head round to the window to see Buzby rooted to the spot, paralysed with fear, his eyes rolling wildly. We had to get out of here. One of the trees could fall at any minute. I felt sick with fright, and knew I'd done the wrong thing coming here. I should have listened to Jodie.

I rushed to the door, but was just a stride away when it crashed shut, cutting off most of the the light. I blinked in the sudden darkness then heard the bolt scraping against wood.

"No!" I flew forward, groping for a handle – anything. Footsteps shuffled and then the bolt slammed across with a sickening thud. Somebody had locked me in.

"No, let me out! There's someone in here! Let me out!" I was screaming at the top of my voice, fighting to be heard over the noise of the storm, but no one came back. Crazy with fear, I turned and banged my fists against the window.

Buzby twirled round and round under the trees, as trapped as I was. There, on the edge of the clearing, I caught a glimpse of somebody. Yes, whoever it was turned and hesitated, then moved away, ducking under the low branches. Their coat snagged on one of the brambles – a kind of purple mac with chevron stripes. And then nothing. Just a blur of trees and a heavy curtain of pounding rain.

My lips began to tremble. I hunched my shoulders and let my head droop, feeling suddenly weary. I pressed my forehead against the cold glass of the window, trying to work out what to do next. I'd been locked in here deliberately. Of that I was sure. And whoever had done it, was a very sick kind of person. Because there was an innocent pony at risk, not just a brainless girl who shouldn't be here in the first place.

The second crack of thunder sounded as if it were splitting the earth. My mind was numb. I was cold to the core. I felt like someone else as I stared at the terrified pony under the trees, jerking against the lead rope, struggling now in a blind panic to break free. I'd let him down. I was putting him through a nightmare. I had to do something.

Groping wildly round the shed my hands brushed one of the wooden crates. My only chance of escape was through the window which meant shattering the glass. I picked up the crate and dragged it over to the window. It was too heavy and I knew I wouldn't be able to swing it with enough force. If only there was more light.

A jagged streak of lightning dazzled the sky. It illuminated Buzby, who was cowering and drenched. His saddle had slipped to one side. At that moment I felt as if my heart had been torn apart.

I was just about to sling the crate at the window in a desperate attempt when there was another crash of thunder on the far side of the wood. I could almost feel the ground tremble. Dropping the crate I fell against the window and stared out with my hands cupped to my face. Buzby had gone. There was no sign of him. He could put a leg in a rabbit hole and injure himself! He could get lost in the woods! He could run into a car!

I had to calm down. Stay calm. Get a grip. I reached out to steady myself, fumbling against the wall, feeling a narrow shelf and something hard and cold – a hammer.

Chapter Five

The muscles in the back of my legs were burning and I felt as if my heart was going to burst, but I kept on running.

The storm had rolled away, leaving a steady downpour of rain and a greyness that matched my spirits. I'd followed Buzby's hoof marks back to the track where I'd left Jodie and Rachel but after that the rain had washed them away. He could be anywhere. Please, please let him be OK. Let him be tucked up in his stable back at Brook House. Let no one notice that we had disappeared. But I knew that was an impossible wish; they probably had search parties out right now. Guy was going to go beserk. He'd already given me a warning.

I knew I would never feel quite the same again. Something had changed inside me. I wasn't the same young girl any more. I had grown up a lot in a short space of time.

There were no cars in the stable yard and no one was around. I cut through between the barn and the manege and headed towards the office. Sophie ran out of the saloon, her face white.

"Oh thank God!" She threw her arms round me. "You're drenched," she gasped. "They're all out looking for you. Apart from Guy. He's ringing the vet."

"What?" My blood ran cold. "W-what's happened?"

Sophie shrank back, hesitating, scrabbling for a way to soften the blow. "It's Buzby, he came back. B-but he's in a bad way – he ran into some barbed wire."

"Where?" I barged towards his stable but Sophie grabbed my arm. "No, Em, he needs stitches."

"No!" My voice spiralled upwards in disbelief.

Guy hurried out of the house, his face tight with worry. "What happened? Why didn't you stay with the others?"

There were no words. No explanations. I just stared.

"The vet's on his way." Guy's voice was strained. "He needs stitches and it looks as if he's chipped a bone."

I lurched back in shock. "I must see him," I croaked.

"Just go and sit down, Emma. You've done enough damage."

"But he's my pony."

"He's a riding school pony," said Guy, walking away.

Sophie put her arm round my shoulders. "He's just upset," she reasoned, "he's got a soft spot for Buz and he's worried about losing his job. He'll be all right once the vet's been."

My knees crumpled under me and Sophie supported me towards the saloon. Once inside I thought I was going to faint. I covered my face with both hands, determined not to cry. Sophie insisted on peeling off my wet coat and the squashed toadstool fell out onto the bare floor.

I sat shivering, hugging myself with my arms. "Oh Sophie, you'll never believe what happened to me," I sobbed. And the whole bizarre nightmare came rushing out.

Just about everybody wrote messages for Buzby and pinned them up on the saloon noticeboard:

Get well soon, Buz, you're the best. Love Kate.
We love you heaps. Amy and Ben.
Thanks for always being so kind. Ebony Jane.
You're the best stablemate ever. XXX Archie.

With a shaking hand I added my message in the bottom left-hand corner.

I really love Buzby. He is one of my best friends.

I'd been frozen out by four of the girls who rode him regularly at weekends – as if I wasn't already being torn apart by guilt and remorse. Guy had grudgingly let me go to the stable once the vet had left, and I had been deeply shocked.

Buzby's head sagged down between his knees. He didn't come to the door like he usually did but stood hunched up. All down his near hind leg was a zigzag of black stitches which had been covered with antiseptic powder. He was holding it slightly askew from the hock downwards which filled me with a gloomy dread. If the X-rays showed a fracture Buz might never be able to be ridden again. At best he would be off work for months and it would cost the earth. Mrs Brentford might decide it was kinder and cheaper to have him put down.

I couldn't bear the thought. I tore myself away and locked myself in the outside toilet and cried and cried until there were no tears left.

Sophie eventually tapped on the door and hissed through the crack that there were people waiting.

"We're having a Six Pack meeting in Rocket's stable," she urged. "Please, Em, you've got to be there. We're starting in half an hour. . ." Her voice trailed off.

Sophie had believed me when I'd told her I'd been deliberately locked in Rhododendron Shed, but would the others? Of course they wouldn't.

They'd say I was exaggerating as usual. I stood up and groped around for another toilet roll to use to blow my nose.

It was only then that I noticed the supermarket carrier bag pushed out of sight behind the toilet pipes. Immediately I thought it must belong to one of the riding school pupils – kids often came straight from school and got changed for their evening lessons. I'd give it to Sandra and she could put a notice on the lost-and-found board.

I grabbed the bag and gasped in horror when I saw what was inside. I couldn't believe it. With trembling hands I pulled the wet garment away from the clinging plastic. Just the touch of the material made my skin crawl. It was a purple coat with very definite chevron stripes.

Whoever had locked me in the shed had realized they'd been seen and quickly hidden their coat behind the toilet pipes. It was frightening to think that it could be anyone at the stables.

"Oh come on, you know what Emma's like for exaggerating – it'll be another one of her fantasies." Steph's spiteful high-pitched voice floated over Rocket's stable door, but somehow it didn't really register. I was walking in a daze, clutching the plastic bag under my own riding mac. The wonderful, friendly riding school had suddenly become an ominous place. Just a moment earlier I'd bumped into Sandra shaking up a fresh straw bed in Panda's stable and complaining about Guy being more interested in showjumping and Cindy Morell than in the riding school ponies. We'd suspected for ages that Sandra suspected was secretly in love with him. Nobody seemed straightforward any more. I left her coughing and spluttering as she forked up the straw banks moaning about the dust and spores.

Everybody on pony week had gone home for the evening. It was past five o'clock. The winners of the treasure hunt had collected eighteen items – we wouldn't have won anyway. There was no sign of Craig.

I walked into the stable feeling like a zombie. "We were just talking about what happened," explained Sophie, "about what you told me."

There was an awkward pause. My five friends shuffled uneasily, full of doubt. Kate was the first to speak. "Are you sure you didn't imagine it, Em? I mean, it's a pretty nasty thing to do."

I waited for a moment, then dug into the bag and pulled out the coat. Kate's mouth fell open. Rocket swivelled round, stretching his lead rope, sensing the tension. I told them where I'd found it and what this must mean.

"But – but who'd want to do that?" Jodie's face crinkled into an expression of disgust.

"The only person I've been able to think of is Craig." I leant against the stable wall drained of energy.

"But you've been so nice to him," said Rachel.

"You didn't see his face after I'd beaten him in the Chase me Charlie." I could still picture Craig's cold eyes and knew he was capable of anything.

"Look, all we have to do is prove who this coat belongs to," said Kate. She picked it up and busily examined the pockets and lining, but I'd already checked it for a name-tape.

"Never mind that, let's go straight to Guy." Sophie was already marching for the door.

"No way." I said firmly. "He won't believe me, he'll think we've made it all up. I'll just be in worse trouble."

"So what do we do? Let *you* take all the blame?" Sophie was really rattled.

"Wait till he cracks," said Jodie, levering herself up from where she was sitting in the straw. "He'll see that the coat has gone from his hiding place and it'll unnerve him. If he's got an ounce of decency in him, he'll own up."

"We'll be waiting till hell freezes over," Steph stated flatly.

"Oh, I nearly forgot," cried Rachel, her hand

193

flying to her mouth. "I heard the girl with the plaits talking earlier – Craig was playing the dunce at first because he wants to win the Most Improved Rider Trophy. He's quite experienced really."

"Hence the sudden improvement in the jumping," Kate snarled. "God, Em, you certainly know how to pick 'em. He really is the ultimate nightmare pen pal."

We all joined hands and agreed to say nothing, at least for the moment. "You may regret it," warned Sophie as we filed out of the stable. I glanced across to the office and saw Guy deep in conversation with both my parents.

"I can't for the life of me understand why you left that pony tied up." Mum was in the passenger seat going on and on. Dad was hunched over the driving wheel, staring straight ahead.

"This is my point, Wendy, there's not enough discipline at that riding school, they're allowed to run wild. There'll be an accident, mark my words, and it won't just be one of the ponies."

I glared out of the window, not bothering to explain that Buzby's future was hanging in the balance.

"This is why she'd be so much better off doing another sport – hockey for instance – and she'd meet some nice people." Mum and Dad had never actually said it but they looked down their noses at Steph, Kate and Rachel for not living in good areas. Mum and Dad were terrible snobs.

The houses rolled past, one after another, all neat and tidy as we turned into our avenue. I didn't want to play hockey. I wanted to keep going to Brook House where people lived life to the full, where jeans were acceptable and horses were everything. I wanted to become a riding instructor one day and live in a cottage with a paddock and stables.

I ran up the stairs to my bedroom and slammed the door. It was painted lilac with horse pictures all over one wall. I'd wanted purple, and lilac had been a compromise. Mickey, my hamster, was running like mad on his wheel. He always woke up at four o'clock when I came in from school. He shot inside a toilet roll tube and peered out from the other side.

Mum came in with a mug of tea and a pile of biscuits an hour later. "Listen, don't take too much notice of your dad," she said smiling. "You know he's all bark. He just worries about something happening to you – he can't help it. He thinks another sport would be less dangerous."

"Less expensive," I forced out through gritted teeth.

"Now Emma, that's not fair, we've always done our best for you."

"Yeah, sorry . . ." I hesitated. "But Mum, I'm growing up, I'm not six any more. I should be able to make my own choices."

"I know." She held my hand and I squeezed hers hard, watching her eyes soften with affection and crease at the corners. "But you'll always be our little baby."

I drank the tea and threw the biscuits out of the window. I didn't know what else to do with them. Two blackbirds pecked at them viciously until a crow swooped down from next door's roof and scared them off.

I pulled my "Milton" duvet over my legs, opened up *Horses from A to Z: The Manual* and started reading. It was the only thing that would take my mind off Buzby.

I knew it was a nightmare before I'd even opened my eyes but I still sat up with a start, my breath tight in my chest. Light was streaming through the curtains but when I fumbled for the alarm clock it only said 4.30 a.m. It was still the middle of the night.

I'd dreamt that Buzby was going to be put down and Guy and the vet were huddled in a corner, talking about injections and humane methods of killing. Everybody at the riding school was blaming me, whispering "Murderer, murderer." I flung back the duvet and sat with my head between my knees, recovering. On the far wall was a colour picture of Buzby with a rosette for clear round jumping at the Horseworld Show. He looked so happy and healthy. I knew I couldn't stay in bed a moment longer. I had to see him.

I pulled on an old grey tracksuit and trainers and reached for the door handle. I crept slowly down the stairs and slipped out of the back door. The air was sharp with a freshness only possible in the early hours.

It was three miles to the stables and I planned to take my mountain bike. The spare key to the garage winked cheerfully at me from underneath the mat where we kept it. Mum was always saying we shouldn't keep it in such an obvious place. There was the bike, all ready and waiting. Not long now, Buzby. With a sudden feeling of dread I realized it was only four hours before Guy would be ringing the vet to discover the results of the X-ray.

The stable yard was shrouded in a hazy grey light and the dawn chorus was in full swing as I gently slipped off my bike and pushed it up the drive. Quarter to six. It seemed to have taken for ever. I realized I'd be in trouble later, but when I saw Buzby's stable, tucked away behind the saloon, I knew I couldn't have done anything else.

He was standing at the back when I peered in. He lifted his head and blinked a few times and then tried to move forward but changed his mind. I welled up again. Buzby always dashed to his door – he always knew there would be a special titbit on offer.

The stitches were still in place, clotted with congealed blood here and there. Bits of straw clung to the hairs and I spent ages trying to pick them off, delicately catching them between my fingernails and tweaking them out. It was all my fault. How could I even think about having a pony of my own? I wasn't responsible. I wasn't even a good rider.

A racking cough from the next-door stable brought me back to reality. A horse was coughing badly. It didn't seem to be able to get its breath. It was Panda, of course – Cindy Morell's gorgeous dun mare. I remembered Sandra making up a straw bed for her and saying they were moving her into that stable because it was the biggest in the yard.

I hurried from one stable to the next. What if she had something stuck in her throat? What if she was choking? She was standing with her head slung low, her eyes unfocused and glazed and her jaw half open, waiting for the next heaving spasm.

I didn't have a clue what to do. She hardly noticed me as I rushed to her shoulder. Her flanks and stomach muscles were tensed and clenched into knots.

"Panda, what is it, what's wrong?" She stared at me, her eyes full of fear, then tried to stagger forward as if to escape the pain. I had to get help. I had to go to the house.

Whirling round, I fled out and across the yard towards the rickety garden gate and the cottage where Mrs Brentford would be tucked up in bed. It was twenty past six. Old people weren't supposed to sleep that well. Maybe she was already up?

I banged urgently on the front door. Then I noticed the doorbell and kept my finger on it. Where was she? I was making enough noise to raise the dead.

"Mrs Brentford!" I yelled up at the top window, which was half-covered in creeping ivy. Suddenly a bolt rattled on the inside of the door. She was here! She was here! The door creaked open a few inches.

"Mrs Brentford, it's Emma Parker."

She fiddled for ages with the safety chain and then appeared, still in her dressing gown, looking wide-eyed with alarm. "It's Panda," I shrieked, "Guy's new horse – I think she's choking." The words tumbled out.

Mrs Brentford was sixty-nine and no bigger than me. She'd been running the riding school for years, long before Guy arrived or Sophie's dad bought in as a business partner. She'd put horses first all her life and I really admired her.

She took the catch off the door and we hurried back across the yard, not daring to speak, imagining the worst. I knew from watching *Animal Kingdom* every week that animals could very quickly choke to death.

The silence from the stable filled me with an icy dread. What if something terrible had happened? What if she was lying lifeless in the straw? Mrs Brentford took charge and pulled open the door. I forced myself to look. I didn't want to scream, I must not scream.

Panda was standing tugging gently at her hay net. She swung her head round to look at us, unperturbed.

"But, but . . ." I couldn't believe it. There was no sign whatsoever that she'd been ill. I rushed forward, running my hand down her huge neck and shoulder, desperate to find any trace of the atttack. But she wasn't even warm. Her breathing was regular and normal.

Mrs Brentford's face had tightened with annoyance. She looked ridiculous standing in a stable in her nightwear. "I think we'd better go back to the house and you can tell me exactly what you're doing in my stable yard by yourself at six o'clock in the morning."

But my brain was racing along a million different channels. Something was wrong. Panda had been gasping for breath. She couldn't recover so quickly. Something had to be wrong. I knew Mrs Brentford checked all the Brook House horses last thing at night . . .

"Supposing," I blurted out, desperate for an answer, "supposing a horse was coughing in the middle of the night, would you hear them?"

Mrs Brentford turned round and stared at me. "Don't be silly, girl, I'm partially deaf," she said flatly, as if it was common knowledge.

Chapter Six

"Can you put me straight through to Mr Nielsen?" Guy turned his back to me so I couldn't see his expression. "Yes, it is important."

Sophie and Rachel were in the office, sitting on either side of me. Guy was ringing the vet for Buzby's results. I felt sick with fear. The thought of Saturdays and holidays without Buzby threw me into despair. I wouldn't be able to cope.

"Don't worry, Em," said Sophie, "if it is the worst, we'll raise money, we'll do whatever it takes to make him better."

"Yeah, sponsored swims, silences, anything," said Rachel, nodding in agreement.

"I see." Guy's voice was cold and unreadable.

"I can't face it," I gulped, leaping up. I rushed out of the office and made for Buzby's stable. I wanted to run my hands through his mane one more time as if everything was normal. What would Mrs Brentford do with him? He wouldn't be any good for anything. We'd be a matching pair.

I heard Guy's footsteps behind me.

"I don't want to hear," I said in a hard, bright voice that wasn't mine.

"Oh. Not even if it's good news?"

I turned round ever so slowly, to see the gently teasing expression in Guy's soft brown eyes. "He hasn't damaged any bones," he said grinning. "He's torn a muscle. He's going to be fine."

I was speechless.

"I'll leave you to yourself." Guy hesitated and then turned and walked back to the office. I buried my face in Buzby's thick spongy coat and cried tears of relief.

"You don't do it like that, you do it like this." Kate, in her usual bossy fashion was showing Rachel how to apply a tail bandage.

"There's no need anyway because Rusty doesn't rub his tail."

"Excuse me," said Kate raising her eyebrows, "but it's supposed to be to flatten down the hairs – you know, make him look presentable."

Rachel stared pointedly at Archie's tail which was sticking up like a toilet brush.

"Well I didn't say it worked for all ponies, did I?"

We were sitting on the grass near the saloon talking horses and generally mucking about. It was our official lunch break and Sophie was swinging her riding crop, pretending to play polo.

"You look so uncool," said Steph, wincing as Sophie sent a tennis ball hurtling across the grass.

"I don't care," she said. "If I don't practise I might hit Rocket's legs."

At two o'clock Guy was giving everyone a polo lesson with proper mallets and balls borrowed from the Pony Club. Sophie was insisting that I share Rocket with her for the rest of the week, but I didn't mind not riding. I was just so grateful that Buz was OK. I proudly held up the massive daisy chain I was making for him which would probably be devoured in thirty seconds.

Mrs Brentford had amazed me by driving me home at seven o'clock in the morning and dropping me off at the end of our avenue. All she'd said during the whole journey was that she'd once run away for three days with a Welsh mountain pony that her parents had wanted to sell. She said it was up to me whether I told my parents – it was our secret, but in her opinion the truth was better out than in. Jodie had always said that Mrs B was a really special lady and now I could see why.

Overwhelmed with gratitude, I got out of the car and ran down the pavement vowing I wouldn't sneak out in the middle of the night again. When Dad came shuffling to the door, dazed with sleep,

I bottled out and made up a bizarre story that I'd been sleepwalking and had locked myself out. Sometimes the truth is just too hard to tell.

"Crikey, Em, that's the first time I've seen you nibble the chocolate off a Mars Bar instead of devouring it whole". Steph's voice interrupted my thoughts and I quickly put the chocolate back in its wrapper and slung it into my bag.

"What's up with you? Has your stomach suddenly shrunk?" said Steph biting into a crisp. She didn't miss a thing.

I'd been watching Panda out in the paddock, playfully nudging the besotted Frank, then turning and clipping up her heels, swirling round and cantering off. She didn't have anything wrong with her now, in fact she was a picture of health. I couldn't mention the coughing attack to Guy because I'd then have to explain why I'd been in her stable in the early hours of the morning. Mrs Brentford quite clearly thought there was nothing seriously wrong. So why couldn't I just forget it?

"It's ridiculous," said Sandra, tightening up Ebony Jane's girth, "she's only hiring her for hacks yet she's insisted on changing her diet, and her tack. Next she'll be wanting her in a side-saddle or something equally stupid."

Cindy Morell was not one of Sandra's favourite people, especially since lunchtime when she'd rung twice to say she'd like the mare in a different bit if possible. Poor Ebby looked uncomfortable with the new jointed snaffle and flash noseband. "You know what an angel she is," said Sandra as she brushed the straw out of Ebby's tail. "You could ride her in a head collar and she'd still be as good as gold."

I reached up and stroked the bay mare's pretty forehead with the zigzaggy star slightly off centre. I wouldn't want Cindy Morell on my back at any cost.

"Of course Guy is so taken up with Panda he'll say yes to anything. Do you know that he's even taking out a bank loan to pay for her? He must be out of his tree."

I knew Sandra shouldn't be gossiping about her boss like this but I couldn't help worrying about Ebby. Sandra did a good job at looking after all the horses although sometimes she'd cut corners and we'd hear Guy asking her to do something again.

"Anyway," she went on, looking up and rubbing at her freckled nose, "when are you going to wise up and tell Guy what really happened in Rhododendron Wood and drop that cocky, jumped-up, so-called friend of yours in at the deep end?"

I stiffened in alarm and then dropped my eyes as Sandra continued to stare straight at me. "How did you know about that?" I gulped.

Sandra tossed her dyed bobbed hair. "Walls have ears you know," she said. "And grooms are a bit like waiters. People carry on talking and forget they're there."

"The whole idea of polo is to hit the ball and keep it moving." Guy surprised us by jumping onto Archie to give a demonstration. The wily Palomino was goggle-eyed and for the first time in his life behaved impeccably.

"I never knew he could move so fast," said Rachel, shielding her eyes with her hand.

"It doesn't say much for your riding, Kate," Steph giggled. "You turn beetroot just getting him to trot."

"Ssssh." Two girls on our right who were taking it mega-seriously scowled at us.

"Are you sure you don't want a ride, Em?" Sophie swivelled Rocket round to face me.

"The assets of a good polo player are an eye for the ball, physical strength, courage, fitness and mental alertness," Guy boomed out.

"Does that answer your question?" I glanced up at Sophie who was fiddling with one of her knee-pads. Rocket took the opportunity to sneeze all over me. I was secretly glad that I'd missed the polo training because the last time someone had tried to teach me eye-ball contact I'd accidentally hit them with the racket.

I clasped my arms over my chest and looked at my feet, suddenly aware that Craig was staring at me from the other side of the circle.

"The best ponies for polo are usually gymkhana ponies so, Rachel and Sophie, we'll have you out first. Now you must stand up in the stirrups to hit the ball and lean towards it." Guy gave a demonstration and smacked the ball down the field where it bounced off a tree.

Steph was busy picking at her chipped nail varnish and didn't notice Monty nibbling at her mallet.

"Excellent!" shouted Rachel, weaving Rusty after the ball and doing a fantastic job of neck-reining.

"I think I ought to call it quits now." Jodie started circling Minstrel. "Have you ever seen an Arab stallion doing a polo tackle?" She sounded worried.

"You mean riding someone off," I corrected vaguely, feeling increasingly uncomfortable.

When I next looked up, Craig was riding towards me on Foxy.

"Is it OK if I change my helmet?" he asked,

already tipping it off his head as I stared down at the pile of equipment around me. Guy had called everyone into a line to practise strokes and I felt alarmingly alone.

"I'm really pleased that Buzby's going to be all right."

"I bet you are," I snapped, thrashing around for another hat to pass to him.

"No, really I am. It would have been terrible if . . ."

"What? If he'd have had to be put down?" I glared at him.

Craig's voice came stiffly through his pale lips. "I hoped we might be friends."

"Oh please. Is that all you wanted to tell me? Isn't there something else you want to get off your chest – a confession perhaps?"

For the first time there was a crack in his coolness. His eyes hardened to a cold watchfulness. "I don't think so." His lips had gone very pale.

"You'd better get back to the group." Even as I said it I realized I was letting him off the hook. "Let me know if anyone's lost a coat," I shouted to his departing back, but he didn't turn round.

Ebony Jane's stable stood empty. Somehow I wasn't in the mood for polo any more so I'd decided to go back and check on Buzby.

Sandra was sitting in the sunniest spot in the yard, supposedly cleaning tack but going to great lengths to catch the sun on her legs.

"Her Majesty left about an hour ago to go on a hack," she volunteered, splashing lotion on her freckly arms. "Anyone would think I was her lady-in-waiting the way she had me running around."

I could visualize Ebby's steady walk and Cindy nudging her on, demanding more and more from her.

"I'll be in Buzby's stable if anyone wants me," I said.

Buzby was confined to box-rest for a whole month and he was already throwing the water bucket round the stable in boredom.

"Now you've just got to put up with it," I told him, tapping his nose, and then felt guilty for reprimanding him. He immediately nuzzled my jeans pocket and sniffed out a boiled sweet.

Why had pony week turned into such a huge disaster? A heaviness kept dragging at my spirits despite the joy of knowing Buzby was all right. Lack of sleep had stretched my nerves to breaking point. Why was it that the things we looked forward to the most, often didn't live up to our expectations? I vowed to expect little from life in the future; then anything good would be a pleasant surprise.

Buzby started to chew my hair as a subtle indication that he was passing out with hunger.

"OK, you win." I jumped up, grabbing hold of the empty water bucket. "I'll find you a gourmet meal which will shut you up, at least until the vet arrives."

The verges on either side of the front drive were tropical paradises of lush grass. Buzby would truly be in heaven once he got his nose lodged in the bucket. Juicy green stains spread across my hands as I methodically snatched clump after clump of grass and pressed them down.

From the age of three my ears had been trained to pick up horses' hoofs like radar, so it was no surprise that I heard Ebby before she was even in sight. I jerked upright and waited tensely for her to round the corner.

She appeared on the grass verge trotting forward stiffly, Cindy's powerful seat driving her on. I was about to step forward to go and meet them when something happened which made me stop in my tracks.

For no apparent reason, Cindy raised her arm and her whip cut through the air and cracked into Ebby's quarters.

Chapter Seven

"Why didn't you tell someone?" Sophie sat next to me on a straw bale, quietly listening as I poured out the whole story.

"I'm in enough trouble as it is," I explained. "Nobody's going to take my side against Cindy Morell." Even Sophie didn't disagree. I'd told her about my secret trip to the stables and Panda's mystery cough and then, most importantly about Ebony Jane.

"This is Six Pack business," Sophie said solemnly. "Anything that involves the welfare of the riding school horses means we have to stand united. I'll call a meeting straight away."

"Do you think they'll believe me?"

"Oh Em, do you really have to ask?" And of course I didn't. On anything really serious my friends had never let me down.

"But I think now we'd better go and watch Guy showjumping Panda. It's the first time she's been exercised since the coughing attack. We may pick up some vital clue."

Guy was trying Panda out on the arena over some really high showjumps. The polo training had finished and everybody had been told to groom their ponies and clean their tack before they went home.

But everybody apart from Craig was glued to the arena watching Cindy put up the jumps and the beautiful dun mare soar over them. Rachel and Jodie had drawn the short straws and were staying in the stable yard to keep an eye on Craig in case he was getting up to some mischief.

"She looks fantastic." Steph moved a seat closer to get a better look. "How high do you think she can jump?"

"Six foot at least," Sophie answered. "That spread over there must be five foot three and she's making nothing of it." Guy was such a good rider that Panda took off at exactly the right spot every time. We were too inexperienced to do that but since Guy had explained about keeping our legs on and sitting still until the very last stride we'd all improved enormously.

Panda's black ears cocked forward as she bunched for the upright which Cindy had raised. "I told you she was good," she said. Her clipped voice made my skin crawl after what I'd seen her do to Ebby.

Panda had been a successful event horse doing

dressage and cross-country as well, but she was so good at jumping that Cindy had decided to sell her as a showjumper.

"She looks fine so far." Sophie was watching Panda like a hawk. There was no sign of a cough. I didn't know whether to be relieved or disappointed.

"I think that's enough for today." Cindy's voice suddenly took on a hard edge.

Guy circled Panda and pulled to a halt obviously wanting to do more but not arguing. "I definitely want her," he said grinning, "she's sensational."

"A world beater." Cindy patted the golden, muscle-packed neck. "I wasn't exaggerating, was I?"

Guy disappeared under the saddle flap to loosen the girth and a triumphant smile flickered over Cindy's face. "Perhaps you could write out the cheque over dinner?"

"A waste of time." Jodie came out of the saloon with Rachel, struggling with a pile of clean tack. "Craig hasn't put a foot out of place, he's got no intentions of owning up, Emma. You've got to tell Guy about Rhodedendron Shed before it's too late, before he tries something else."

"I don't think he'll be trying any more stunts," said Kate, running up, breathless and excited. "I've just seen him leaving the toilet, obviously going back for the coat. He was as white as a sheet – he knows he's been sprung."

The vet arrived soon after Guy had finished riding Panda and both Guy and Cindy went with him into Buzby's stable. It was only supposed to be a routine check-up but they'd been in there for ages. I could see their dark outlines moving around through the stable window.

Just about everybody had gone home apart from Kate and Steph who were doing a horsy jigsaw in the saloon, killing time waiting for Kate's mum. Everyone was meeting in town at the ice rink at seven for the pony week social outing. Kate's mum had organized it together with a couple of the other mothers and Guy. They'd even laid on a special minibus. The Six Pack would have rather gone to a horsy demonstration but had been outvoted.

I picked up the yard brush and absent-mindedly swept two blades of straw back and forth. I couldn't stand not knowing what was going on. Somebody put a hand over Buzby's door to pull back the bolt and then hesitated and carried on talking.

I felt as if I was going to scream. Then I noticed a trickle of water spreading from under Panda's door. She'd knocked over her water bucket . . . And her stable was right next to Buz's. It was the perfect excuse to get closer.

"Of course in my opinion the Conservative government brought about their own downfall. Now when I get elected as councillor . . ."

I couldn't believe it. They weren't talking about Buzby at all. They were talking about politics. I was crouched inside Panda's stable listening at the wooden divide. Guy was making every attempt to escape but Mr Nielsen was obviously on his favourite subject.

"Well at least Buzby is making a full recovery," Guy butted in.

I closed my eyes and felt the warm relief surge through me. Buzby was OK. I shuffled slightly as I felt pins and needles in my left leg. My concentration settled on Panda who oddly hadn't come across to snuffle my hair and look for titbits as every horse usually did. Sandra had forgotten to put on her cooler rug. My eyes drifted over her strong shoulders and deep girth to her powerful quarters and then back to her flanks. She was standing near her hay net but not eating. Was it my imagination or was she . . .? I studied her ribcage more closely. It was rising up and down in a rhythm but every time she drew in air there seemed to be a double movement, like a double breath. I could see it clearly – there was something wrong. I stood up quickly and banged my head on the manger.

There was a silence from next door. I had to take the bull by the horns. I had to go and face them.

"I think there's something wrong with Panda," I blurted out.

Cindy Morell glared at me as if I was a worm crawling about on the floor. Mr Nielsen took a step forward but she shot out her hand and snatched his arm. "Don't listen to her, she keeps making things up. She even said I was being cruel to one of the riding school horses."

I gaped in shock, completely thrown. I'd only told Sophie about Ebby. She was obviously convinced I'd tell and had decided to beat me to it and discredit me.

Guy looked puzzled and then reddened with growing embarrassment. He walked foward and glanced over Panda's door, then broke into a relieved smile. "She's just got a chill – that stupid groom's left her rug off."

"There you are then." Cindy manoeuvred Mr Nielsen right away from the stable. "Nothing to worry about."

"Well I suppose I'd better get onto my next

call . . ." He hesitated for a brief moment then picked up his bag.

"What's got into you lately?" Guy hissed a few moments later. "All these fantasies of yours, Emma, are just not on. This is a riding school, not a setting for a novel. Get your feet back on the ground before I completely lose my patience."

My eyes filled up and I gulped back a sob. "Guy Marshall, I hate you," I mumbled to his departing back. Panda pushed her nose against my shoulder as if to thank me for trying. "What is it, Panda?" I stroked her kitten-soft nose. "What's wrong with you?"

The car park at the ice rink was packed so Sophie's dad pulled his Jaguar right up to the main doors. Half the Six Pack had travelled together which had been a nightmare in a way because Sophie had telephoned everyone earlier to tell them about Ebony Jane and Panda but we couldn't under any circumstances discuss it in front of her dad.

Steph irritated everyone by playing the same Spice Girls song over and over on the CD player until Sophie threatened to strangle her with the seat belt.

We spotted the minibus parked over by the fence. Kate's mum and a troop of other mums were harassing Guy as to whose daughter was the best rider. Rachel rolled her eyes and we smothered giggles as we dived through the rotating doors. It was the first time I'd laughed in ages.

Jodie and Kate were already putting on their skates and had ordered ours.

"Listen," I said, feeling really lighthearted, "let's forget about riding school business tonight and concentrate on having a really good time. What do you say?"

"Count me in," agreed Rachel collecting everybody's coats. "Let's skate till we drop."

"Er, who invited her?" Steph made a face as Cindy Morell stalked in through the doors in front of Guy. I noticed Craig was directly behind them with his head slung low, avoiding eye contact.

"It doesn't matter." I forced out the words. "We'll just ignore her. We're not going to let her ruin our night."

Sophie was the best skater, followed by Steph and then me. I was thrilled that my new pair of boot-cut trousers which I'd had for my birthday were actually loose around the waist.

Steph suggested we all link hands which we did for a while, then Kate had the idea of pretending we were doing dressage tests on ice which was hilarious, especially as we got Guy to do the judging. Sophie did the best centre line and I did the best ten metre circle.

Rachel swished across and nudged my arm, discreetly pointing to where Cindy was trying out a pair of skates and clinging onto the boards, glowering like a bull.

"I dare you to go and annoy her," she said grinning. "Go on, it'll get right up her nose."

I skated past Cindy keeping my chin in the air and my eyes fixed firmly ahead. I could feel her seething. Funnily enough it gave me a wonderful feeling of exhilaration. Turning round, I set off back, moving in even closer so I'd blast past her feeble efforts.

She grabbed my arm and before I even realized, I felt myself being hauled round and saw the boards crashing towards me. I stuck out my hand to save myself and my knuckles crunched painfully as the weight of my body slammed into the boards. Pain soared up my arm.

"Don't think I don't know what you're up to," Cindy hissed. "Don't meddle in things you know nothing about, OK?" She was so close my nostrils were twitching from the smell of her nauseating perfume.

"Leave her alone for God's sake, Banny." I jumped back, startled by Craig's voice. He was pushing her away, his face burning with anger. But he'd called her Banny. My mind struggled through the fog searching for the relevance. I'd read a personality profile once ... Yes, that was the nickname her family called her ... Family.

"Yeah you've sussed it," said Craig looking straight into my eyes, his mouth settling into a resigned smile, "Cindy is my cousin."

Chapter Eight

The quiz started first thing the next morning which left no time for us to have a proper Six Pack meeting.

Steph had brought along her plastic model of a Haflinger pony which she swore brought good luck and Rachel had spotted an Eddie Stobart lorry on her way to the riding school which she insisted was a good sign. Jodie said we were a superstitious lot and refused to have five lucky mascots on our table. We'd called ourselves the Equine Warriors and were determined to do the best we possibly could. When someone answered three questions wrong they got knocked out so that eventually there would be just one winner left, who would pick up the special achievement points and rosette. I tried to visualize the pages of *Horses from A to Z*, but only got as far as section C.

"If everybody's ready we'll begin." Guy rustled his thick pile of papers. "When is a Thoroughbred's official birthday? ... What was the name of the first mare to win the Hickstead Derby? . . . Which brush should be used on a pony's mane and tail?"

I'd shoved my hand up in time for question two and got it right. Bluebird.

"Most greys are born black or brown. True or false? . . . A Falabella is the smallest breed of horse. True or false? . . . What is a gag?"

Most people were too keen to stick up their hand and were eliminating themselves with the wrong answers.

"How would you describe a Trakehner? . . . All ponies should be fed immediately before being ridden. True or false? . . . The poll is to be found on which part of the horse's body?"

My brain was leaping around with excitement. I knew most of the answers. It was almost as if I had so much on my mind worrying about Buzby and Panda and Ebony Jane, not to mention my parents and Cindy and Craig, that I was functioning on automatic pilot. I didn't have any nerves fizzing around and clogging up my head. Steph was studying me with muted surprise. I wasn't Emma Parker, thick and hopeless any more. I was carrying our team. I'd got five questions right.

Sophie groaned as Rachel and Steph got knocked out in quick succession. People were falling like flies now. In fact there was a reluctance to put up hands. The questions were getting harder.

"What are the symptoms of strangles?" Jodie flew up her left arm and then clapped her hand over her mouth. She gave the wrong answer and got knocked out. We were down to just Kate, Sophie and me.

"A Palomino is recognized as a breed in America, but elsewhere is only classed as a colour. True or false? . . . How many inches in a hand? . . . What is a skewbald? . . . Is ragwort a poisonous plant?"

The questions were getting easier again. Craig fired off three out of four of the answers. I was still hanging on. Then Sophie was knocked out too. There was only a handful of people left in. Craig was at the opposite side of the room concentrating like mad. I couldn't look at him or he'd put me off.

"Which side should you plait up a horse's mane? . . . Which side should you lead a pony from? . . . What is laminitis caused by?"

"Goodness, Emma, it's just you and Craig left in!" Sophie was so excited she was shouting at the top of her voice. I must stay calm. I musn't blow it. I fixed my eyes on Guy and waited for the next question.

"A pony who rubs his mane and tail raw in late spring and early summer could be suffering from what disease?"

"Sweet itch!" I shot out the answer as soon as Guy had finished the sentence.

Guy nodded and moved onto the next. "Removing droppings from a pony's field helps to control what?"

"Worms!" Craig beat me to it by seconds.

The tension was becoming unbearable. Everybody was so quiet you could hear a fly land never mind a pin drop. My mouth had turned desert-dry. For the next five minutes Craig and I shouted out answers, one after the other. It was a dead heat.

"This is no good." Guy looked flustered. "I'm going to give you each a pen and paper and you're to write down the answer to a very difficult question. There's to be no help whatsoever from your team members."

He passed us a single sheet of notepaper and I picked up the black biro which slipped through my sweaty fingers. Craig looked as if he were about to run the one hundred metres.

"Is there such a thing as a bog pony and if so where does it originate?"

I'd seen something on telly about this. Ancient bog ponies were thought to be extinct but a stallion had been found and now they were breeding them. They were called bog ponies because of their ability to pick their way through the Irish bogs. My hand scrawled the answer at a delirious speed.

Sophie passed the folded pieces of paper to Guy and we waited for the result. The Six Pack had crossed their fingers and legs and Steph was even trying to cross her eyes.

"The winner is . . ." Guy hesitated with a look of amazement. "Emma Parker."

The Six Pack went absolutely crackers. We'd won. I'd won. I pinched myself and the dream still didn't go away. Guy was walking towards me with an orange rosette. I saw Craig disappear out of the louvred doors looking tired with disappointment. I should be glad that he'd lost but I felt nothing one way or the other. All I knew was that something wonderful had happened. And for the first time in a long time I was starting to like myself again.

"I want to apologize." Craig leaned over the stable door where I was grooming Buzby. He'd got thousands of hay seeds in his mane where he'd been rubbing against his hay net. I tapped the curry comb against the wall and started again.

"Emma, are you listening?"

I shrugged and kept up the regular sweeping strokes. Buzby closed his eyes and leaned into the brush. "What are you sorry for?" I asked simply. "For being a rude pig? For lying about your riding?

Or for lying about your famous relative? Or let me think, maybe there's something else?"

"OK, you've made your point, but you know what for. I never meant it to go that far. I was just messing about."

"With other people's lives?" I stared straight ahead at Buzby's rounded withers. "Is that it with you, Craig? Is everything just a lark, regardless of the consequences?" My voice was low and almost toneless now.

"I'm going to Guy and I'm going to tell him everything." He made a sweeping gesture with his arms as if he was doing me a big favour.

"Well don't expect a medal. It's taken you long enough." I glared at his carrot-red hair and snubby nose almost with revulsion. "If all pen pals were like you, Craig, the Post Office would be out of business."

"Look," he said, clenching his fists and taking in a sharp breath, "I admit, I was wrong, I was angry that I lost the jumping and I shouldn't have locked you in that shed. But I can't change what's done. I can only attempt to fix it."

I stared at him with cool appraising eyes. "If you really want to fix things, you'll tell me what's wrong with your cousin's horse."

His face suddenly went rigid. "You've got it wrong," he said, obviously flustered. "There is nothing wrong with Panda. Do you honestly think Guy would be considering buying her if there was?"

"I don't know . . ." I hesitated, my mind racing back over the events of the last few days.

"Well if you're so right," he snapped, "why has she got an up-to-date veterinary certificate saying she's in perfect health? Answer me that."

But I couldn't. My mind was blank. Any thoughts on Panda had suddenly dried up.

Sandra was mucking out Ebony Jane's stable swinging in time to her walkman. A cold feeling of dread skittered through me. Ebby wasn't there. We'd devised a plan where Jodie and Minstrel would be ready to follow Cindy as soon as she came to the stable, to try and catch her out.

I pushed mindlessly passed Craig and ran across the yard. Two hens squawked from under the wheelbarrow but Sandra still didn't hear me.

"Sandra!" I lifted up one of her earphones and yelled at her. She dropped the pitchfork in fright. "Where's Ebby?" I said lowering my voice, my face tight with worry.

"Cindy's taken her," she said. "She came when you were all doing the quiz. She's been gone ages."

"Have you any idea where she's gone?"

She shrugged her shoulders. "Haven't got a clue."

*

"This is the worst," said Steph. "Poor darling Ebby, she could be anywhere by now."

I blinked hard to shut out the picture of Cindy cracking her whip down Ebony's side. "It's my fault," I whimpered. "I should have said more – told Mrs Brentford. I shouldn't have been frightened to upset Guy. Horses should always come first."

"We'd better tell the others," Steph smoothed down her hair which immediately sprang back up again.

We found everyone except Sophie in Minstrel's stable with Jodie tightening his girth and Rachel brushing his silken tail with the body brush. Minstrel was so highly bred that he still came in at nights because otherwise he got a chill. He pushed his wonderful dished face against my coat sniffing out horse nuts.

"There's nothing we can do now," said Jodie when I told her what had happened.

"If that woman hurts one hair on Ebby's body..." Steph stopped, unable to finish her sentence.

"I know." Jodie kept her voice level and looked at her. "But we can't do anything until she gets back."

"Emma, I've got some fantastic news." Suddenly Sophie thundered towards me, not slowing down, her breath rasping in her throat. "Craig's told Guy what happened. In fact Guy's looking for you right now . . . But that's not the best bit. You're in line to win the Most Improved Rider trophy. Guy said so. You're the only person to win two special achievement rosettes. So . . ." She broke off and steadied her breath, the colour in her face calming down. "There's something I want you to do. I want to stand down. I want you to ride Rocket in the cross-country."

Chapter Nine

"I can't do it, I can't. Rocket's 14.2 hands. He's massive compared to Buzby."

"Don't be silly, of course you can. He's an angel, he'll carry you round."

Cross-country practice was starting in five minutes and Rocket was tacked up, observing me with a mild gaze. He was a chestnut with a zigzag blaze down his nose and one white sock. He was the best pony in the riding school. It was like upgrading to a Rolls Royce after riding Buzby who was only 12.2 hands. Despite my nerves I felt a tremor of excitement.

"But it's not right for you not to ride," I said for the hundredth time. Sophie gave me a stern look and prepared to hoist me up into the saddle.

I glanced back at Buzby's stable, only to see him stuffing himself with hay, not minding in the least. "OK," I squeaked. "I'll give it a go."

Rocket stood beautifully as I gathered up the reins and felt for the stirrups. The Six Pack were waiting in a line: Kate on Archie, Rachel on Rusty,

Steph on Monty and Jodie on Minstrel. I hadn't realized just how much I'd missed being part of the gang. We all clunked our crops together and doubled up into pairs to ride down to the wood.

Guy was waiting by the gate, his thoughts obviously elsewhere. "Has anybody seen Ebony and Cindy?" His voice was tight. Everyone shook their heads and I avoided his eyes by focusing on Rocket's rubber reins.

"He's fantastic," I whispered to Sophie as we walked towards the first few rustic jumps. Unlike Buz, Rocket didn't snatch at the reins and try to pull me out of the saddle. I could concentrate on sitting up straight and using my legs to best effect.

"Now remember," Sophie instructed, "he doesn't like to be rushed into a jump and you must give him his head. He'll do the rest."

Guy started off over some low jumps, straw bales and a palisade followed by a slip rail. I was the second to go and felt my heart lurch as I pushed Rocket forward. Everybody was watching. "Please don't let me down," I whispered into Rocket's floppy ears.

Rocket saw the jump ahead and lengthened his stride. I closed my eyes and held my breath. He cleared it effortlessly and automatically turned for the next. I pulled up gasping for breath and flung my arms round Rocket's neck.

"Well done," Guy shouted and then set the next rider off.

I jogged back to Sophie on cloud nine. "He's incredible," I shrieked. "He just flies them."

We had to wait for ages before it was our turn again. Guy moved on to a small ditch with a log over the top which is called a Trakehner, then two banks which you had to step up, and a mini-coffin which Buzby had always refused point blank to jump. A coffin is a jump down to a ditch followed by a jump uphill. It filled me with terror.

"Rocket could jump it in his sleep," Sophie whispered.

But that was without me bouncing around on his back and hindering him.

Jodie made it look easy and Steph went too fast but was still clear. Three of the other riders had refusals.

"OK, Emma, your turn."

I trotted Rocket forward and then circled.

"Look up, look up, look up . . ." I said to myself as I rode down to the Trakehner in a shaky line remembering that you mustn't look in the ditch but straight ahead at the top part of the jump. Rocket ignored my aid to go faster, jumping out of his stride and giving it a wide berth.

"Good boy, brilliant boy!" I patted his neck, ecstatic with pleasure. He popped up the banks as nimble as a cat. It was incredible. I felt like a professional. I had to remind myself to breathe and hastily took in gulps of air.

The coffin was next. I looked across to find my line and that's when the dizziness hit me. The ground wouldn't stay still, everything was reeling. Rocket eased back to a trot, sensing something was wrong and I slumped forward over his neck. I could feel myself slipping helplessly to one side and grabbed at a chunk of mane. Somebody was running towards me, but I couldn't hang on.

The ground was whizzing towards me and I knew it was just seconds before I'd hit it. I remembered thinking that I was falling off wrong, that I should have rolled away from Rocket's hoofs in a tight ball. And then a wave of blackness swamped me and I passed out before I crashed to the ground.

"You fainted." I recognized Sophie among the blur of faces. They were all pressing down, anxious and tense. I struggled up on my elbow and blinked hard. There was a huge grass stain all down one side of my jodhpurs and a rip across the knee.

"OK everyone, move back, give her some air." Guy shuffled forward. "Now Emma, I want you to tell me how many fingers I'm holding up."

I blinked again and did as I was told on automatic pilot.

"And what's your name and address?"

I told him and screwed up my face in confusion.

"I'm checking for concussion, Emma. Do you think you could get to your feet?"

Guy and Sophie walked me back to the stables with Kate leading Rocket from Archie. The cross-country practice was postponed for the day. I just concentrated on putting one foot in front of the other, feeling as weak as a kitten.

Once in the office, Guy said he must ring my parents. I didn't appear to have concussion but I'd certainly have to go home and rest.

"But I know what's wrong with her," Sophie blurted out, gripping the back of a chair.

Guy turned round in surprise.

"She's been secretly dieting." Sophie glanced at me, aching for forgiveness for telling. "She's hardly eaten anything for days. I should have said something but I didn't know how."

My face flushed to a deep crimson.

"Is this true, Emma? When was the last time you had something to eat?"

Mum arrived to pick me up twenty minutes later, her face creased with worry. We sat in silence all the way home finding it too awkward to talk.

"Why Emma, you've always had such a good appetite," Mum burst out as soon as we got into the house. "This is my fault, I'm your mother, I should know when you're upset."

"But you weren't to know." I rushed across the room and flung my arms round her waist. "I've been really stupid," I said, my mouth crumpling with emotion, "I thought I was getting too fat to ride. I didn't realize not eating for a few days would make me ill. I know I've been really stupid."

We clung to each other, really close, and ended up laughing as Mum pushed my hair back off my forehead and picked out bits of straw.

"Oh Emma, you're such a lovely, healthy girl. How did you ever get it in your head that you were overweight?"

The Six Pack arrived in force at 4.30 armed with bags of Mini-Mars Bars, crisps, a tub of chocolate chip ice cream and a packet of cashew nuts.

"It all adds up to over four thousand calories," Steph boasted as Mum pulled a face and praised the virtues of wholesome home cooking. We piled into my bedroom and ripped open the bag of Mars Bars.

"From now on people can take me as they find me," I said grinning, and decided that chocolate had never tasted so good. "It's what's inside a person that counts. I'm never going to be so stupid again."

"We're glad to hear it." Kate wagged a finger. "The Six Pack is not for the faint-hearted." I laughed and threw my chocolate wrapper at her.

"How did you know?" I whispered to Sophie when the others went down to fetch soft drinks.

Sophie crinkled her nose. "I think it was when I caught you throwing a sausage roll out of the saloon window that I realized something was up."

I smiled, feeling slightly embarassed. "I've been a fool," I said. "But I've learnt my lesson."

"We've got something important to tell you," announced Rachel as she came back in the room followed by Steph balancing two drinks in one hand.

Everyone found a seat apart from Jodie who was holding Mickey in the palm of her hand.

"After you left, Cindy came back on Ebby," said Kate. "She'd been out two and a half hours and Ebby was exhausted. And she was in terrible pain with her arthritis."

"Sandra could hardly get her in the stable," Rachel added.

"Guy went mad saying that she should only have been walking and trotting. Anyway Cindy started shouting back and Mrs Brentford came out and nearly had a fit when she saw Ebony Jane. She said that no horse should go out unsupervised and that Guy had better start looking for another job

– he obviously didn't care enough about the riding school horses."

"Wow," I mumbled, wishing I hadn't missed all the drama.

"And then," said Steph taking over the story, "Kate and I went into the office and told Guy that unless he started listening to you about Panda, the Six Pack were going on strike. There'd be no more help at weekends and holidays."

I flinched in surprise, twisting the duvet in my fingers. I was all too aware that there were hundreds of girls who'd love to step into our shoes. I could see Jodie thinking the same thing. Also, we were supposed to vote on important decisions. It was another case of Kate taking over if she was given half a chance.

"What did Guy say?" I ventured delicately.

"Nothing," Steph answered. "He just stared at us with his head in his hands."

Dad came home from work at 5.43 exactly. I knew because I was counting the minutes on my digital alarm clock. And I also knew that at this precise moment Mum would be telling him about me falling off Rocket.

I heard raised voices and clapped my hands over my ears. Then I decided that was being childish. I was desperately wondering what to do when the doorbell rang and Mum went to answer it. It was probably someone collecting for a charity or the boys from next door to say their football had gone into our garden.

"Hello. Mrs Parker?" The deep, controlled voice was unmistakeable. "I'm Guy Marshall. I teach your daughter at the riding school."

They went into the sitting room and I waited to be called down, but nothing happened. I paced back and forth wondering what on earth was going on. Guy must be here to talk about me falling off. It was the only explanation . . . Or to say I wasn't welcome at the riding school any more.

I sneaked halfway down the stairs and crouched, listening, but they'd moved into the kitchen and all I could hear was muffled voices. I was convinced it was something bad.

After what seemed like a lifetime the front door opened and shut and I heard Guy leaving down the front path. He hadn't even wanted to see me.

I was desperate to find out what he'd said but a dark feeling of gloom kept me in my bedroom. After a few minutes of silence I heard Mum and Dad on the stairs.

"Can we come in?" Dad peered in awkwardly and they both came across and sat on the edge of the bed.

"That was your riding instructor," Mum said

tentatively. "He told us about this Craig boy who's been calling you names."

"Oh," I mumbled, not knowing what was coming next.

"But we'll talk about that later," said Dad quickly, a twinkle in his eye. "Mr Marshall was here to tell us how much your riding has improved."

My mouth dropped open in sheer surprise.

"It seems you're a bit of a star," he added, grinning. "What's this about winning rosettes and not telling us?"

I glanced to where the orange rosettes were slung on my dressing table. "I've had other things on my mind," I said truthfully.

Dad laughed, thinking I was cracking a joke, and then grew more serious. "We're really proud of you, Emma. Neither of us had any idea how seriously you take your riding." He touched my head softly.

"Thanks, Dad."

"You've grown up a lot, Emma, and we've both decided to support you with your riding as much as possible."

Mum nodded, a tear sliding down her cheek. She always got emotional at important moments.

"We want you to do this cross-country and

enjoy every minute of it. If you don't do very well it doesn't matter – it's the trying that counts."

"Maybe we could be your grooms or something," Mum said. "Anything to help." I giggled, remembering that last time Mum had gone near Buzby he'd grabbed hold of her coat and wouldn't let go.

As they closed the door, reminding me that *Animal Kingdom* was about to start on telly, I felt a warm, fizzy happiness rushing through me. They may not be my biological parents, but they were the best Mum and Dad in the whole world.

Chapter Ten

"I can't help it, I can't stop them shaking." I glanced down at my hands which were quivering like two jellies. I'd never known fear like this: I was petrified.

"If this is what cross-country does to you, I'll stick to flatwork," groaned Kate as she came out of the toilet for the third time looking dishcloth grey. She'd only recently started jumping Archie and before that she used to make up any excuse to avoid jumping. "I don't mind telling you, I'm a nervous wreck." She sat down on the stone manger and put her head between her knees.

"Where's Steph?" Sophie rushed up carrying a pile of back protectors. Monty's grey head was sticking out over his stable door, trailing hay. "All of the Six Pack follow on after one another. Jodie's already warming up Minstrel. Come on, you guys, get a move on!"

Guy had rigged up a commentary system with a loudspeaker which kept everyone informed of what was happening. Kate and I agreed this was just going to make it extra-embarrassing when we fell off.

Mum had cooked me a massive breakfast which was sitting in my stomach like a layer of lead. Mum and Dad had set up their fold-up seats by the coffin which just made me doubly nervous. The professional photographer had arrived and moved his equipment to the water jump. There were fourteen ponies competing and as many sets of parents walking round and getting in the way.

"OK, let's strut our stuff." Kate pushed Archie forward. I mounted Rocket and gathered up my reins, trying to send him calming vibes. His back was as tense as an ironing board.

So far only two people out of seven had gone clear. There was also a timed section which Sandra was supposed to be monitoring with a stopwatch.

Rachel was walking Rusty round near the start, keeping him alert. Considering she hadn't been riding for very long she had a really neat position. Suddenly I felt like a sack of potatoes.

Minstrel was the first to set off. Jodie touched him lightly and immediately he started cantering on the spot, snorting through wide nostrils.

Rocket observed everything with a look of superiority. He felt as solid as a table and I'd convinced myself his extra-height would just make the fences look smaller.

Minstrel scorched off, Jodie grabbing hold of him and anchoring him back, not daring to go at more than a steady canter. Rachel moved Rusty up. As he was the oldest pony in the riding school she was just going to do half the course and no jumps over two foot six.

Kate was following Rachel and then it was me. I patted Rocket's neck and asked him to look after me. I tried to visualize the course; straw bales, palisade, tyres, parallel, chair, banks, coffin, water, slip rail, tiger trap, Trakehner, telegraph poles. Home.

"Good luck," called Rachel as she set off at a trot. Archie lined up, his eyes squinting, no doubt thinking up some mischief. Kate tapped him with her heels as a warning to behave.

"Three, two, one . . . Go. Good luck."

I jerked upright, swamped with nerves as Archie thundered off.

"Emma!" I suddenly registered Craig's voice. He was leaning over a rope on Foxy, his face tight and drawn. I scowled at him, warning him not to ruin my moment, angry that he'd already broken my concentration.

"Did you get the letter?" he asked. "I left it in your grooming box."

"What?" I shouted, convinced he was deliberately winding me up.

"The letter, it's important. About Panda."

My brain whirred but the cross-country was the only thing I could think of.

"If you'd like to step forward . . ."

Rocket gnawed at the bit, anticipation building up.

"Three, two, one . . . Go!" Rocket shot forward, living up to his name.

I grabbed at the reins and leaned foward, trying to remember everything Guy had taught me. Rocket surged over the bales and palisade as if they were nothing. We stood off for the tyres effortlessly and I started to relax and enjoy myself. It was the most incredible feeling of power and freedom. Riding a proper course was so different from schooling over one jump at a time.

We turned into the woods for the chair, fighting back to a slower canter.

"Stop!" Suddenly Sandra appeared from among the trees and blew on a whistle, making Rocket swerve to one side. Luckily his head came up and threw me back into the saddle.

"Archie's playing up," Sandra shouted. "You'll have to wait."

I spotted Archie's solid, immovable bulk in the trees, refusing at the chair. Kate was pulling at the reins trying to upset his balance. She yelled and kicked and suddenly Archie flung himself over the fence and charged on to the next as if he hadn't made any fuss at all. A great whoop of delight went up from the parents who had converged round the jumps.

"This is the timed section," said Sandra patting Rocket. "I'll set the stopwatch and say go."

Suddenly I knew I was going to go as fast as I could. I was going to give it my all. Rocket bristled, bunching his muscles. We were united in one purpose – winning . . .

We soared over the chair, checked back for the steps and balanced up for the coffin. I leaned back and made Rocket bounce into it just as Guy had told us. I'd never been so determined to clear anything in my life. My legs were set like concrete.

Rocket didn't hesitate once. I saw Mum and Dad in a blur and then I was leaping out over the other side. Clear!

We eased back after the timed section and that's when I made my first mistake. My legs went slack as I entered the water and Rocket pecked on landing, sending me sprawling onto his neck. Water shot up into my mouth and eyes and I lost my line. We brushed against a tree, my stirrup crashing into the bark. Amazingly, I stayed on board and rode like a Trojan over the slip rail and tiger trap. By the telegraph poles I knew we'd cracked it and wanted to thrust my fist in the air like Frankie Dettori. Sophie was waiting at the finish, jumping up and down on the spot, hugging herself.

I'd done it. I'd gone clear and fast on a strange pony and proved to myself and everyone else that I could ride. I wanted to keep the happiness inside me for ever.

"That was brilliant!" Sophie gave me a bear-hug that would have knocked the breath out of a sumo wrestler.

I jumped off Rocket and loosened his girth, ready to walk him round and cool off. Mum and Dad came across in a flurry of excitement, patting and fussing over Rocket as if he were their own.

"Thanks," I whispered to Sophie, "for everything."

It was ages before I was able to break away from everybody and lead Rocket back to the stables. Guy announced on the loudspeaker that the last rider was on the course and had fallen off at the water. I was sure it was Craig.

Sandra was walking towards me leading Panda who was all tacked up with protective boots and a martingale. "Guy's popping her round the course now everyone's finished," she mumbled, looking bored. "I suppose her snotty owner will be turning up soon. She's got some nerve after yesterday."

I decided to give Ebony Jane an extra carrot and

some fuss. Then it hit me like a thunderbolt – what Craig had said about a letter.

I searched through my grooming box and found the envelope under the hoof-oil tin.

Dear Emma,
I'm truly sorry for the way I've treated you. I couldn't face the idea of a girl pen pal being a better rider than me. Unfortunately it was me who left the pitchfork in the stable and the lid off the feed bin. I've learnt my lesson about pranks. The only person they hurt is yourself. I should have told you about Cindy being my cousin and I should have told you about Panda. She has some kind of breathing disorder caused by the spores in hay and straw – obstructive pulmonary disease or something. It's also known as broken wind. Please don't let Guy buy her – he's being ripped off.
    Craig.

I was running flat out across the field, my lungs burning and my arms flailing. Guy was walking Panda round near the start. If I took a short cut through the wood I could block them as they approached the first fence. It was my only option.

Bright green nettles stung at my bare arms as I ran through the undergrowth, tripping and nearly falling. I could hardly get my breath now, it was coming in shallow bursts. This was how Panda must feel, I realized with dread, and forced my legs on, climbing the last bank on my hands and knees.

I was too late. I could see Panda's golden body glimmering between the trees – she was already on the course. I had to do something. In one last desperate attempt I levered myself up and ran out in front of the first jump. As I turned to position myself all I could see in the dim light was Panda's legs hurtling towards me.

"Watch out!" Guy's startled voice seemed to tear out of his throat. Panda slammed in her heels at the last minute, scuffing up the loose sandy earth and throwing her off balance. Her near shoulder crashed into my body, tossing me to one side like a feather-light pillow.

Intense, stinging pain shot across my chest as the breath was knocked out of me. But it didn't matter. I'd stopped Panda. She was staring at me with a look of concern in her huge liquid eyes. All I had to do now was explain why.

During the next hour things took a bizarre turn. Amid the confusion Cindy turned up, but not alone. She was accompanied by the instantly recognizable vet from *Animal Kingdom* who was shooting thunderous looks at her.

There was a wave of excitement at the presence

of a famous person but it passed me by. I'd learnt that if someone was famous it didn't mean they were automatically nice. You had to judge people on what they were and not who they were.

We learnt a lot about Panda's illness. It was the dust in hay and straw which caused her to cough and made her short of breath. The double breathing was an effort to get more air into her lungs. Panda only suffered mild symptoms of the disease which was why it had passed unnoticed by so many people. However it still meant she wasn't a hundred per cent sound or capable of galloping and cross-country.

Cindy had known this all the time. She'd deliberately tried to con Guy after Craig had told her about my letters and about an up-and-coming showjumper and riding instructor who was looking for good horses.

The vet from *Animal Kingdom* was her fiancé and unknowingly he'd signed a piece of paper which he'd thought was just a form from the newsagent's, but which turned out to be a veterinary certificate which Cindy had taken from his files. As soon as he'd found out, he'd made every effort to track her down.

"You've not only lost your fiancé," he spat at her, "you've lost the only real friend you had. Don't bother giving me back the ring."

They left in silence, with a wall of bitterness between them. Even Cindy had enough of a conscience to look shamefaced.

Guy was devastated and walked quietly down to the office, shutting himself in. He'd been so obsessed with Panda, so blinded by her good nature and talent, that he hadn't looked at the whole picture. The tell-tale signs had always been there but he'd chosen not to see them.

While everybody was talking non-stop and repeating the facts over and over again, I sneaked back to the stables with one clear purpose. Pulling out some carrots from my coat pocket I went first to Rocket's stable and thanked him for the day. Then I went to Ebony Jane, gave her bony neck a good pat and blew up her nostrils which she loved. inally I went to Buzby, pulling open his stable door and going in, wrapping my arms round his thick, strong neck until I was covered in grey hairs from head to foot.

"Dear, darling Buz, thank you for teaching me to ride." He eyed me with a look of disapproval, until I fished out his favourite sweets, liquorice allsorts, and he ate them happily from my open hand.

"Even when I outgrow you, I'll never forget you," I whispered into his woolly ears while he slurped away happily. "You're not fast and you're not showy but it doesn't matter because you've got an elephant-sized personality." He glared at me for being soppy but I carried on.

"Horses always make the best listeners." Guy appeared in the doorway, his face strained but smiling.

I jumped slightly, feeling a prickle of embarrassment. "What will happen to Panda?" I blurted out with a need to know.

Guy shrugged. "She'll be put on woodshavings and given dust-free hay and six weeks rest, then she'll probably become a show horse or a brood mare. The good news is Mrs Brentford has agreed to keep her here and find a suitable home for her when she's better."

"That's brillant!" I perked up, genuinely thrilled. Panda was a top horse and deserved the best.

"I guess we've all made a few mistakes this week." Guy studied his feet. It was his turn to be embarrassed.

"My mum says it's not how many mistakes we make but whether we learn from them that counts."

Guy nodded, understanding. "I'm going to keep working here so you'll have to put up with my bad temper a little longer."

"I think the Six Pack can cope with that," I said grinning.

"Oh here, I nearly forgot." He brought his hands out from behind his back and passed me a beautiful crystal horse engraved with the words, "Brook House Riding School Pony Week. Most Improved Rider."

I swallowed hard not knowing what to say. I clutched the statue as if I was holding something rare and priceless.

"You've earned it, although at the beginning of the week I would have sworn you were a 200–1 outsider."

"So would I," I laughed, marvelling at the way things could change. "It just proves that where there's life, there's hope." I fingered the delicate glass in awe. "If at first you don't succeed, try, try, try again. But most important of all, more than anything – *believe in yourself*!"

Answers to the Quiz in Chapter Eight

When is a Thoroughbred's official birthday?
  Ist January.

What was the name of the first mare to win the Hickstead Derby?
  Bluebird.

Which brush should be used on a pony's mane and tail?
  A body brush.

Most greys are born black or brown. True or false?
  True.

A Falabella is the smallest breed of horse. True or false?
  True.

What is a gag?
  A bit with leather straps running through the bit cheeks. Useful for a strong horse.

How would you describe a Trakehner?

A cross-country jump with a log suspended over a ditch.

All ponies should be fed immediately before being ridden. True or False?

False.

The poll is to be found on which part of the horse's body?

The top of the head, behind the ears.

What are the symptoms of strangles?

Thick discharge from the nose, a high temperature, coughing, and a typical stance where the neck is extended and the nose poking out.

A Palomino is recognized as a breed in America, but elsewhere is only classed as a colour. True or False?

True.

How many inches in a hand?

Four.

What is a skewbald?

A horse or pony with brown and white patches.

Is ragwort a poisonous plant?

Yes.

On which side should you plait up a horse's mane?
    The right side.

From which side should you lead a pony?
    The left side.

What is laminitis caused by?
    Usually by too much rich grass or by hard feed.

Steph

Chapter One

Dad came out of the riding school office and gave me a quick wave before driving off. Thoughts scrambled over each other, racing around in my brain. Dad never came to the riding school, let alone to have a private meeting with the riding instructor.

Monty, my grey pony, nudged me in the back, irritated that he was no longer the centre of attention.

Monty was on loan from a girl who'd outgrown him. Dad had organized for him to be kept at the riding school free of charge in return for being used for lessons and hacks. Even though he was sort of my pony, he wasn't really – until now . . . possibly. It all seemed to fit together; the phone calls from his real owners, the questions from Dad, the talk of me having a very special birthday present . . .

I couldn't bear it any longer. Hurtling along the newly painted row of stables, I crashed into the saloon, which was an extended stable decorated in a Western theme where everybody hung out.

"Dad's buying Monty for my birthday!" I yelled, practically breaking the sound barrier, grinning from ear to ear. Then I proceeded to pirouette down one side of the saloon, did a cartwheel and finally tripped, lunged forward, and collapsed into a chair in a fit of giggles.

Kate glanced up from a horsy crossword with a blank expression. Jodie, who was cleaning a bridle, gave me a hard stare. "And exactly how do you know this?"

It was so typical of Jodie to try and burst my bubble.

"I just know." I made a sweeping gesture with my arms. "All the signs are there – it's so obvious."

Emma, who was the youngest, showed the most enthusiasm. "You're so lucky, Steph. My parents would never buy me Buzby – not in a million birthdays."

I couldn't stop a satisfied smirk. Steph Richards – Pony Owner. I would be able to do exactly what I wanted; picnic rides, jumping, horse shows – I might even try dressage. One thing was for sure – I wouldn't let any more beginners bounce around on him yanking at his mouth. The only person who was going to ride Monty was me.

Jodie carefully squeezed out her sponge and rubbed on just enough saddle soap without causing a lather. I could see she was working up to saying something. She always furrowed her brows when she was thinking.

Jodie, Emma and Kate were three members of the Six Pack. I was the fourth and Sophie and Rachel brought it up to six. We'd initially formed the Six Pack to save Brook House Riding School from being closed down. Now our mission was the continued welfare of the horses and ponies and learning as much about horses as possible. We were determined that Brook House would eventually be voted Riding School of the Year. We all helped out at weekends and holidays in return for free lessons. Guy was the riding instructor and Sandra a full-time groom.

Jodie scraped dried grass off a Pelham bit. "Don't you think you're jumping to conclusions?" she asked.

It was the last thing I wanted to hear. A sudden streak of spite shot up inside me. "Why do you always have to be so jealous? Just because there's no chance of you ever owning Minstrel, you can't bear anyone else to have anything. You've always got to be the best, Jodie Williams. If you're not top dog, you're not happy."

The words came out in a rush and Jodie's face crumpled with hurt. Kate and Emma looked stunned. A flash of remorse swamped me but it was too late now. Besides, Jodie needed taking down a peg or two.

263

"If you'll excuse me," I said in an acid voice, "I'm going back to my pony."

By lunchtime everybody knew.

Georgie Fenton was the third person to mention it. "I hear you're getting a pony for your birthday. Welcome to the select club of pony owners." She flung her brand new saddle onto the tack room floor, not even bothering to run up the stirrup leathers.

I grimaced with dislike. Georgie Fenton was probably the most unpopular girl at the riding school. She'd recently moved her pony, Sultan, to Brook House at full livery. The Six Pack had rallied round in an attempt to make her welcome but she soon made her feelings quite clear. She didn't want anything to do with kids who drooled over riding school ponies, and in her book, if you didn't own a pony you weren't worth knowing. She wouldn't even let the school ponies near Sultan because they were common and ugly and he might pick up bad habits.

"If you ever fancy a hack some time, let me know. And I mean a *proper* hack, not messing about doing square halts every five minutes."

I knew what Georgie's idea of a hack was – galloping flat out, non-stop, regardless of traffic and hard roads. I stared at her tall, lean figure, her blond hair shaved up the back and her dangly earrings, which you weren't supposed to wear around horses. Her mouth curved into a small, fleeting smile as she waited for me to jump at the offer. She was only asking because she thought I was going to be a pony owner.

"I don't think so," I muttered and turned my back so I couldn't see her smile vanish. She didn't say anything at first, just seethed silently. I could feel her eyes boring into me.

Her voice was high-pitched when she eventually spoke. "I don't know why you have to hang around with that Six Pack lot. They're so wet, such goody-two-shoes. You don't know what you're missing out on – you could be having some real fun . . ."

"Like I said, no thanks."

"Well have it your own way," she snapped. "But I'm warning you, don't expect me to ask you again. One day you'll be begging to be my riding partner and then you'll be sorry."

"What do you get if you cross a horse with a skunk?" Emma leaned on the fence post rattling off her latest batch of horsy jokes.

I shrugged.

"Winnie the Pooh, of course."

"What horse can't you ride?"

"Milton?"

"A clothes horse."

"What's the definition of a zebra?"

"Emma, this is stupid."

"A horse crossed with venetian blinds."

I had to smile at that one.

"Gotcha!" Emma's face lit up with delight. "Now that you're actually looking human again, what's the score? Why did you bite Jodie's head off? If I was getting a pony for my birthday I'd be hugging everybody to death. I think you owe her an apology."

I sighed heavily, not knowing where to begin. How could I tell any of my friends what had been upsetting me for weeks? They weren't in the same situation. They wouldn't understand. How could they?

"Come on, tell me." Emma poked me in the ribs with her riding crop.

"Ouch, that hurt." I grabbed some grass and stuffed it down her shirt.

"Mercy, mercy!" she cried, rolling around and clutching her neck. Suddenly she sat bolt upright, obviously remembering something important. "I nearly forgot," she gasped. "Guy wants to see you in his office – as soon as poss."

This was it. This was when Guy was going to tell me that Monty was no longer needed in the riding school. He wouldn't tell me that Dad had bought him; that would be kept secret right up until my birthday. And of course I wouldn't let on that I already knew.

"Ah, Steph, good, come in and take a seat." Guy gestured towards one of the hard plastic chairs hugging the wall.

I had to catch my breath after running across the yard. I swallowed hard and sat down, clasping my hands in my lap. I waited.

Guy shuffled some papers around the desk. He seemed on edge, almost nervous. "Um, it's about your lessons . . ."

There was an awkward pause. A tiny flutter of anxiety flickered in my stomach.

"I've decided to move you down to the lower group."

It was like a bombshell. I shook my head as if I hadn't heard properly. As if I'd got water in my ears.

"You've been falling behind for a while now," Guy continued. "It's got to the stage where you're holding the others back and it's not fair to them."

I sat swaying, feeling the first wave of horror hit me. I was frozen to the seat. For over a year I'd been in the top group with Sophie and Kate and now Jodie. How could I bear the humiliation of being dropped? My head started spinning in a frantic spiral.

"You can always move back up if and when you start to improve." Guy sat down, relieved that he'd got it over and done with. "I've spoken to your dad and he agrees."

My heart sank. I was too stunned to react, to even shake my head. I knew I hadn't been trying as hard as I should, especially with the flatwork, whereas the rest of the group took it all ultra-seriously and talked passionately about turns on the forehand and serpentines. I'd been late for nearly every lesson and half the time I didn't listen. But to be put in the baby group! I'd never dreamt that Guy could be so heartless. He was making me a laughing stock.

"You know if something's bothering you, Steph, anything at all, if someone's bullying you at the stables, you must tell me." Guy leaned forward, his dark eyes flooding with comfort, inviting me to open up.

That's how much he knew. I stood up stiffly. He'd ruined my credibility and now he wanted to play agony aunt to ease his own conscience. Well, if I wasn't good enough for his precious top group then he wasn't good enough to be my instructor. I stomped out of the office resolving never to have a lesson again.

The first person I ran into was Jodie. "Look, I'm sorry," she said, catching hold of my arm and turning to face me. "I shouldn't have doubted you about getting Monty for your birthday. It wasn't very nice. I think it's fantastic that you're getting your own pony."

I stared at her in despair. When she'd gone I shut my eyes and sighed. How on earth was I going to face everybody now?

Chapter Two

"It's all her fault!" I marched into my brother's bedroom and slammed the door.

James glanced up, crouched over a model aeroplane, carefully applying glue from a tiny tube. James was fourteen and behaved as if he came from another planet most of the time.

I collapsed onto the bed and started fiddling with the frills of the duvet. "That girl is ruining my life!"

James gave me a cold, hard stare. "Have you ever considered for one fraction of a second how difficult it is for her?"

I glared at him. This was not what I needed.

"I never asked for a stepsister," I threw back, feeling my mouth start to tremble. "I never asked for a complete stranger to take over our house, my bedroom, our dad. I never asked for this to happen."

"Hey, come on, it's not that bad." James moved forward, still holding the glue, and put an arm round my shoulder.

Abby Barratt had moved in with us two weeks

270

ago. We'd known about it for two months but that hadn't made it any easier. Abby was ten, a year younger than me, and she expected us to get on like a house on fire, even though we'd only met once, at the wedding when our dad and her mum had got married. I felt as if my life had been turned upside down; I couldn't concentrate on anything, I was totally disorientated.

"I like her," James volunteered, staring at the opposite wall.

Abby was pushy, untidy, rude and never stopped talking. I couldn't see how James could possibly like her.

"You don't have to share a bedroom with her," I pointed out. From the very first night she'd eaten packets of crisps under her bedcovers, kept the light on and asked constant questions about Monty.

"All I'm saying . . ." James began, searching for the right words, " . . . is give her a chance. She might not be as bad as you think."

The whole situation was a nightmare for me. It had taken ages for me to accept Margaret, and even after she got engaged to Dad I still refused to eat any of her cooking or hold a conversation of more than one sentence with her. Just as I was getting used to her, Abby had arrived on the scene. It was too much for anyone to bear.

"Where is she now?" asked James, flicking back his curly brown hair.

"At the garage – with Dad."

"Well just try to put yourself in her shoes. She's the one who's left her home and her brothers and friends. She must be feeling like a fish out of water."

Despite everything, I felt myself soften and reluctantly agreed to be more understanding. I could see that Abby probably didn't like the situation any more than I did.

"Here's your moment to put it into practice." James got up and walked across to the window, peeling back the net curtain.

Dad's pick-up truck had just pulled up outside. I heard the familiar engine cut out and a car door shut. Dad's husky voice was unmistakeable. And so was Abby's. Her cackling laugh drifted up and in through the open window.

They both fell through the back door, holding their sides and giggling like two hyenas. Nobody ever laughed at Dad's jokes; they were too corny. I arrived downstairs with a fixed grin on my face.

"Oh, Steph, just the person I want to see." Dad swooped a great arm round my neck and pulled me closer, then locked the other round Abby. "We've come up with a great plan." His eyes were twinkling with excitement. I expected a trip to the amusement park or something. He hugged me closer and planted a kiss on top of my head. "You're going to teach Abby to ride."

"I will not," I hissed two hours later when I caught Dad alone. We were in the kitchen making hot chocolate. "It's not fair, Abby's never been to riding school, she won't know what to do. Sh-she'll hold me back."

Dad turned round, leaning against the units, his face drawn into a tight line. "It's nice to know I've got such a charitable daughter."

"You don't understand, Dad." I raised my voice, clutching at straws. "Ponies are dangerous and Abby's never been near one before – she's never even had a goldfish. She's not athletic enough. *You've* seen her – she's the ultimate couch potato." I bit my lip, knowing straight away I'd said too much. Blushing, I looked away and stared at the clock.

Dad was glowering. "How do you expect her to know how to ride a pony when she's lived in the middle of Manchester all her life?"

I felt awful. I wanted to rake the words back in, but I just stood there, sullen and still, any words of apology stuck in my throat.

"You should think yourself lucky going to riding school and having a pony on loan. Right now, you don't deserve either." I'd never seen Dad so angry; he was literally shaking.

Upstairs, on the landing, we saw Abby quickly disappear into my bedroom. She must have heard every word.

Dad turned back, his eyes hard and cold. "Are you satisfied now?"

Abby arrived at Brook House Riding School in a pair of my old jodhpurs and a scruffy brown jumper which she said belonged to one of her brothers and which looked as if it had never been washed.

She leapt out of the pick-up as soon as we pulled into the yard, and ran up to the first horse she saw. I cringed with embarrassment as she slapped a hand on its rump and said she'd seen them do that in cowboy films. Sandra, the groom, smiled and carefully explained how you should approach horses quietly and always from the front.

Jodie and Emma came out of Minstrel's stable just as Sophie led in two ponies from the nine-thirty ride. Their eyes immediately lit up with interest. I swallowed hard and tried not to go red as they came hurrying across.

"This is Abby," I mumbled, staring at the concrete drive. "She's staying with us at the moment."

"What's she like?" Abby tutted and stepped forward, beaming from ear to ear. "I'm Steph's stepsister," she boomed. "No doubt you've heard all about me. Steph's going to teach me to ride."

274

She said it with such pride that I felt sick inside. My mouth went dry and I tried to avoid my friends' eyes which was practically impossible. The tension between us was electric. Abby's eyes misted over with disappointment but she brushed it aside and started gabbling on about Shire horses.

"I'll show you Frank," said Sophie, linking arms with Abby and leading her off to the field where Frank was grazing with the rest of the riding school horses.

"You never told us you had a stepsister." Jodie's voice was quiet and loaded with disapproval. Emma was looking completely agog.

"It never came up . . ." I groped around for an answer. "Besides, I hardly know her and she's not horsy at all."

"Well she seems really nice," Emma remarked. "You're so lucky to have a stepsister." Emma was adopted and an only child so it was natural that she'd think any family was great. "And for someone who's not horsy, she seems incredibly keen to learn."

That was the trouble. Abby never stopped. Question after question. She wanted to be involved with everything. I gave her a guided tour of the riding school ponies, telling her about different colours and breeds and sizes.

"Rusty is a strawberry roan." I pointed to the

ancient 12.2 hand pony dozing under a chestnut tree. "That's the name of his colour. Can you see how the brown hairs are mingled with white?"

Abby poured all her concentration into listening to every word.

"That pony there is a Palomino. He's called Archie." I pointed to the golden pony who was rubbing his tail on a fence post. "And this is Buzby." I showed her a pretty dapple grey who was trying to kneel down to reach for a dandelion under the fence. "He's the stable rogue," I said, rubbing his head affectionately. "He's so naughty – his favourite game is forcing riders off by rubbing them against the holly bush in the arena."

Abby scoured the group of ponies, some kicking up at flies and others scratching at each other's withers.

"But where's Monty?" she burst out. "I've been here an hour and haven't seen him yet."

I was taken aback by her enthusiasm. "He's used in the riding school in the mornings," I quickly explained. "He'll be finished in quarter of an hour. If you like we can head back to the stables. I thought you might like to spend some time grooming Blossom. She's really sweet."

"But I came to ride Monty."

Her voice was direct and precise. Of all the cheek, I thought, irritation beginning to bubble and boil under the surface. He was my pony, after all. Who did she think she was?

I stomped back to the yard and made straight for Monty's stable. Maybe once she'd seen him and realized that horses were hard work, unpredictable and dangerous, she might give up on the idea of riding. We arrived just as Sandra was leading him in from the arena. His reins were hooked back under his stirrups and his head was arched. The sun, breaking through a bank of cloud, glinted on his grey coat.

Abby's face drained of colour. Her eyes were suddenly huge in her face. Her hand flew to her mouth and she drew in a sharp breath. "But he's beautiful," she murmured. "I've never seen a white horse before."

"He's a pony," I corrected. "And the right term to use is grey."

We groomed for half an hour, brushing the dried sweat from his neck and chest and setting his mane straight with the water brush. Abby was useless and continually dropped the brushes which clattered near Monty's hoofs, sending him jerking back against the lead rope.

When she was brushing his legs she let out a shriek of horror and fell back in the straw. It took me ages to get through to her that the hard, horny growths on the sides of Monty's legs were called chestnuts and perfectly normal. She was convinced he had some terrible disease.

"Are you still grooming?" Kate poked her head over the door, her eyes latching onto Abby, alert with curiosity. Kate was the oldest in the Six Pack at thirteen and tended to boss everyone around. Nothing happened without Kate knowing about it first.

"Hi, I'm Kate." She smiled confidently at Abby and ran her hand through her dark hair while scanning the scene like a radar. "Now for goodness sake, let me fetch you a riding hat. I think it's about time Steph got you up in the saddle, don't you?"

It was boiling hot. Monty was more interested in kicking up at flies trying to land on his flanks. My shirt was sticking to my back and Abby made things more difficult by constantly asking what she could do to help. I jerked up Monty's girth and groaned when he blew himself up like a beach ball.

"I'll give you a leg up." Kate marched through the thick sand of the arena acting like an instructor. Jodie and Emma had come to watch and were perched on the fence, their shirts rolled up so they both had bare midriffs.

Abby went round to the left side as Kate instructed, and bent her left leg back at the knee.

"After three," she said, chucking her up and into the saddle. I winced as Abby's right leg crashed across Monty's hip. He stood quietly, gazing into space, used to all this.

A wave of irritation swept over me. Monty was meant to be my birthday present. How could Dad let me down like this? I didn't want him to stay in the riding school. I wanted him to be mine.

I grabbed the reins, pulling them out of Abby's hands without even looking up.

"Gee up," I heard her say in a sing-song voice. When was she going to realize we weren't playing cowboys?

I walked forward, measuring each stride, keeping my head down. Abby whooped and tried to flap the loose loop of rein across Monty's neck.

"Just sit still," I snapped. "And don't do that again. You squeeze with your legs to make him go forward." Her face closed up and she sat as quiet as a mouse.

"You look good," Jodie shouted, cupping her hands round her mouth.

Kate's voice travelled better. "Keep your shoulders back and your heels down."

Abby immediately sat up ramrod straight like a guardsman. Emma and Jodie clapped enthusiastically and she gave an ecstatic grin, then leaned forward to touch my shoulder.

"Can we go any faster?" she asked.

I definitely wouldn't have let her if Emma, Jodie and Kate hadn't been watching. Clicking my tongue, I urged Monty forward, jogging alongside. Abby's face lit up with excitement. "This is fantastic!" she shouted, waving at the girls, bouncing non-stop. I did a circuit of the arena and then slowed for a breather.

"Again!" Abby beamed, her face red and her hands clasping the reins like lumps of clay. "Let's do it again."

I ignored her and continued to walk down the long side of the arena.

"Let me off the lead if you can't keep up," she said, nudging my arm. "Go on, Steph, Monty'll look after me. He's cool."

In a moment of madness I pulled Monty's head towards me and chinked off the lead rope.

"Well go on then if that's what you want. If it's so easy, do it yourself." I was hot and bothered and irritated. I let my hand drop and Monty immediately slowed his pace. I didn't expect anything to happen. I thought Monty would just grind to a halt.

But I didn't account for two things. Firstly, that Sandra would be clattering feed buckets in the shed off the stables, and secondly, that Abby would lift up both her legs and, in a determined effort, slam them down on Monty's sides.

He burst into a trot, skidding away from my outstretched arm and trundling up to the gate. He wasn't doing anything really wrong, but Abby wasn't prepared for the sudden spurt of speed. Caught unawares, she lurched to one side, lost a stirrup, grabbed some mane, but couldn't stop herself from sliding. Monty shied round a jump wing and Abby sailed over his shoulder and, with a sickening thud, crashed to the ground. She crumpled into the sand, heaving for breath, her face drained of colour and contorted with pain. Katie, Jodie and Emma were already running forward. I stood motionless, a cold, guilty sweat prickling my skin.

"What did you think you were doing?" Kate flared up, her black eyes flicking over me with a sudden contempt. "You know complete beginners don't go off the lead rein."

Jodie helped Abby to her feet. She'd got her breath back but she still looked deathly pale. Emma ran across and caught Monty who was gazing yearningly at a yellow feed bucket. I stood like a lemon, helpless and useless.

Abby's mouth crumpled and a film of tears began to form over her eyes. Then she drew herself up straight and seemed to physically shake off any hurt.

"It was my fault," she said, her voice wooden and shaky. "I asked to go by myself. Don't have a go at Steph. It was my fault – I should have known what to do."

A cold chill settled on my three friends as they

turned and stared at me as if I was a complete stranger. Jodie was the one to voice their feelings, talking to Abby but looking directly at me. "And how can you possibly be expected to know what to do, Abby, if somebody doesn't have the decency to tell you?"

Chapter Three

"Hey, Em, what's up with everybody?" I ran up behind her and pulled lightly on her ponytail. "Have I suddenly developed the plague or something?"

"What?" Emma swivelled round, looking uneasy. "I don't know what you mean."

"I mean there's an arctic wind blowing in my direction. Like the cold shoulder. Get my drift?" I had to laugh at the pun.

Emma smiled back but it was half-hearted and didn't show in her eyes.

"Oh, don't say you've gone peculiar as well," I complained, not really believing it.

"Everyone's just wound up over this road safety test," she said. "There's a lot to learn." She glanced towards the saloon where a knot of people were already gathered. "And if we don't get a move on we won't get a seat for the meeting."

Inside the saloon the plastic chairs had been arranged in rows and the main table pushed back against the far wall. When I'd first come to Brook House the saloon had been nothing but an empty stable. Now it had a distinct Western flavour with a real lassoo coiled on the wall, a life-sized poster of Billy the Kid, and an American show bridle – which belonged to Sophie – hanging near the window. What we really needed to finish it off was a Western saddle but they cost the earth. Even so, we were pleased with what we'd achieved.

The Six Pack were sitting in the front row, Jodie at one end and Sophie at the other, scribbling notes. Almost as if she could feel my eyes on her, Abby swivelled round and stared straight at me, her mouth curving up into a smug smile. Rachel whispered something in her ear and they both dissolved into smothered giggles. Rachel took ages to get to know somebody, she was usually so shy, it wasn't like her at all. Irritation quickly became real hurt as I glanced down the rows of seats and realized nobody had left a place for me.

Sophie's dad who owned a half-share in the riding school and had agreed to take charge while Mrs Brentford, the owner, was away on holiday, stood up and addressed the twenty or so riders in front of him. "Road safety is probably the most important test you'll ever take on a pony. The test, as you know, will take place this weekend and those who pass will receive a certificate. The written test will commence at eleven o'clock on Saturday morning, so it's important you know your highway code by then." Mr Green coughed awkwardly as if he expected a reaction.

Everyone remained quiet, their eyes fixed on the person standing next to him.

"If there are no questions, I'd like to introduce you to the District Commissioner of Sutton Vale Pony Club who will be able to explain everything in more detail."

A ripple of excitement ran through the room as the woman in the smart suit stood up. The Sutton Vale Pony Club was famous for its Prince Philip Games team and one of its past members, Alex Johnson, was now a famous eventer.

The woman smiled confidently. "If everyone's ready I'd like to run through what will be expected in the practical test."

A knot of nerves twisted in my stomach. I saw Jodie and Kate draw in sharp breaths. This was our chance to prove that we were capable riders, every bit as good as the riders at Sutton Vale.

"There'll be a number of hazards, such as roadworks, noisy pedestrians, parked cars, a zebra crossing. You'll be judged on how you respond to each of these, as well as on turning left and right and trotting a short distance in traffic. You'll also be required to dismount, lead and remount. Essentially we're looking for a quiet, controlled test and a good knowledge of road craft."

Jodie stepped forward with a pile of papers,

looking very official. It was Jodie who had written to the district commissioner requesting permission to take part in their annual road safety test. She'd done nothing but preach about it for weeks as if it was her own personal crusade. We'd all got roped into entering and just about every pony in the riding school had been hired for the day.

Two and a half years ago, Jodie had been involved in a terrible road accident which had left her with a shattered left leg and very little hope of ever being able to ride again. She'd fought back with physiotherapy and was now determined to face up to her fear of traffic. As she sat down again, I could see the anxiety flickering behind the confident mask she'd fixed on her face. Kate squeezed her hand as if she could see it too. It was Jodie's determination to get things done and her ability as a rider which made us all slightly jealous.

"It's impossible," cried Emma, rushing out of the saloon as if she needed a breath of fresh air.

"Not impossible, just incredibly difficult," said Rachel as she followed her out, looking gloomy.

The District Commissioner had spent an hour explaining all the pitfalls of the test and how only twenty per cent of Sutton Vale members passed in any one year. Abby had had the cheek to ask the most questions when she wasn't even taking part.

"Well, you lot just sat there like wet lettuces," she had complained when I challenged her.

Outside, a frenzied clattering of hoofs caused the horses to run to their doors and the conversation to break off abruptly. Georgie Fenton and two of her friends came haring into the yard, their ponies foaming white with sweat and blowing heavily. Georgie tilted back her riding hat and smiled menacingly.

"Well, if it isn't the goody-two-shoes Six Pack, out to save the world."

"Give it a rest, Georgie," Sophie said sourly.

"Ooh, touchy, aren't we? What's the matter? Have you all been given L-plates to wear?" she taunted.

The girl on the chestnut pony behind her sniggered.

Sultan suddenly whirled round and tried to gallop off, his eyes popping with fear.

"Hold him," one of the girls shouted.

Georgie yanked on the left rein, carting him in a circle, his head practically touching her toe. Then she rammed her heels into his sides and drove him forward. Her two friends watched in open admiration.

"You wouldn't get much chance to ride like that on your riding school donkeys," she sneered. Sultan stood trembling, his black coat drenched and glistening like oil. Georgie's eyes glittered with enjoyment. "But I suppose you have to take a road safety test to learn how to get those nags moving."

"Oh, wake up you stupid, stupid brainless girl." Jodie cannoned forward, her eyes blazing with anger, the muscles in her neck standing out like cords. "Have you any idea about the accidents that can happen on roads and how they can wreck people's lives?" She stood rigid, outraged, shaking from head to foot.

Georgie's face registered surprise, and her mouth dropped open.

"This is what it can do to you," Jodie went on, bending down and fumbling and clawing at her jodhpurs. She peeled back the material in a frenzy, then pulled down her sock and yanked her jodhpurs up higher to expose the white flesh of her calf.

Everyone stood deathly still, frozen into silence.

The jagged, mauve-blue scar trailing the back of her leg held everybody's focus. It was hard to look away from the dented hollow as big as a fifty pence piece, or the bridge of stitch marks, still vivid. The scar had a grim fascination.

"Go on, look, feed your eyes, because that could happen to you, to anyone."

Georgie's mouth tightened but for once words had deserted her.

The Six Pack had all seen Jodie's scar before – in fact, once at a horse show, she wore shorts to

288

prove she could face people, but usually she kept her leg covered because people invariably stared or made rude comments. I could only imagine how much courage it must have taken to show it to Georgie.

Jodie stood up looking drained. Her hands were clenched together, white with tension. "OK, that's it, the freak show's over," she said, and walked away stiffly, keeping her head down and not looking back once.

"Don't you think you ought to rub Sultan down?" Kate rounded on Georgie as soon as Jodie was out of sight, her eyes flicking over her as if she was inspecting a dead fish. "Everyone knows you're supposed to walk the last mile home. If you leave him in the stable like that he'll get a chill."

Georgie leaned forward in the saddle, resting her forearms on the pommel and smiling lazily, back to her usual self. "You just worry about that yellow hairy thing you ride with the odd legs and I'll look after my own pony, because that's the difference, you see – Sultan's mine. I can do exactly what I like."

She obviously hadn't listened to a word Jodie had said.

"You've not done under the rim," I said as I inspected Monty's feed bucket, itching to find a trace of dirt.

Abby wrinkled up her face obstinately and pulled off a rubber glove. "I'm not your slave, you know, even if you do treat me like one." Monty peeled back his top lip and nodded his head up and down as if he was laughing. "Even the horse agrees with me."

Despite myself, a flicker of humour touched my lips. "Well if you want to learn to ride, you have to be prepared to do all the jobs that go with it. It's not about just sitting there and saying 'gee up', you know – it's hard work."

"Yes, boss." Abby's eyes darkened with boredom. It was working. She was already getting tired. All I had to do was keep this up and she'd never want to set foot in a stable again.

"Now, I'll just get the grooming kit which needs scrubbing, and then there's the tack. I'll show you how to clean it properly – there's quite a skill to it." I slipped the feed bucket back into Monty's stable. It had never sparkled so much.

"Why don't you take your riding boots off and I'll scrub them as well?" Abby grunted, rubbing her knees.

"You know," I said, hiding a smirk behind my hand, "I hadn't thought of that. It's not a bad idea. Thanks, Abby."

"You're not supposed to be cleaning that," I snapped as soon as I'd stepped into the saloon and caught sight of Abby. She was leaning over the table, gently sponging the soft leather of Sophie's American show bridle, and stroking it as if it were the crown jewels.

"It looked dusty," she said, keeping her eyes fixed on the ornate silver buckles. "Besides, what else am I to do when you leave me for hours on end?"

My conscience twinged uncomfortably when I heard the hurt in her voice. Had I really left her for that long? Oh dear. Well, at least she wouldn't want to come tomorrow, I thought. It was for her own good in the long run.

"Your dad's here, Steph," said Emma as she crashed through the louvred doors. "He says he's been waiting fifteen minutes and could you please hurry up." Emma flopped into a seat, panting as if she'd just run a marathon. "I just can't wait till your birthday," she gasped. "It's going to be so incredible. I wonder if Monty will have a big bow round his neck?"

Abby glanced up casually, her eyes alert with interest.

"Come on," I snapped. "We're going."

Emma stared at me, puzzled, trying to interpret my body language as I zapped out warnings to her to shut up. The last thing I needed was Abby telling Dad that I thought Monty was my birthday present. Sooner or later I was going to have to admit that I'd jumped to conclusions and I wasn't getting Monty for my birthday after all.

Even worse, it would come out that I'd been demoted to the lower riding group. Just the thought of it made me shudder. The longer I left it the better – I just couldn't face Jodie's smug expression saying, "I told you so."

"It's been lovely meeting you," said Abby, formally holding out her hand to Emma, who, caught unawares, had to wipe hers first on the front of her jeans.

"But you are coming back, aren't you?" Emma checked.

I crossed my fingers behind my back. I couldn't help it. Abby seemed to consider the question before replying.

"Oh yes, I'm coming back as soon as I can." She paused and it felt deliberate. "And the next day and the day after that and every week from then on. Steph thinks it's great that I like horses, don't you, Steph?"

I nodded numbly. She was saying this to get her own back. She didn't really mean it. She couldn't.

"See you tomorrow then," Abby said, her face deadpan. And we both walked to the car without saying a word.

Chapter Four

"When can I have a ride?" Abby nagged for the hundredth time.

Last night, instead of watching TV as usual, Abby had pored over my pony books, asking endless questions. She didn't seem to be able to get enough of horses. Dad and Margaret thought it was great and James found it funny. I thought it was a nightmare.

"Shall I go and tack him up?"

"No!" I barked, and then softened my voice. "We'll go riding after lunch; just be patient." The knuckles of my hands stretched white as I clutched onto the top of Monty's stable door. I felt closed in, trapped, almost claustrophobic.

"Why don't you find Emma and Rachel? I'm sure they're doing something more interesting than grooming," I suggested.

"But I want to brush Monty. He's our pony, isn't he?"

"OK, fine." I closed my eyes summoning up inner strength. "You do that, I'm going for a walk."

I power-marched round the field twice, trying to release the steam that was building up between my ears. This was so unfair. Nobody should be expected to play nursemaid to someone as irritating as Abby. She was taking over my life.

Ebony Jane and Frank, a retired racehorse and a part Shire, both stared at me from underneath the cool cloak of the horse chestnut tree. Frank was so tall, the lowest branches were touching his back, and he was rocking back and forth scratching his withers.

I shouldn't get so upset. This was my riding school, I'd been here the longest. I knew every horse and pony intimately. I shouldn't feel threatened by Abby. Brightening slightly, I turned and headed back to the stables. I didn't see Kate waving to grab my attention. I didn't know that within moments I would feel far, far worse than I ever imagined.

"We're having our lesson now," Kate shouted, but all I registered was her mouth opening and closing. It was as if everything was in slow motion; the weight of her words sinking in, but my reaction delayed as if holding off the moment of truth for as long as possible.

"Steph, are you all right?" Her voice faltered, and she wrinkled her eyebrows, giving me an odd look. "Come on, Guy's slipping us in before the four o'clock ride. He's going to teach us shoulder-in." She sounded as if she couldn't wait. Dressage was Kate's favourite, and Archie was really good at it. They would soon be able to enter competitions.

Sophie was already in the arena, warming up Rocket, trying to get him to bend round her inside leg. She waved. Unaware.

The raw panic which I knew was building up suddenly broke through. I could feel the heat prickling up my neck, the dryness tightening my throat. "I've got a headache," I blurted out. "That's why I went for a walk – to try and clear it."

"Well there's nothing like riding to get rid of that," Kate chivvied, trying to be so adult.

"I can't." My voice was little more than a croak. I could hardly breathe because my heart was hammering so fast. "Just leave it!" I muttered, stumbling forward, my eyes suddenly glazed with a film of tears.

I didn't see Guy until I nearly crashed into him.

"Whoa there, steady, it's not the Grand National." His angular face split into a grin as if everything was all right. As if I was still in the top group.

I wanted to cannon past him, but he propped a hand on my shoulder, anchoring me to the spot. "I've put you in Rachel's group for tomorrow morning. It'll be like a refresher course, just what you need."

Rachel had only been riding for six months.

They were barely cantering, let alone jumping. I could feel Kate's astonishment. The truth was out. Soon everyone at the school would know, and they'd all be sniggering behind my back. A wave of hurt seared through me.

"It's all right." I took a step away, my voice trembling. "I've decided not to have any more lessons, I'm just going to hack, it's much more fun."

Guy's eyes widened. "But what about the road safety test? What about your flatwork? You can't just throw it away."

"It's boring anyway," I lashed out. "I should have packed it in ages ago. From now on I'm going to do some proper riding."

A new sense of purpose coursed through me. I didn't need lessons. I could ride perfectly well. Before Guy had a chance to respond, I swivelled round and stalked off. He didn't see me rubbing at my eyes with my knuckles. Nobody was going to know that I'd been hurt at all.

I didn't notice Monty and Abby until I'd passed the saloon and could see clearly down the drive. Emma and Rachel were on either side, jogging to keep level, as Abby bounced up and down in the saddle, slamming her heels into Monty's sides every time he threatened to slow down.

As they turned to come back, Monty stumbled and Abby shot forward and flopped onto his neck, giggling uncontrollably as Rachel tried to lever her back into position. Emma was shouting instructions but nobody took any notice. Rachel grabbed hold of Abby's knee and they set off again, shrieking with laughter as Monty made a beeline for a tasty shrub in need of some pruning. The sun poked out from behind a blot of cloud and Sophie's American bridle glinted on Monty's head, the silver sparkling and the dark leather contrasting with his light coat. Abby let out a whoop of excitement as she nearly got towed under some low-lying branches.

"What do you think you're doing?" I hardly recognized my voice, it was so distorted with anger. I took heavy steps foward, overwhelmed with jealousy.

Abby tilted her head up, trying to see under the peak of my riding hat which was a size too big for her. I grabbed at Monty's reins just as he decided to veer off into a flower border.

"Get off!" My voice was arctic.

A hollow silence followed.

"What's got into you?" Emma cringed with embarrassment, but I didn't care.

"Get off my horse." I fired out each word like a bullet, staring at Abby until she awkwardly slithered out of the saddle.

"Now give me my hat."

Abby fiddled frantically with the chinstrap, then Rachel helped her, all fingers and thumbs.

"Don't you ever ride Monty behind my back again." I felt as if I was going to explode. It was all Abby's fault. Everything. I stared into her wide-set, brown eyes and felt real hatred. "Isn't it enough that you've taken over my dad, my home, my brother, and now you've started on my friends? Well, you're not having Monty, no way, he's my pony." I snatched at the reins, startling him from a doze.

"How can you be so mean?" Emma glared at me, disbelieving. "I always knew you had a nasty streak, Steph, but this is cruel. She's your sister for heaven's sake."

"That's a joke," I spat, not caring how much hurt I caused. "Sisters? We hardly know each other! If Dad hadn't married Margaret she'd still be in Manchester."

Abby looked up, her hair flattened, her narrow face white.

"Nobody can say I haven't tried," she whispered, suddenly seemingly so much older. "I thought you were someone to look up to. I wanted to be like you in every way." She paused, her eyes empty and resigned. "We could have been friends, but the trouble with you, Steph, is that you want to keep everything for yourself." She walked away, dignified, the only sign she was upset being the slight droop of her shoulders. Rachel went after her.

"Don't count on me as a friend after this," Emma snapped. "You're out of order, Steph, big time." She left me alone in the middle of the drive holding Monty which was what I'd wanted all along.

"It's just you and me, boy," I murmured, pressing my cheek against his nose. And as my anger slipped away, the heavy weight of guilt kicked in.

"Faster!" I urged Monty on, clattering over the loose stones, feeling the rush of speed against my face, my neck. "Go on, go on." We tore up the bridleway, thundering into a near gallop. I crouched closer to the saddle, half aware of the hedge whipping past, my eyes watering as rushing air slapped my face. It was exhilarating. It was the fastest I'd ever been.

I yanked on the reins to slow down as the narrow track petered out. Monty responded by slamming in his heels and jerking to a halt which nearly sent me sprawling up his neck. The breath dragged in my throat from the exertion, but every nerve was set alight from the thrill. Monty pulled and tugged, crabbing sideways, his eyes bursting with the same buzz.

For years, all he'd done was a rocking horse canter up that same track, dropping to trot well before the road. All the hacks I'd been on with the riding school had been slow and controlled. I must have been mad to stick it for as long as I had. I wasn't like Kate and Emma and Rachel. I didn't have to follow stuffy rules. I could do anything I wanted with Monty once the riding school had finished with him.

My lips stretched into a thin smile as I thought of Kate doing shoulder-in and Guy bossing them all around like a schoolteacher. I sucked in a mouthful of air and revelled in the jolting rhythm of Monty, straining to go faster. I was free, away from Abby's constant harping, away from her stupid questions and her trailing after me like a puppy.

"Yee hah!" I shouted up at the blue sky and pushed Monty forward, tapping my heels on his sides and feeling him respond like he never did with the others. It was as if somebody had put a match to a petrol can; he was suddenly all life, all speed, all flared nostrils and foaming mouth.

One, two, three. I counted the tiny drainage ditches as we raced down the grass verge, jumping one after the other. Monty skittered out onto the road when I lost a stirrup, and a car hooted behind me. I pulled him back onto the verge and stuck my tongue out at the woman driver. Starchy old ferret. No sense of fun.

Monty suddenly stiffened like a pointer, his

whole body electric with tension. I tightened the reins and tried to soothe him but his whole attention was fixed on the road ahead. He ran forward taking quick wooden steps and whinnied with a blast of noise that shattered the still air. A shudder of nerves rippled up my spine.

Three ponies surged round the corner, straddling the road. The riders were chatting and giggling but fell quiet when they saw Monty coming towards them. The black pony in the middle threw up its head and neighed wildly. Georgie Fenton took in the scene in front of her and then kicked him forward.

"Well, well, we've not seen you out by yourself before. Where are your precious bodyguards?" Georgie rode up alongside me, hardly able to hide her delight.

Monty was crushed between Sultan and one of the other ponies and refused to leave them. I had no choice but to turn in their direction. Georgie introduced me to the other two girls, Serena and Jane, who immediately plastered friendly smiles onto their faces.

"So you've finally seen sense and left the circles and serpentines behind," Georgie said grinning, and jabbing at Sultan when he tried to break into a trot. Monty settled down and walked out on a long rein, happy to be in horsy company. I relaxed and found myself enjoying their conversation.

"It must be really difficult for you having this new girl living with you," said Georgie, startling me with her genuine concern. "I've got a stepdad and I can't stand his kids."

I suddenly started opening up, all the bottled-up emotion spilling over as Georgie listened and seemed to understand exactly what I was trying to say. "My friends are OK, but they just see Abby's side," I went on. "In fact Emma thinks I should be over the moon about it all."

"Sad girl," Georgie tutted. "They're not giving you much support, are they?"

I felt a twinge of guilt at talking about my friends like that, but I had to agree with Georgie, they weren't even trying to see my side.

"You're getting a bit old for this club thing anyway, aren't you? I mean, it's your life, you can do what you want," she continued.

We broke into a trot, hammering forward, all in a line, Monty stretching into extension, bubbling with excitement. It felt good.

"Look, say no if you like, but I could get rid of Abby for a while. . . . Well, not get rid of her, but give you more space, stop her being your permanent shadow."

A flame of hope leapt up inside me. I was willing to try anything. I didn't think I could bear another day with Abby at the riding school.

"Leave it with me," said Georgie consolingly.

Serena and Jane crossed over to the verge ahead for a canter and we followed. Maybe Georgie wasn't that bad after all. At least she'd listened to my problems. And I was having fun, wasn't I? The Six Pack were getting too serious for their own good. I opened my fingers and Monty rocketed forward, grass flying up behind as he bucked and sprang after Sultan. We were both having more fun than we'd had for weeks.

As we turned homewards towards Brook House, a nagging worry started pulling at my insides. I'd stormed off leaving Abby crying in the saloon and Emma and Rachel convinced I was the most selfish person in the world. No doubt by now they'd have reported everything to the others, and then there was the humiliation of being dropped from the top group. Kate had probably figured that I wasn't getting Monty for my birthday too.

And when they saw me riding home with Georgie, well, that would really seal the rift. I doubted any of them would talk to me again. A stab of anxiety ran through me. There was nothing I could do. I couldn't just wave goodbye to Georgie and start out on another ride. And I couldn't say I didn't want to ride through the gates with them. I was trapped.

I stared down at Monty's coat covered with dried sweat. At least he wasn't hot. I gave him more rein as his head sagged down, weary.

"It's so cool being a pony owner," Georgie struck up, letting her feet loll out of the stirrups and looping the reins through one arm. "I don't know how people stand plodding around on those riding school puddings. They look half dead. I bet you can't wait till Monty is all yours."

She wittered on, swinging her legs back and forth which caused Sultan to half rear. Unlike Monty, he was still pepped up and raring to go.

"I tried having a conversation with that Emma girl the other day," she continued. "All I asked was if she went to shows, if she rode every day and who her blacksmith was, but I soon realized she couldn't answer any of them. She just stared at me blankly. So boring. And that pony she worships, the grey blob – what's his name? . . . Buzby – he looks like a cross between a dog and a camel. Should be quarantined."

I winced at the spite in her voice and wanted to stick up for Emma and Buz but the words died in my throat.

"Listen, I was wondering . . ." Georgie swung Sultan closer. "We're going to see Josh le Fleur's demonstration at Horseworld Centre the night after next. We've got a spare ticket . . ."

The Six Pack had been trying to get tickets for weeks but they were ultra-expensive and sold out anyway. Josh le Fleur was the leading trainer in the country, using new techniques in the vein of the legendary Monty Roberts. People said he could get a horse to do anything. Horseworld Centre was just down the road. It used to be a riding school but now held regular showjumping and dressage classes and different lectures and clinics every month. All we could ever do was ride past and try to catch a glimpse of the action by standing in our stirrups.

"Would you like to come? It's all paid for – you just have to turn up." Georgie's eyes bored into me, not expecting me to say no.

"No . . . I mean, yes," I said. Her comments about Emma, the Six Pack, her bad horsemanship were all wiped away like chalk off a blackboard. All I could think of was Josh le Fleur.

Georgie's eyes crinkled with amusement.

"It's the chance of a lifetime," I raved, blanking out all thoughts of my friends' reactions.

"So you're coming?" Georgie smiled triumphantly.

"Oh yes. Just try keeping me away."

Chapter Five

I was a fool if I thought Georgie was going to keep it to herself. As soon as we got back to the stables she was boasting to anyone who'd listen.

I sneaked Monty back into his stable and quickly rubbed at the sweat which was encrusted all over his chest and outlined his saddle. I didn't want Guy to see, if I could help it.

There was no sign of the Six Pack, or of Abby.

I put the saddle and bridle back in the tack room and then went to find Georgie in the feed room, as arranged. She was waiting by one of the feed bins and grabbed my arm as soon as I entered.

"Look." She pulled the lid off the furthest bin and ran her hand through some flaky white oats. I knew they were oats because they were exactly the same as the porridge Margaret had served up all winter. I stared at them as if they were an illegal drug. All I knew was that oats were energy packed and often unsafe for ponies. Monty always had a feed of pony nuts and chaff, and I explained this to Georgie.

"And that's why he's like a donkey," she scoffed.

"Now here, this is Sultan's feed bin, so help yourself. And here's a special iron supplement which will really get him going. Go and get a bucket now."

She left me alone, trailing my fingers through the oats, feeling like a conspirator. I reckoned that if I was going to take Monty on long rides he'd need more energy. And it was really good of Georgie to give me her feed.

"What are you doing?" Emma blocked the doorway, hands on hips, her face as brightly-coloured as her orange T-shirt. "Honestly, Steph, I knew you could stoop low but making friends with Georgie Fenton? You must be out of your tree."

I jumped guiltily, jerking my hand out of the feed bin. "She's not that bad," I said lamely. "She just needs someone to tell her about pony care."

"And I suppose you think you're that person." Emma grunted.

I didn't answer.

"We're having a Six Pack meeting at four o'clock in the saloon. I might as well warn you, Jodie and Kate are livid about you going to see Josh le Fleur. It's a case of if we can't all go then nobody goes. You know, that little word – loyalty. Has it dropped out of your vocabulary?"

"Oh get lost, Emma."

"And apologize to Abby." Emma stared at me,

making it quite clear what she thought. "She's grooming Blossom."

Irritation raged inside me. I didn't have to stand trial just because I was going somewhere with Georgie and not with the Six Pack. What had happened to free will?

I thumped down Monty's feed bucket – the one with no handle and his name painted on it – and started ladling in oats. I'd show them all what a good rider I was. And just for good measure, I added an extra scoop.

Twenty-five minutes past four. I glanced guiltily at the face of my Mickey Mouse watch. I hadn't gone to the meeting. Instead I'd sneaked off with Georgie, Serena and Jane to the coffee shop, Orchard Mall, in the new part of the village. I'd been before but the drinks there were really expensive and Sophie thought it was a rip-off. I was conscious of the tiny amount of loose change left in my pocket and tried to make my vanilla and banana milkshake last as long as possible.

Serena and Jane were talking about movies and Leonardo di Caprio. Georgie said she'd got her eye on a boy at school who was Leo's double and she was positive that he'd be asking her out as soon as term started. I tried to steer the conversation round to Josh le Fleur but Jane's eyes glazed over and she went straight back to boys.

"We'll pick you up at eight o'clock," Georgie reassured me. "Make sure you give me your address before you go."

I scribbled it down then and there on a paper napkin and tried not to notice Serena giggling and pulling faces at Georgie.

"Have Emma and Rachel ever had boyfriends?" Jane's face took on a gleeful leer as I shrugged my shoulders. Georgie burst out laughing and I tried to join in. I'd never had a boyfriend either but thankfully they didn't guess.

"Oh crikey, I've got to go." I suddenly remembered that Dad picked us up at five o'clock.

"Have a nice night in with your weird step-sister," Georgie sniggered. "And we'll see you tomorrow tacked up at twelve."

I nodded mutely and scrambled out of the shop.

Abby spent the whole night glued to the television watching soaps, and didn't utter a word, even when I accidentally tripped over her pile of books. When Dad asked if she was enjoying riding school, she nodded and added that tomorrow she was helping Emma to bath Buzby. It was news to me. I was amazed she was even going back.

To hide a burst of annoyance I went upstairs to root out my best pair of jodhpurs and riding gloves for tomorrow's ride. The Six Pack only ever wore jeans or scruffy jods, discoloured from too many washes, but Georgie, Serena and Jane all had the latest fashions. Jane must have money on tap to afford suede jods and proper riding shirts. I spent the rest of the night reading one of James's *Top Hits* magazines, trying to catch up on the latest movies so at least I would have something to talk about tomorrow.

The next day Sophie got out of her dad's car and for the first time ever didn't shout hello. Usually we'd have walked up to the stables together.

Abby and I arrived late because Margaret had some shopping to do first and it was nearly twelve o'clock by the time I slipped into Monty's stable. I noticed the difference immediately. He was tense and drawn round the flanks, ready to flinch at the slightest movement. His eyes, usually so placid, were alert and shining. As soon as I opened the door he crushed against me, trying to get out.

"Whoa boy, steady." I held out some mints in the palm of my hand and tried to push his shoulder back. He snatched at them briefly and scattered them on the floor. Georgie was already leading out Sultan whose hoofs clattered and skidded on a grate. Wasting no time, I did up my riding hat and unleashed the reins which were caught up in Monty's throat lash then pinned under the stirrups. He would have already done an hour's work in the riding school. Serena and Jane appeared in the yard next to Georgie.

"And to dry off the tail, you do this." Emma, who had Buzby tied up outside, suddenly grabbed hold of his tail and spun it round so a shower of water sprayed up all over Georgie.

"Watch out, you imbecile, you're not supposed to do that all over people." Georgie flicked water off the arm of her shirt while Abby and Emma doubled up in a fit of giggles. Buzby then decided to join in the fun and gave a huge doggy shake, cascading water all over Jane.

"That pony is the limit," she screeched. "Can't you control it, just for once? It shouldn't be allowed near people."

By the time we set off on our ride I was the only one completely dry and Jane was on the verge of tears because the suede on her jodhpurs might be stained permanently from the soapsuds.

Monty jigged along, snatching at the bit, skewing his head to one side when I wouldn't let him go forward.

"The oats have pepped him up," said Georgie, glancing over her shoulder and smiling triumphantly.

I had to use all my energy to keep him under control. My arms were already aching.

"Now you can really do some riding," Georgie shouted, resting one hand on Sultan's rump.

I didn't answer because I was terrified that if I took my eyes off Monty, his head would disappear between his knees and he'd buck until I came off.

All four ponies thundered down the narrow lane then veered sharply to the right, down the side of a hedge.

"But this is a footpath," I shouted to Serena who was directly ahead and doing nothing to stop her pony from dancing sideways into the farmer's field.

"So what? It's a fantastic gallop," she yelled back. "We've not been caught yet." She let her reins drop and immediately her pony blasted forward.

The sheer surge of speed made me gasp. Monty panicked into a faster gallop, terrified of being left behind.

We hurtled along, soil flying up in a dusty curtain. All I could hear was pounding hoofs on hollow ground. I crouched forward as tight as a jockey, urging Monty on. I didn't think what would happen if he stumbled, if he put a hoof in a rabbit hole; I was completely absorbed in the electric buzz of speed. I closed my eyes, feeling the whip of the wind on my cheeks and in my hair. Nothing in the world felt like this – we were free from everything.

Monty saw the old woman first and threw himself nearer the hedge, reeling off balance to avoid knocking her down. Sharp, stinging brambles smacked at my face and I lost a stirrup.

The woman stood transfixed, trembling from head to foot, clutching a tiny dog who was yapping in protest. I pulled on Monty's reins but he had no intention of stopping. The other ponies were careering on ahead.

"I'm really sorry," I yelled back, but the words were smothered as Monty leapt forward, seizing the bit in his mouth and thundering on. The old lady became just a blur, a dot in the distance, still rooted to the spot and staring after the ponies, probably in shock.

"Did you see that old lady?" I shouted to Georgie who finally pulled up on Sultan. Monty crashed into Serena's chestnut, his sides heaving for breath and his mouth flecked with white foam. For a few moments it was clashing stirrups and yanking reins as we tried to sort ourselves out. Sultan kicked out peevishly as he plunged into the other pony's sides.

"That old lady," I repeated, still in shock myself, "we nearly knocked her down. We must go back and see if she's all right."

Serena and Jane stared at me in amazement. "Are you serious?" said Jane.

"She could have been killed," I croaked. "Or even her dog. We should never have gone on a footpath."

Georgie angled Sultan closer and Monty shuffled back warily.

"Look, if you want to play good Samaritan, go back and find her, but she's nothing but a nuisance. She's always on this footpath and she should know what to expect. It wouldn't hurt her to get out of the way."

"But she's an old woman," I protested, hardly believing their attitude. All three of them glared at me, forming a wall of animosity. I didn't dare say that we were in the wrong. That bridleways were for horses, not footpaths, and it was in the road safety test that you should always walk past pedestrians. There was no way Monty would leave the others, so I rode on behind them, wanting to be back at the riding school, in the saloon, even talking about turns on the forehand and shoulder-in.

After a few moments Georgie slipped alongside me, and gave me a megawatt smile, as if the whole episode was forgotten.

"I'd wear a skirt tonight," she said beaming, "and jazz up your hair a bit. Don't look as if you've just come out of the stable."

Thoughts of seeing Josh le Fleur took over from thoughts of the old lady. I was filled with a warm, fizzy anticipation. It was going to be ace.

"But it'll be in the indoor school," I said, grasping what Georgie was saying. "There's no need to get dressed up – we'll need coats."

"Just do it, OK?" she snarled. "It says so on the

314

tickets." She smiled sweetly and started to praise Monty.

He was still pulling my arms out as we rode into the stable yard, and broke into a ragged trot as he spotted Rocket and Archie by the field gate. Sandra came across, almost as if she'd been waiting especially to see me. I knew Sandra would usually be busy bedding down and a cold shiver of anxiety rippled through me. There was no sign of any of my friends. Or of Abby.

Sandra rested a hand on Monty's reins, her eyes going to the crusted foam and grass on the bit. "Guy asked me to watch out for you," she mumbled, pushing her blond hair behind her ears. "He'd like a word urgently. In the office. I'll take Monty and untack him."

I gulped nervously and swung out of the saddle. My legs buckled on the concrete. I'd never ached in so many places. Monty butted my stomach and snorted loudly. Maybe it wasn't anything bad. Maybe he'd reconsidered and decided to put me back in the top group.

I knocked lightly on the office door and stepped in, twisting my hands together nervously as Guy looked up with a stern face.

"Ah, Steph, there you are. There's something I need to discuss with you."

I stood awkwardly at the other side of the desk which was cluttered high with papers, a bottle of horse shampoo and a hoof pick balanced on top. I gritted my teeth and waited.

"It's about Abby."

I started in surprise.

"To cut a long story short, Sophie's American show bridle went missing this lunchtime, and ... well ... it was found in Abby's bag."

I flinched.

"Abby swore she didn't take it and to be quite honest I believe her. What I really want to find out is how it ended up in her bag."

My thoughts tumbled over each other. Abby loved that bridle and she'd been the last to use it on Monty.

"I know there's been a lot of bad feeling between the two of you," Guy went on. "It would be understandable if you wanted her to stop coming here, wanted that badly enough ..."

"I didn't do it." I couldn't believe what he was suggesting.

"OK." Guy swung his hands behind his head. He looked relieved. "Just so you know, she's gone home with your dad. She was quite upset."

A gnawing sense of guilt twisted my stomach. I'd been so awful to her. I didn't like her but I didn't think she was a thief.

"One more thing."

I was making for the door, desperate to get away.

"Monty bucked somebody off this morning. He was like a different pony. Have you any idea what's got into him?"

I shrugged in reply, then stumbled out of the office, gulping in air, feeling quite sick. If only I hadn't given Monty those extra oats.

"Hey, Steph!"

I glanced up. Georgie was climbing into her dad's car. She grinned impishly through the window in the back seat and stuck up her thumb. There was something in her face, in her eyes. Surely not. No. It couldn't have been. What had she said? *I could sort out Abby. Leave it to me.* I stared at her departing figure waving from the back window. No, I told myself sternly. Even Georgie wasn't capable of being that cruel.

Chapter Six

Blast. That's all I needed. The zip of my only decent skirt well and truly snarled up with my new top. I performed an angry jig around the bed as if that would help then swivelled the skirt round for a better look and groaned out loud. It was hopeless. The whole outfit would have to come off.

Somehow time had run away with me. Georgie would be knocking on the door any minute. Jeans would have to do.

If only Dad hadn't spent so long interrogating me about Abby and the missing bridle. My blood chilled when I remembered his words about Monty. *If he gets dropped from the riding school, I'm sorry, Steph, but there's no way I can foot the bills for shoes, hay, feed and all the rest of it. He'll have to go back to his loan owners.*

I sat down on the bed, watching the colour drain from my face in the mirror. At the beginning of the week I'd been so cocky about owning a pony. Now I was fighting just to keep one on loan. I had to get those oats out of his system, and fast.

The horn tooted outside. I drew in long, slow

breaths. It was time to go. Moving quickly now, I stuffed two five pound notes into my jeans pocket and flew down the stairs.

"Have a nice time," said Margaret appearing in the hallway, tight-lipped because I wasn't taking Abby. The door clicked shut behind me.

"What took you so long?" Georgie leaned over towards the back seat, watching me squeeze in next to Serena. She darted her eyes over my jeans like a hawk. "I thought I said to wear something decent."

I noticed with horror that all three of them were dressed up to the nines, plastered in make-up and wearing platform high heels. I squirmed uncomfortably. Georgie introduced me to her brother who was driving and didn't speak. His hair was scraped back into a lank ponytail and he just sat hunched over the wheel, scowling.

Georgie smiled graciously and said we were going on a picnic ride tomorrow and I was in charge of sandwiches.

"Sounds great," I mumbled, wondering why I felt so heavy-hearted.

"Oh and I fed Monty while you were talking to that Guy Marshall. He devoured the lot. He really loves his oats, doesn't he?"

"Yeah," I croaked, feeling my stomach clamp into tight knots of hopelessness. "I think we're going in the wrong direction." I was starting to get nervous after sailing through another set of traffic lights I didn't recognize.

The atmosphere was suddenly heavy. Something was wrong somewhere. Nobody had so much as mentioned Josh le Fleur.

"I wonder if he'll use a round pen and work them loose?" I volunteered, feeling the air turn ice-cold. Serena nudged Jane and Jane eyeballed Georgie.

"Actually, we couldn't get the tickets. They'd double-booked." Georgie kept her eyes focused on the dashboard.

My brain was whirring as I uttered the next sentence. "So where are we actually going?"

It was a few moments before Georgie spoke. "A party. Some friends of my brother's," she mumbled. "They've hired a youth club." She stared straight ahead but I saw the sly smile flicker on her face through the rear view mirror.

So that was it. There never were any tickets for Josh le Fleur. It was all a set up. Georgie just wanted to get me away from the Six Pack, to break us all up. I'd fallen for it hook, line and sinker.

Suddenly I felt claustrophobic. I just wanted to go back home. I didn't want to be in the middle of nowhere, heading for a youth club. Dad would go absolutely berserk – he'd ground me for years.

"I want to go back," I said, pulling my seat belt away from my body, panic rising.

320

"Don't be so silly," Georgie snapped. "You'll enjoy it. Besides, we're already here."

The car juddered to a halt outside a grey building with an old sign saying Community Youth Club. A thickset man with a moustache was taking invitations from a group of girls, all wearing very short skirts.

"Look, there's Toby." Georgie's brother suddenly came to life, switching off the engine and pushing the door open with his foot. "Hey, Tobe, over here." Swarms of people appeared round the corner, forming a queue at the entrance.

"Come on." Georgie grabbed my arm and literally hauled me out of the car. "This is going to be the party of the century."

I stood shaking, feeling sick with disappointment I didn't want this. I didn't want any of it. I'd been such a fool, so gullible.

"Sorry, no jeans I'm afraid," said the organizer as I walked through the door.

"What?" I stared at him, motionless.

"Sorry, but rules are rules. It does say on the invitations." He was already taking invitations from other people.

Georgie and Serena glanced back to see what had happened.

"I can't get in!" Panic dragged at my voice.

Georgie shrugged but didn't make any effort to

move. "I did warn you," shouted Georgie above the noise. "There's a bus stop down the road."

"But you can't . . ." The knot of people in front crushed forwards and the three girls disappeared into the crowd.

I was left alone on the pavement, hugging my arms. I didn't have a clue where I was. Cars rushed past on the main road. A sudden chill cut through my thin shirt and I realized my riding jacket was still in the car.

"Can you point me in the direction of Carlton Estate?" I asked the organizer, but he was too busy dealing with the queue of people, and ignored me. "Oh don't bother," I mumbled, and set off down the road, marching to keep myself warm.

I couldn't find the bus stop.

I turned down a side street, tight and cold with fear. I could be out here all night. Terrible thoughts kept leaping into my mind. I had to get a grip. I couldn't buckle now. Angrily, I brushed away hot tears from my cheeks and trudged on. I could always ring for a taxi. I had some money. But Mum had always told me never to get in a taxi alone. Ninety-three, ninety-four, ninety-five. I counted my strides and concentrated on avoiding the cracks in the pavement – anything to stop panic breaking out.

I walked faster. The narrow streets gave way to tree-lined avenues. Then I saw a park on my left.

I would find a phone box and call Dad. As soon as I'd decided, I felt better, warmer. I looked up and down the road so he'd know where to come. Coronation Parade.

I pulled up short, my heart starting to beat faster. Surely it couldn't be. I ran forward, dashing round the next right-hand bend. There was Sophie's house, standing back from the road with a huge willow tree in the garden. I wasn't lost at all. I knew exactly where I was. I flew up the drive, and rapped the familiar brass knocker in the shape of a lion's head.

"Come on, come on," I said to myself, hopping from one foot to the other, determined to tell Sophie everything. To admit I'd been a stupid, foolish idiot.

"Hello." Natalie answered the door. Sophie's older sister.

"Is Sophie in?"

Natalie arched her perfectly shaped eyebrows. "She's gone to Jodie's. I thought you'd have been there. Didn't you know, they're having one of their meetings? I heard Sophie talking to your stepsister on the phone." Natalie's mouth carried on moving but I'd ceased hearing. They were having a Six Pack meeting without me. They were going to chuck me out. It was so obvious. They were going to ask Abby to take my place.

"Are you all right?" Natalie peered into my face.

"It's too late," I mumbled, feeling tears trickle down my cheeks. "They won't forgive me now. They won't even talk to me."

"I think you'd better come inside." Natalie grabbed my arm and pulled me into the hallway. "You can start by telling me exactly how you got here."

"Were you OK?" Georgie's voice crackled down the phone. "Sorry we had to leave you, but we didn't have a choice."

Oh yeah, I thought savagely, gripping the phone harder.

"We're riding at eleven o'clock. Make sure you bring marmite sandwiches, cheese and pickle, and ham if you've got any."

"The cheek," I mumbled under my breath.

"What was that?"

"I'll see you at eleven," I said firmly and replaced the receiver. What was the point of falling out with her? Then I'd have no friends at all. I couldn't bear the thought of spending endless days at the riding school and having no one to hang out with.

Abby hadn't said a word since breakfast. She was already home by the time Natalie dropped me off in her Fiesta last night. Natalie had promised not to say a word to Sophie. I was still rigid with disbelief that they'd all gone behind my back.

I sat down heavily on the stairs and remembered

what Georgie had said about feeding Monty more oats. He'd been hard enough to ride yesterday and today he was only booked in for one hour in the riding school. For the first time since I'd started learning to ride, I felt a real prickle of fear.

"He snores his head off," said Emma, smiling at the young visitor who couldn't have been more than six. "And he dreams – sometimes his legs move as if he's running a marathon. I have to go in and wake him up." Buzby stuck his huge grey head over the door and yawned at the little girl, giving a full display of his molars.

"He's like a crocodile," she gulped, stepping back.

I walked forward, towards Monty's stable, not knowing whether to say hello to Emma or to keep my head down and pretend I hadn't seen her. For one awful moment our eyes clashed and we both looked away sheepishly. It was as if there was a huge wall between us. I scurried into Monty's stable and bolted the door behind me.

Immediately he crushed against me, his chest pushing into my hip. "Monty!" I pushed him away and he turned and clattered round the box, skidding on the concrete floor which had the bed piled in one corner so the floor could dry out. His blue-black eyes looked as if they were popping out of his head.

"Monty!" My voice froze to a whisper as I advanced with the lead rope. He ducked to one side and crashed towards the door, thudding against the solid wood. Somehow I had to get a bridle on him.

"Are you ready in there?" Georgie's steely voice cut across the yard.

"Nearly," I croaked, taking deep breaths. "Perhaps you could give me a hand."

After threats of rain, a pale sun pushed its way out and the whole hillside lit up in a warm ray of light. I pushed my sleeves up and tilted my chin so I could feel the heat on my face. Even the ponies settled, stretching out their necks so we could relax the reins. I found that if I kept Monty tucked directly behind Sultan he stayed at a sensible pace and didn't pull my arms out.

We'd stopped for a picnic and taken it in turns to hold the ponies. Serena brought a special horsy rucksack which she'd won in a pony magazine and which carried all the food.

"This is so cool." Jane gazed down the hill where sheep were tugging at the croppped grass and rabbits scuttled between covers of bracken and gorse. I sighed deeply, drawing in the sweet country air. Monty hadn't been so bad after all. And Georgie and the others had been falling over themselves to make up for last night. Maybe the ticket mix-up had been genuine. Maybe they hadn't lied at all.

Georgie pushed Sultan on down the gritty track and we all followed. Ahead was the road that led to the riding school. We'd been out for two hours, cutting across the golf course and along a bridleway which Georgie had found on a local map. Down below, the road looked toy-sized. A lorry tooted, trying to get past a caravan, and I shuddered, grateful that Monty was good in traffic.

Further along, heading towards the disused railway line, was the two o'clock ride, obviously going home. Sandra was out in front on Frank who was easily recognizable because of his size. Seven, no, eight ponies followed, all in a neat line. I could pick out Buzby, Archie and Rocket. I didn't want to bump into them. My hands instinctively tightened on the reins, shortening Monty's steps.

"Last one down is boring," Georgie whooped, and holding one hand in the air like a rodeo rider, she urged Sultan on down the steep track. Serena followed at a thundering canter and Monty threw up his head. I swallowed back a wave of nerves and closed my legs round his sides.

Very soon we were all going at a breakneck gallop. I clung onto a fistful of mane as Monty plunged downwards, helter-skeltering over the rough stones. Sultan skidded to a halt in front of a five-bar gate and whirled round, his eyes rolling in a frenzy. Georgie leapt off and started tugging at the chain which held the two posts together.

"I think Jake's got a stone in his hoof." Serena dismounted and gingerly picked up his leg.

"It's hardly surprising," I gasped, feeling as if every joint in my body had been jolted out of its socket.

Georgie's features blackened. "He's fine, Serena, stop fussing." She swung back onto Sultan and grabbed at the reins. "And leave the gate. Nobody knows we've been here."

"You can't do that," I exclaimed, already noticing the sheep inching closer.

Sultan spun round and dived through the open gateway, doing half leaps on his hind legs. Georgie laughed, enjoying every minute. I stared down at my hands, hating myself for being there, for not telling Georgie what I really thought of her bad riding. For not having the strength to have no friends instead of the wrong friends. Why was I such a fool?

Monty followed the others, ripping the reins effortlessly through my raw fingers. I didn't have any energy left to control him. Tears of frustration burned in my eyes.

"Come on." Georgie's harsh voice grated. "I want to get back to the stables to see if your sweet little stepsister's copped it."

"What do you mean?" Something deep inside

me knew exactly what she meant. "Abby didn't take that bridle. She's not a thief."

"Ooh, so protective all of a sudden." Georgie swung round, her eyes glistening dangerously, annoyance flaring up. "I thought you'd have been thanking me. It was what you wanted. Only you didn't have the guts to do it yourself."

I slumped forward, sickened. If only I'd given Abby a chance. If only I hadn't been so stupidly possessive of Monty. Now I'd ruined any hope of us ever being friends.

Monty suddenly sensed my lack of concentration. In a lightning movement he sank his weight back on his quarters and reared up. I lost a stirrup and floundered desperately, trying to catch hold of the reins.

"Watch out!" Serena's face quivered with fear as Monty stepped back towards a ditch.

"Monty!" I screeched, paralysed with terror. The black hollow behind seemed to be rising up to meet us. Not a moment too soon he swung down onto all fours, blowing and snorting. We could have been upside down. Seriously injured. And all Georgie could think of was galloping on down the stony track.

"Wait!" I was still grappling to find my stirrup. Sultan took off in a blaze of speed. Monty fretted and yanked at the reins, crabbing sideways. It was hopeless. Soon all four ponies were careering down the track. Hard hoofs pelted along the ground, chippings flying up in all directions. My breath locked in my throat. I was totally out of control.

"Georgie! Monty!" Words screamed in my head. I leaned back and hauled at Monty's foam-spattered mouth but his neck was fixed hard and rigid. I saw the others easing back to a canter but Monty thundered on, relentless. We were approaching the road. I blinked back tears and started battering my fist against his shoulder – anything to get a response.

It didn't work. "Help!" I found my voice just as Serena and Jane turned round in their saddles to see why I wasn't slowing down. My lungs burned as if on fire.

Monty cannoned through the other ponies, not even faltering. Then I realized why. Out of the corner of my eye I could see the riding school ponies bunched together on the verge, watching my mad dash towards the road. Monty was racing to join his friends. If I could just turn him into the hedge before he reached the road. I was already looking to each side to see if any traffic was coming. The end of the track loomed close.

In a split second Monty shied violently to the left. I didn't expect it. I collapsed forward, flopping over his neck and felt gravity pulling me down-wards. I hit the ground with stunning force, shoulder first, and felt the pain rush up my neck.

Monty galloped on, straight into the road, in a blur of flying stirrups and hoofs. He skidded as soon as he hit the tarmac. His hind legs collapsed beneath him and he crashed heavily onto his side.

"Monty!" I was running now, gripped in a vice of panic which I'd never known before.

He didn't get up. His neck swung upwards and he grunted, his eyes glazed. He was winded.

"No!"

The grinding hum of a vehicle broke through my terror. To the left I saw the riding school ponies gathered together in a ragged clump, their riders staring in disbelief. And to the right ... Oh no. My blood froze. There was a lorry, hurtling along in top gear. And Monty was still in the middle of the road.

Chapter Seven

The screeching of brakes went on and on.

I ran into the road, waving my hands, watching the huge cab draw closer. The wheels locked and grabbed at the road surface, but it was still going too fast. There wasn't enough time.

"Stop!" I yelled, "Just stop!"

Someone ran into the road. I saw a bike abandoned on the verge, wheels spinning. And there was Abby. She went straight to Monty's head and pulled at the reins, coaxing him up.

That's what I should have done.

"Come on, boy. Up you get. Quick now." Her voice was as cool as a cucumber and her whole concentration was focused on Monty. The wild terror in his eyes abated. Gingerly he placed one fore leg in front of the other and heaved himself up.

"Quick!" I shouted, shuddering with fear. The lorry looked as if it was about to jackknife. I could see the driver's face, strained and white, as he gripped the wheel. The noise of the squealing engine was deafening.

A moment later, the lorry sailed past the spot where Monty had fallen. It skidded and spat and ground to a halt a hundred metres or so further up the road. The driver levered himself out of the cab on shaky legs, amazed that nobody had been hurt.

Abby was still holding Monty, talking nonsense to him, stroking his sweat-stained coat with a rhythmical motion. A silence fell over everybody. It was a combination of relief and shock. I reached for Monty and buried my head in his warm, sticky coat, closing my eyes to the nightmare that had just happened. Abby stood next to me, breathing steadily. Monty owed his life to her courage and clear thinking.

"I don't know how I can ever thank you," I mumbled, starting to tremble.

"Don't." She shrugged her shoulders. "I did it for Monty."

"What did you think you were doing?" said an angry voice. I jerked my head up, staggered to see Mr Green in his Jaguar, his head out of the window, his dark eyes blazing. He must have seen everything. I swallowed down a new wave of horror, but just ended up shaking.

"Is this what you get up to behind our backs?" Mr Green leapt out of the car, about to slam the door, but changed his mind when Monty shied away. A muscle twitched violently under his left eye and his hands were clenched white with tension.

"Is this what Brook House teaches people? To ride like maniacs? To be a danger to the public?" I wanted to crawl into a hole. I couldn't cope with much more. I hated myself enough already.

"Dad, I can explain." Sophie was trotting Rocket down the road, her face awash with anxiety. "Are you all right?" She scanned my dishevelled appearance, ripped jods and blood-spattered shirtsleeve. "Dad, she's just had a bad accident. This is no time—"

"Don't tell me what's right and wrong." He was literally hopping from one foot to another, colour scorching up his neck.

The lorry driver, seeing someone acting with authority, came striding up. "I want the name of your insurance company. If there's any damage to my truck . . ."

Sophie jumped off Rocket and wrapped an arm round my shoulder. The sudden kindness was too much and I burst into tears.

"How did it happen?" asked Sandra as she rode up on Frank with the rest of the ride behind her. Frank's big Shire nose nudged the lorry driver in the ribs which half scared him to death. Traffic held up by the disturbance started tooting, which set all the ponies barging into each other. I glanced round for Georgie but she'd disappeared. There was no sign of Serena or Jane either.

"Here." The lorry driver passed me a hanky with an oil stain in one corner. "I can't stand seeing people cry. Are you all right?"

Mr Green ran his hand down all four of Monty's legs, checking for damage, then turned to me. "I'll take you back in the car. Did you hit your head? Are you hurt?"

"No, no," I yelped. "I can ride, honestly." The thought of sitting next to Mr Green and his boiling wrath made me shrink inside.

"This pony is no use to a riding school. I've no choice but to let him go. He's dangerous."

"But you can't," I pleaded, desperation crashing through me. "He's not usually like this. You don't understand."

"You've got to give him another chance." Abby wrapped her arms protectively round Monty's neck.

"Dad, don't be so awful. You can't make a decision like that without consulting Mrs Brentford."

"I'm running a business, not a charity, and in Mrs Brentford's absence I have full authority here." Mr Green's face tightened with resolve.

"Even so, it does seem a bit severe." The lorry driver was softening and even reached out to stroke Monty who had recovered and was tearing at some cow parsley.

"What's it got to do with you?" Mr Green glared at him. He pushed his grey-black hair off his forehead and squared his shoulders. "OK, prove to me he's safe. Let me see him pass the road safety test. And not with an experienced rider. I want a complete beginner on board. Someone like this girl. What's your name?"

"Abby."

"Can you ride?"

"No."

"Well, here's your lucky chance. You've got four days to learn."

"Dad!" cried Sophie.

"It's my final offer. Now, if you'll excuse me, I'm going back to the office." Mr Green manoeuvred his car round the lorry and a backlog of vehicles flowed past, all carrying angry drivers, one even shouting abuse.

I turned back to Monty feeling drained. For a moment Abby's eyes clashed with mine. The bitterness and hurt were undeniable. There might as well have been a hundred miles between us.

"So it's all right for me to ride him now you need me?" Abby crossed her arms defiantly, hugging her chest.

We were in the saloon, trying to absorb the

336

bombshell. Sophie had called a Six Pack meeting as soon as we got back to the stables which really surprised me. Jodie, Kate, Rachel and Emma had listened to the story in silent amazement. I had had to confess everything – even feeding oats to Monty.

"I could try to get Dad to change his mind but there's not much hope." Sophie pressed a finger to her forehead and closed her eyes. "You're totally sure your dad's not buying Monty?"

I nodded briskly, not daring to speak. It was going to be the worst birthday ever.

"At least she won't have to learn to canter." Rachel piped up. "That'll cut the work down a bit."

"I haven't said I'm doing it yet," Abbey answered obstinately.

"I can't say I blame you." My voice quivered with hopelessness. My shoulder ached and I wanted to crawl into a hole.

Emma started to read out Leo from the horoscope page of *In the Saddle*. "There's a horsy challenge in your life which you need to face up to. Take the plunge and it'll all work out OK. That fits you too, Abby. You're Leo as well, aren't you? No wonder you don't get on – you're both too alike." Emma went quiet when she realized she'd said too much. Abby looked furious.

"I can't believe you were so stupid," Jodie burst

337

out suddenly, unable to hide her feelings. "You've seen what happened to me in a road accident. Doesn't that mean anything?"

Jodie had fallen in with a bad crowd at her old riding school. It had seemed fun at the time to try and ride along the white line in the middle of the road. Now she had a metal plate in her leg.

"I didn't think I had any friends left," I croaked, my teeth chattering. "You were going to give my place in the Six Pack to Abby, p-probably still are. You all met up last night without me."

"You were going to see Josh le Fleur!" Jodie retaliated. "Or had you conveniently forgotten?"

"Stop it!" Sophie raised her voice. "There's been enough falling out. And Steph, if you must know, we called a meeting last night to discuss you and Georgie. How we could get you to see sense. Because we were worried about you."

A stony silence followed.

"I-I never realized," I said, feeling ashamed. Hot tears ran down my cheeks. The last ounce of strength drained out of me and I sat down in a battered old armchair and sobbed uncontrollably. Rachel and Emma immediately came across and wrapped an arm each round my shoulders. Kate thrust a tissue in my face.

"Whether you like it or not, the Six Pack stick together." Sophie pulled a mock stern face. "We're friends for life through thick and thin, remember?

That's the pledge we all made to each other. Now, just because you temporarily messed up, doesn't mean you're not one of us any more." She held out her hand for our special handshake and we all placed our hands on top, palms downwards.

"Six Pack for ever," everyone yelled.

"Where's my riding hat?" Abby asked, standing with her hands on her hips and a piece of hay in her mouth. "If I've got to become a Harvey Smith in four days we'd better get on with it, don't you reckon?"

Monty danced and skittered sideways as Kate led him into the arena and Abby followed, turning pale at the sight of him. "What have you done to him? Put rockets in his hoofs?"

"He'll calm down in a day or two," I reassured her. "Just as soon as the oats get out of his system."

Jodie suggested we lunge him before Abby mounted and I raced back to the stables for the lunge cavesson and long whip. Lunging is when a horse goes round in a circle on a long line, held by someone standing in the middle. It's really good for making horses more obedient and supple, but if you aren't careful it can make you dizzy. Also, it's dangerous if you get the lunge rein caught up in the horse's legs. Jodie was the only one who could do it properly.

Maybe, just maybe, this crazy plan would work.

I flew into the tack room, at least feeling that we were doing something positive. I wasn't prepared for running slap bang into Georgie.

"Well, look who it isn't," she leered, her face immediately lighting up. "It didn't take you long to go running back to your old crowd. What was the matter? The pace too hot with us? Couldn't you keep up?" She glanced back towards Serena, looking for support, but Serena kept her head down and fiddled with the velcro straps on a pair of brushing boots.

I stepped back. Just the sight of Georgie made me remember my recklessness, my stupidity, and the glaring horror of seeing that lorry hurtle towards Monty. And she didn't care. She hadn't even apologized.

"I'm back with the Six Pack because they're my real friends," I burst out, surprising myself with a sudden surge of strength. "You only wanted to hang out with me to get up their noses, to break us all up."

Georgie smiled drily, confirming everything I'd just said. "And it worked, didn't it? You were sucked in. You, who said you never would be." Her eyes glowed with triumph as if she'd achieved some special feat.

"More fool me," I mumbled, despising myself. Only this time Georgie couldn't get to me. I had her measure. I knew what she was about. I turned

340

back, not in the least bit riled. "The sad thing about you, Georgie," I answered, keeping my voice low and feeling almost sorry for her, "is that you'll go through life and you'll never really know what true friendship is."

"Legs, legs, more left rein," Jodie shouted. Abby was so busy concentrating on her hand position that she didn't realize she was tipping to one side.

"You're still bouncing up and down." Kate urged Monty on from behind with her riding crop. "Your hands keep shooting up round your chin." Abby grunted something, but it was swept away as Monty lunged forward, half rearing, and she bounced along like a rubber ball, clinging tightly onto the saddle.

"Try gripping with your knees," Rachel shouted, moving a jump wing out of the way.

"That's throwing her out of the saddle," Sophie argued. "Just think of yourself as a jelly, Abby. Let yourself go."

"Your heels have shot up again," Jodie commented.

"What do you think I am? A contortionist?" Abby pulled up, crimson in the face. "You're going to have to sort yourselves out, because I can't cope with six instructors. It's worse than being at school."

Of course she was absolutely right. Even Kate looked sheepish.

"Who can remember how to do rising trot?" asked Rachel as she jumped off the fence and walked across with Emma who was writing everything down as if it was a school assignment.

We all looked blank.

"I think we ought to take it in turns to lead her," said Sophie sensibly. "We're not getting anywhere like this."

"We could position ourselves like a relay race," Emma suggested. "That way no one runs out of puff."

"And when do I get a break?" Abby said drily, but nobody heard. Emma was already allocating positions around the field.

"Steph, you can be on the last run. From the chestnut tree to the gate."

The sheer task ahead of us was beginning to hit home. How could we possibly get Abby to ride properly when she barely knew the difference between walk and trot, never mind anything about sitting and rising? A cold feeling of hopelessness settled over me.

"Before we start," Abby added, pushing back her hat and accidentally dropping the reins, "I think my pedals are too long."

"Up, down, up, down, up, down." Kate dragged Monty on, trying desperately to stop him from breaking into a canter. Abby bumped along methodically, heaving herself up and then plopping down like a sack of potatoes.

Sophie took over from Kate. "Up, down, up, down, up, down." They trotted along the bottom side towards Rachel, and then onto Emma. Abby didn't look remotely like she was doing rising trot. In fact, she just seemed to be bumping more and more.

"Hold onto the front of the saddle," Emma advised between gasps. They were trotting towards me now, getting faster and faster. Emma's face was bright red.

"Here." She thrust the reins at me, bending down with her hands on her knees.

I kept at Monty's shoulder, trying not to interfere with his stride. Abby was bumping totally out of rhythm but looking straight ahead, her face rigid with concentration. I couldn't believe her determination.

Monty stumbled and she grasped hold of his mane to stay on. Abby was still fighting to win back her balance and I was just about to slow down to walk, when a parcel van rattled up the drive, close to the fence. Usually this wouldn't have caused a problem so I didn't think anything of it. But Monty's recent bad experience with traffic had obviously had a damaging effect on him. In a split second, he'd lurched back onto his quarters, eyes popping out of his head. The reins scorched through my fingers as he shot up on his hind legs, fear oozing from every pore of his body.

Abby didn't stand a chance. Monty smashed his neck into her face and she was tossed backwards like a discarded doll. Instinctively, she curled up into a ball as Monty screamed in panic and went right over, slamming down hard on his right side, just centimetres away from Abby. It all happened so fast. If Monty had fallen the other way, his flailing legs would have . . . It didn't bear thinking about.

"*Abby!*" The Six Pack raced towards us, electrified with terror. Abby didn't move.

"*Abby!*" Now I was shouting. I stumbled across, trying to remember my first aid from school. Her face was white. I didn't move her. Leave that to the paramedics. But what if she was choking? What about the recovery position? I peered down, straining to see any sign of life. "Oh please, Abby, don't let anything be wrong. I'd never forgive myself. You've got to be all right. Abby?"

Her eyes flicked open and she grinned impishly. "I didn't know you cared so much, sis."

Relief made me dizzy. She propped herself up on one elbow and blood surged from her nose, which was already swelling up.

"Thank goodness!" Sophie was the first to reach

us, and squatted down, telling Abby to pinch her nose and lean forward.

"Who said you're not a proper rider until you've had your first fall?" Abby managed to splutter even though Sophie was urging her to be quiet.

Kate held up three fingers for Abby to count. I went to tend to Monty who was shaking, his head flopped down between his knees. The sweat was pouring off him. It was obvious he was still traumatized.

"We ought to get her to hospital. She might be concussed," Emma said, coming over.

"No way!" Abby struggled to get up, overhearing us. "Do that and Monty'll be on the first truck out of here."

"I'm hunky-dory anyway." Abby stumbled to her feet, still dripping blood. "Just give me two minutes and I'll be back in the saddle."

Rachel passed her another tissue. I marvelled at her courage and determination but a new depression was pushing me close to the edge. Not only did we have to teach Abby to ride, but we had to cure Monty of traffic-phobia. It was too much. Sophie stood grim-faced beside me, obviously thinking the same thoughts.

"So where do we go from here?"

Chapter Eight

"I can't move," groaned Abby, peeking out from under the bedclothes. We'd gone through this ritual for the last three mornings. I had to support her shoulder while she swung her legs out and gradually shuffled onto the floor. Then I had to help her get dressed because she couldn't lift her arms over her head.

"I've heard of being saddle-sore, but this is ridiculous," I said rooting out a sock from under the bed.

Abby was having to pretend that everything was OK in front of Margaret and Dad. James knew something was up but was too absorbed in his model aeroplanes to say anything. After endless riding Abby still hadn't mastered rising trot. We were now in a state of total despair. It was the theory test that morning and the practical the next day – my birthday. Short of a full-blown miracle there was no way Abby or Monty would pass. Abby insisted on green socks for good luck and started counting magpies out of the window.

"Why don't we throw in a black cat and a

rabbit's foot as well?" I groaned and picked up the road safety manual for the thousandth time. "On which one of the following can you ride or lead? A. A motorway. B. A footpath. C. A bridleway."

"Give me a break." Abby screwed up her face. "I'm not that thick."

"OK, OK, something less obvious. If you are riding one horse and leading another, where should the led horse be? A. On your left. B. On your right. C. Behind you."

"Oh, you can't fool me. That's a trick question. You shouldn't be leading a horse at all."

"No, Abby! The answer's on the left!"

"OK, keep your hair on. It's not the end of the world. Try another one."

"Can I just say that it *will* be the end of the world to me if you don't pass this test!"

We both collapsed on the bed wondering who we were trying to kid. We were almost pretending it was a school spelling test or something, not Monty's future hanging in the balance.

"Here, you might as well have this now." Abby passed me a grubby envelope which looked as if it had been stuck down with superglue. Inside was a thin piece of white card with a drawing on the front of Monty and me looking out over a stable door. It was a caricature done in pencil and it was absolutely brilliant.

347

"I'm a bit of a dab hand at drawing," she said, embarrassed. "Pity I'm not as good at riding, eh?"

I was still too stunned to speak. All the time she'd lived here I'd treated her like an idiot and acted superior, when actually she was really talented.

"It's really special," I whispered, finding my voice. "And . . . I'm really pleased you're here . . . as part of the family."

"Yeah?" Abby raised her eyebrows. "You know, if you look at that drawing long enough, we even look like each other – especially the snub nose."

"Don't push it." My face broke into a grin and I rammed her in the back with a pillow.

"Ten minutes to go!" Rachel shot back into the stable holding a carrier bag over her head to keep off the rain.

The test was being held in the saloon and Sutton Vale Pony Club members were still turning up in expensive cars with horsy-looking parents and enough knowledge to go on Mastermind.

"What's the sign to get a driver to slow down?" Kate was having a panic attack and scouring through Jodie's memory cards.

"Easy. A rider moves her right arm up and down with her palm facing the ground."

We were all convinced Sophie had a photographic memory.

"What if we all fail?" Emma wasn't exactly inspiring confidence.

"With all the lucky mascots you've brought along, you won't even be able to see the test paper." Kate picked up a Kermit which had faded to yellow.

"I can't do this." Abby stood by the window looking as if she wanted to climb out and escape. Her teeth were chattering and her skin was shining with beads of perspiration. Monty wafted his head up and down as if to disagree.

"What do you mean *can't*? You'll breeze it." Kate shut up when she realized she sounded like a schoolteacher.

"Please Abb, for Monty," I said. Her eyes followed mine to where Monty was gently nibbling at a hay net, shaking off a fly without a care in the world.

"Why does it always have to be me?" she whimpered, her eyes glued to Monty's innocent, unsuspecting face. The mere thought of the gnawing sense of loss that I'd feel if Monty went back to his loan owners practically knocked the breath out of my body. I felt numb.

"If everybody's finished you can now put down your pens."

Abby's face creased into a megawatt grin as she stuck up her thumbs in triumph. "We did it! We did it! We did it!" She started hopping about on the spot as soon as we got out of the saloon. Emma joined her and various lucky mascots went shooting all over the yard.

Sophie was holding the test sheet against the answers in the manual, her knuckles rigid and white with tension. Jodie leaned over her shoulder, moving her finger down the page. "The correct answer to question one is . . ." I held my breath. We all dived forward because none of us could remember the question. A roar went up when Jodie said C.

"A, D, B, C, A, A, B, C, D, A."

A gush of relief swamped me when I saw the joy in Abby's face. We'd all passed, Jodie and Sophie with top marks.

"This is as good as winning a cross-country," said Emma. "Shouldn't we get a rosette or something?"

"That comes later," Sophie pointed out. "When we prove we can ride in traffic."

Instinctively, I glanced across to where Monty was standing, ears pricked forward, alert to something in the distance. What was going through his mind? How was he feeling? We'd given him some time off from even seeing a car after he nearly scrabbled across the bonnet of Rachel's mum's car two days ago. The truth was, none of us knew what to do. The best we could come up with was to give him time to forget the accident. To make sure no one hassled him. None of us would admit to each other that we were scared to handle Monty, that Sophie's dad was possibly right, that Monty was too dangerous to have in a riding school.

"OK. Lead him forward." Sophie stepped away from Guy's horsebox, leaving the ignition key in and the engine gently thrumming.

My fingers immediately tightened on the lead rope. "Come on, boy, walk on."

There was no response. Monty had already thrown up his head, eyes rolling. The veins in his neck stood out like cords, and fear surged through his body.

We were in the stable yard, near the barn, where there was enough room to lead Monty past the vehicle. He'd been fine when the engine was off, calmly walking past, more interested in raiding my pockets for horse nuts.

Now it was a different story. Abby caught my eye. A streak of nerves rippled up my spine. I could feel Monty arching his back, tensing, digging his heels in. "Please, Monty, please walk forward, walk on." I forced myself to take a step, bearing down on the lead rope.

"Come on, Monty, come on, baby." Kate held out her hand encouragingly. For a second I really thought he was going to go. He seemed to lower his neck and relax, trusting we weren't going to hurt him.

"That's my boy." Sophie's voice rose with hope.

Then it was all over. Nostrils wide, eyes bursting from his head, he charged backwards, the lead rope scorching my bare hands.

"Watch out!" Jodie's face was white with terror.

Monty swirled round, knocking me off balance, and then, desperate with panic, lashed out with both hind legs. The sound of broken glass filled my head. The left headlight was out.

Jodie rushed forward, grabbed Monty's bridle and dragged him away. Already his coat was streaked with sweat. His flanks were quivering and drawn in like a greyhound's. His eyes were dilated in a way I'd never seen before. Even worse, Guy and Sophie's dad were running towards us. Guy looked absolutely furious.

"Who gave you those keys?" He glared all around, his jaw fixed and his eyes narrowed to tiny slits.

Kate blanched as if she'd seen a ghost. She'd told us she'd asked Guy's permission to take the keys from the office.

"I took them," Sophie blurted out, trying to cover up.

"Don't lie, Sophie, you're so transparent." There was no fooling her dad. "That pony is dangerous.

I want you to turn him out in the bottom field and leave him there until we decide what to do."

"It's not for you to decide," I said, and immediately regretted it. His eyes were as cold as ice.

"While I'm in charge of this riding school, young lady, I'll make the decisions."

"No." Sophie drew herself up. We all knew how much she loved her dad, how she always wanted to please him, how difficult it was for her to go against his authority. "You gave us till tomorrow afternoon. After the road safety test. You can't go back on a deal."

Mr Green's heavy, dark eyebrows shot up in amazement. Guy quickly tried to diffuse the tension by examining the shattered headlight. Sophie remained resolute, meeting her dad's fierce glare. In exasperation, Mr Green mumbled under his breath, "OK, have it your way. But mark my words, it'll take an act of God to get that pony right."

Sophie threw her arms round his neck. "Thanks, Dad, thanks a million."

"Um, sorry to interrupt," said Guy, shuffling his feet anxiously, "but who exactly is going to pay for this completely wrecked headlight?"

"He's right though, it is going to take an act of God." I was plaiting Monty's mane to keep it lying on the right side just for something to do and to

353

try and stay sane. Abby was pulling bits of celery out of a salad sandwich and offering them to Rusty who was dozing in the next door stable.

"What we need is some kind of horse doctor, someone who can speak Monty's language." Abby was just rattling on, not realizing the importance of her words. Not until my mane comb went crashing to the floor and she turned and saw the grin splitting my face.

She smiled a slow smile, beginning to read my mind. We both shouted out into the charged silence at the same time: "Josh le Fleur!"

Chapter Nine

"It's crazy, it'll never work," said Rachel once she'd listened to the plan which we'd cobbled together.

Abby had already rung Horseworld Centre and discovered that Josh le Fleur was doing his last matinée performance that afternoon. But it was fully booked – not even a single cancellation.

"He has to go in and out of the indoor school, doesn't he?" Kate said. "All we have to do is hide somewhere until we see him alone, then spring out and plead for his help."

"And he's just going to come running to do our bidding, even though we have no money and he doesn't know us from Adam." Jodie wrinkled up her nose in disbelief.

"Well can you think of a better plan, Einstein?" Emma leaned forward, clearly not wanting to dwell on negative thoughts.

We were all sitting on the fence waiting for the twelve o'clock lesson to come in. We always did jump duty which entailed putting up the poles which were endlessly falling, even though the jumps were only two foot six.

Rocket was the first to come in, carrying a nervous rider called Sandra who rode every Saturday but never seemed to improve. Archie, Kate's favourite, came next, glued to Rocket's tail, doggedly refusing to turn right and setting off at a trot to the far corner where his best friend Buzby was grazing.

"She's got her reins all over the place again," Kate tutted. "How can I attempt to get Archie on the bit when he gets ridden by lemons like that?" Actually Kate was a very good rider and extremely adept at putting Archie on the bit and executing complicated dressage movements.

"Look who's coming next." I had to do a double-take to be absolutely sure. Georgie Fenton rode in on Sultan, keeping her eyes fixed on her hands and her mouth in a tight line.

"After all she's said about lessons." Sophie let her breath whistle out in amazement. We were all gobsmacked. She walked stiffly round the arena the opposite way to everyone else, hopelessly trying to stop Sultan from jogging.

"She doesn't even know how to form a ride," Emma bitched. "And look at her elbows – she could do a chicken impression with them."

I felt hot and sick at being so close to her. Since the accident, I'd purposely stayed out of her way, ducking behind feed bins if I had to, to keep out of sight.

356

"Sssh," Sophie put her hand over Emma's mouth as Guy walked in in a steaming mood.

"He's still angry about the headlight," Rachel whispered. "I feel sorry for this ride – he'll really put them through it." Guy was well known for working riders until they were blue in the face at the best of times. Now he asked everyone to trot, glowering like a bull when Archie stuck his head down to try and roll.

"Shorten your reins and keep your leg back," he yelled.

By the time the jumping started, the atmosphere was laden with bad feeling. Guy had already had words with two sets of parents who had tried to take over the lesson and instruct their own children. This happened every Saturday and Guy had some great put-down lines like: "This is what I'm paid to do. Will you kindly let me get on with my job?"

Rocket was a brilliant jumper and there was no excuse for his rider collapsing on his neck and then bursting into tears when she realized she hadn't fallen off.

"What a wimp," Kate tutted.

Minutes later an irate parent told Guy that she'd only just come out of plaster from her last fall and angrily accused him of being a slave driver.

Then it was Georgie's turn and all credit to her, she did quite well, although Sultan was pulling like a train. Emma and Rachel put up the jump following Guy's instructions and that's when things went wrong. Archie decided now was the time for a quick exit and scuttled straight out of the open gate and back to the stables with his rider screaming her head off.

Guy started shouting at the girl on Rocket for cantering past the other riders instead of waiting her turn. Poor little Blossom was cowering into the hedge, frightened to move.

Georgie was walking down the long side waiting for the ride to reform and before I knew it, she was there, trying to talk to me. I stiffened and my mouth dried up.

"I know you don't want anything to do with me," she started. I was holding a yellow and black pole with the paint peeling off at one end. I concentrated hard on it, trying to push all thoughts from my mind. I could sense the Six Pack behind, overprotective, wondering what was going on.

"I don't want to cause trouble, here," she began again, rooting in her jods pocket, digging down deep and standing up in her stirrups. Eventually she pulled out some tickets, limp from the heat of her body. She leaned down, imploring with her eyes for me to take them. I reached out and stuffed them awkwardly into my jeans pocket without looking at them.

"They're for the Josh le Fleur demo this afternoon. Dad got them for me, but I figured you'd appreciate them more. I'm selling Sultan, you see. That's why I'm on this lesson – to try and get him going better. I'm not interested like I used to be. It doesn't seem to be any fun any more." She ran on, tripping over her words. Somehow it was important for her to tell me this.

The Georgie Fenton spark had vanished. It was almost as if she'd been putting on an act all along and this faded, quieter version was the real her. It struck me quite suddenly that her drive to split up the Six Pack had been fuelled all along by jealousy. She didn't belong at the riding school, never had. Probably, nobody had ever invited her to join a club before. She'd been on the outside, shunned because of her attitude, an attitude developed from bitterness because she was never really one of the in-crowd.

"Are you planning on letting go of that pole, Stephanie? Or are you going to treat us all to a tango?" Guy was waiting with his arms folded.

I climbed back onto the fence with a warm, leaping sensation coursing through me. Just to be totally sure I pulled out the tickets, feeling the grainy texture of the damp card, and read the official words. Three tickets. It wasn't a hoax. Three of the Six Pack had first row seats at the Josh Le Fleur lecture-demonstration. It was a godsend.

*

"We're going to be late." Sophie sat on the bus, nervously twiddling her hair, as signs for Horse-world flashed past. Jodie was staring out of the window, her chin set in a rigid line which was a tell-tale sign that she was nervous. I'd got to choose who went with me and I'd picked Sophie and Jodie because they were the most mature and sensible. Kate had been put-out because she was the eldest and naturally thought she should be in charge.

I stared out of the window thinking about the legendary Monty Roberts who had started off the phenomenon of talking to horses in their own language. There had been a series of articles in *In the Saddle* about talking to horses. The Six Pack had spent hours in the field trying to achieve the same bond. We'd all been to see *The Horse Whisperer* four times and knew it off by heart. Please, Josh, be able to sort out Monty's problems. If only this total stranger knew he was our very last hope. I spent the rest of the journey pretending to jump telegraph poles in my mind's eye, getting the striding spot on. I'd done this since I was six years old.

"It's packed," said Sophie as we arrived and pushed our way down to the front row, looking for seats twelve, thirteen and fifteen. None of us wanted to sit in seat thirteen but Sophie eventually agreed and plopped herself down saying we were stupidly superstitious.

The indoor school was buzzing with excitement. Slap bang in the centre was a see-through metal pen which was where all the training took place. Somebody was talking on a microphone, going through all Josh le Fleur's achievements. He'd even been working with wild zebra and antelope in Africa. He'd worked on racehorses for royalty and famous showjumpers and once retrained a killer stallion who used to attack anyone who set foot in his stable.

There were lots of oohs and aahs and an electric current of anticipation. The speaker announced there would be refreshments in the break. The most we could run to was a coffee between the three of us.

We weren't prepared for Josh le Fleur. He was about the size of Frankie Dettori with a mop of unruly brown hair and a down-to-earth, almost shy demeanour. It was as if he was embarrassed by his own success.

Two men were leading a huge, heavy Irish Draught horse down the side of the school, keeping a really strong hold on brass chain lead ropes.

"I recognize that horse," said the woman in the next seat, ferreting on the floor excitedly for her programme and turning to the man next to her. "That's O'Riley – belongs to Pip down the road. It chased the vicar out of the field the other day. Nobody can do a thing with it."

She leaned forward intently as the men released the horse in the pen and it immediately took a swipe at one of them and thundered round in a rage. Jodie, Sophie and I exchanged startled looks and wondered what would happen next.

Josh stepped inside the pen with nothing but a lunge rein. Everybody in the building fell silent. The horse snorted and stared like a bull. We were convinced it was going to charge him.

And then the magic started. Josh began by quietly driving him away, looking him straight in the eye. O'Riley seemed stunned that someone had the guts to stand up to him and paddled off in the direction Josh wanted. He kept this up for a few minutes and miraculously Josh predicted what he would do next. When O'Riley started lowering his head and making chewing movements with his jaw, that was when Josh dropped his eyes and half turned his back.

The audience gasped as this huge bully of a horse immediately walked after Josh like an innocent baby, zigzagging round the pen after him, his nose touching his shoulder. Everybody clapped like crazy and O'Riley stood stock-still like a transformed horse, enjoying the attention and flapping his rubbery lips as if to say how pleased he was with himself.

After that there followed a procession of different horses. There was a Shetland pony with a terror of horseboxes. A show horse who hated male judges, a racehorse scared of starting stalls and a beautiful Arab who bucked like crazy every time the rider tried to tighten the girth. Josh had them all cured within minutes and could give a detailed account of what had made them so traumatized in the first place. It was as if he could read their minds and talk to them in a way the average person couldn't. He was truly gifted. We were all transfixed. We didn't notice time passing, and had no idea that the bay dressage horse, carefully going through his paces, was the grand finale. And then Josh was summing up, advising owners on how they could get more out of their horses and develop a special bond.

I was in a daze, trying to memorize each word. Suddenly Jodie was leaning close, pointing at her watch. We had to get out of there. Quick.

I leapt up and immediately knocked over a carton of popcorn. Jodie grabbed my coat and we started inching down the aisle, scrabbling over feet and handbags.

"Hurry up," Sophie hissed, bringing up the rear.

There was various tutting and some disapproving faces. Josh was still talking. Everyone was now aware of three girls frantically trying to leave the building. I could feel my face flushing brick red. The last man in the row had to stand up to let us pass which took for ever, and in the mean-time Josh was leaving the arena.

"Where now?" I asked frantically. We slid out of the main doors earning an angry look from a woman in a grey suit.

It was dark and cold outside and extremely quiet. We could still hear the microphone: "Unfortunately Mr le Fleur has to leave straight away in order to catch a flight to Los Angeles where he'll be working on a film due out next year. However, there are various books, videos and signed photos on sale, and experienced assistants in the foyer who'll be able to answer any questions." There was a groan of disappointment.

"Come on!" Jodie grabbed my arm. "Run!"

The car park was jam-packed but there was no sign of Josh.

"The back doors," Sophie breathed.

We ran at full pelt down a row of stables, disturbing horses, clattering over a bucket. Sophie streaked ahead – she wasn't a champion cross-country runner at school for nothing. There, by the gate, was a set of headlights, dipped into the hedge.

"It's got to be him!"

We thundered across, my lungs gasping for air, and a stitch searing through my side. The car was black and sleek with someone in the driving seat reading a paper by the interior light. He got out as soon as he saw us. Behind, we heard the click-clack of high heels. It was the woman in the grey suit. And behind her, draped in a cream riding mac, was Josh.

"Mr le Fleur!"

"Oh no, it's those kids again." The woman wrinkled up her face in distaste and hurried her step. "Mr le Fleur is a very busy man. If you'd kindly step aside."

Jodie and Sophie were blocking the car doors – not intentionally, but they didn't move when they realized the delaying tactics of their position.

"Mr le Fleur!" I stepped forward, every nerve in my body zinging with urgency. "Please help us!"

The woman's face set hard. Her voice was raw with irritation. "Would you please step aside."

"It's my pony," I blurted out. "Well, he's a loan pony, but he'll be sent back if . . . Please, Mr le Fleur, he's terrified of traffic. We've only got until tomorrow." I babbled on, frantic, desperate.

"I'm sorry, but I've got a plane to catch." He said it firmly, trying to smile.

"You're our last chance," I pleaded, pushing my hair back behind my ears, wishing I wasn't so young, so insignificant. "You said you wanted to help horses and ponies all over the world, and not just the expensive ones."

He paused, faltering for the first time in his hurry to get to the car.

"Please, Mr le Fleur. Monty needs help. He's screwed up. I don't know what to do to help him." I felt my voice start to shake. My eyes filled with tears and I brushed them away impatiently.

"Monty, you say . . ." He was thinking, considering.

"We really must get a move on," said the woman, fidgeting, panicking, trying to urge him on.

Seizing the moment I spilled out the story of Georgie Fenton, the accident, the Six Pack, Abby and the test tomorrow.

"You're our last chance," I pleaded. "I know you can cure him." At that moment I would have gladly gone down on my knees and begged.

"How far away is this riding school did you say?"

Relief washed over me in great waves.

"We really need to be at the airport . . ."

"Later," Josh waved his hand dismissively, his eyes bright with sudden excitement and urgency. "I think you and your friends had better get in the car, don't you?"

Chapter Ten

"My brain feels like scrambled eggs." Abby shot up in bed, clearly remembering what day it was.

I dragged myself out of sleep, suddenly feeling sick with nerves. Abby's test was at 2.30 p.m. Then we'd know for definite whether the training had worked.

"Happy Birthday," said Abby, looking pale as she headed for the bathroom.

I glanced at the lovely glossy photograph of Monty on my dressing table and counted off twelve years on my fingers. "Happy Birthday – *not*," I mumbled, feeling my stomach flip over.

Josh's visit to Brook House had been incredible. Everybody knew who he was and I couldn't believe we'd got his sole attention. He treated Monty as if he were a racehorse belonging to the queen. Other girls in riding hats and jods hung around, hoping to get a look in, but Josh got straight on with the job in hand, totally focused on Monty's condition.

To start with he worked at gaining his trust,

without even going near a car. Very soon Monty was following him around like a devoted puppy. He looked like the old Monty, his brown eyes relaxed and fearless.

Sophie clutched my elbow. She was as excited as I felt. Abby was screwing up her face, watching the whole procedure in awe. This was Monty's chance to be normal again.

When Josh finally asked the woman in the grey suit to switch the engine on in his car we were all so nervous we could hardly breathe. Rachel and Emma were so obviously star-struck, they hadn't said a word since Josh had arrived.

"I wish he could do this to humans," Kate whispered. "I'd ask him to stop me from being scared of jumps, and to be able to pass exams without throwing up."

"He's a top class horse trainer," Jodie hissed, ultra-serious. "Not a genie in a lamp."

"All right, don't get uptight. I was only saying."

"Well don't."

Monty was approaching the car. At first he seemed tense. He snorted once. Josh circled round him, not looking him in the eye, and then walked closer, waiting for him to follow. There was no pressure on the lead rope. Monty shrugged, almost as a human would, and clamped onto Josh's shoulder, as close to him as was physically possible.

"Come on, Monty," I whispered, crossing my fingers.

Monty tentatively stepped closer, his forelegs shaking as he lifted each one from the ground. The soft purr of the engine seemed to roar in my ears, louder and louder. Monty was right next to the car and he still hadn't pulled back.

Amazingly, Josh opened the bonnet so Monty could see the engine whirring, hear the noise more loudly, smell the oil. Still he didn't pull back, but just pushed his nose into the crook of Josh's arm, seeking safety.

Josh asked for a bucket of feed which Sophie ran off to fetch. I desperately wanted to go up to Monty but knew I'd break the magic spell. Monty was totally focused on Josh. If a jumbo jet had landed I still don't think he'd have flinched.

Sophie quietly passed the feed bucket to Josh who placed it on the bonnet of the car. Miraculously, with a little encouragement Monty started eating from the bucket, his chest only inches from the sleek bonnet. All the time, Josh talked to him, ran his hands all over his body, under his stomach, his back, down each leg. We could all see Monty relaxing. All the tension of the last week draining out. In fact, by the time he'd finished the horse nuts, he looked half asleep.

Josh then got his assistant to drive the car back and forth past Monty, revving the engine as loud as she could. The whole Six Pack braced themseles anxiously. Even Rocket, or Buzby or Rusty wouldn't tolerate that. In fact no horse or pony at the riding school would. Monty blinked curiously and then even rested a hind leg! It was a miracle! He was cured!

Josh finally let us go up to him and pat him and hug him. Then Sophie, being the most socially confident of all of us, hugged Josh, and Kate asked for his autograph which he scribbled on a match-box. I buried my hands into Monty's thick mane and didn't know whether to laugh or cry.

"Now I really do have a plane to catch," said Josh glancing anxiously at his watch.

"How can we ever thank you?" I felt dizzy with emotion.

"No, thank *you*," he replied, rubbing Monty's nose one more time, "for asking me to help. For going to such lengths."

The car pulled away, turned right and quickly disappeared. All we had to worry about now was the test. And whether Monty would remember what he'd just been taught. Or anything at all.

Margaret had cooked a full English breakfast with mushroom, sausage and the crispiest of bacon. Beside my place was a birthday card and a tiny present which, when I opened it, held two tiny gold earrings in the shape of horseshoes. Just what I wanted. Inside the birthday card was a simple message – Good Luck for today.

I carefully stood it up next to the ones from Dad and Mum and glanced across to the door handle where my black show jacket was hanging, brushed and cleaned to perfection.

"Thanks," I said and meant it. "For everything."

Then I picked up my knife and fork and tackled the huge breakfast. I cleaned my plate for the first time since Margaret had married Dad and she flushed with pleasure. Everything wasn't totally OK yet but at least we were all heading in the right direction. We wanted to be a family and that's what mattered most.

We were determined to give Abby one last chance to get the hang of rising trot. As soon as we arrived at the riding school we tacked up and headed for the field. We were going to position ourselves as before, but this time Sophie was going to ride Rocket alongside in the hope that Abby might fall in with her rhythm.

It was a clear, fresh morning and Monty shone like the sunshine itself. Abby tightened her reins and, lost in concentration, drew level with Rocket. Kate clipped a lead rope on Monty's bit and led him forward.

"Up, down, up, down, up, down. Come on, Abby, up, down. One, two, one, two." She was bumping valiantly, her face grim with determination. Rachel took over, chanting the rhythm. Abby fixed her eyes on Sophie, watching her rise up and down on Rocket. She looked as if she was about to burst with frustration.

"Come on, Abby!"

Jane and Serena happened to be riding down the drive, legs loose, out of the stirrups, shoulders slack, slouched in the saddle. They started tittering and I knew why. Rage ripped through me and I fixed my eyes on Abby bouncing towards me.

"*Abby. Up. Now!*"

Her head darted up, her riding hat slipped down and she levered her seat up just at the right moment. One. Two. One, two, one two. She'd got it. She was doing rising trot. Her face lit up incredulously and Kate yelled out in sheer disbelief, "She's got it, Abby's doing rising trot!"

After that it was easy. She walked, trotted and cantered round the field by herself, in perfect balance. Monty didn't put a foot wrong. I'd never seen anybody so ecstatic. She showered him with pats and kisses and slithered to the ground with dimples showing in her cheeks from grinning so much.

"Wait till I tell my mates back home about this. I can ride, really truly ride, and not a plod either – a proper horse." I didn't pull her up about Monty being a pony, not a horse because I was too taken

372

aback. It was the first time she'd ever mentioned her life "back home".

An outline of the road safety course was pinned up on the saloon noticeboard. It was marked in a red pen. Red for danger. Abby suddenly seemed to have turned a very funny colour.

I was to take my test on Blossom, a cute little Welsh Mountain who could be awkward if you didn't show her who was boss from the very beginning. Emma groaned when she saw we had to ride down a stretch of road with luscious grass verges on each side.

"Buzby will stick his head down for sure. I'd better superglue my hands to the reins."

"That pony needs his jaw wiring up," Kate said matter-of-factly, somehow finding the appetite to eat a cream bun.

"By the looks of it, so do you."

The test was divided into two parts, one on the actual roads, and another in the back field, which was a mock test with lots of hazards – pretend roadworks, traffic lights and noisy pedestrians. There was even a mock road junction where we had to use arm signals.

"What do they think we're riding? Police horses?" Jodie was looking increasingly alarmed, mainly because she was riding Minstrel, an Arab who spooked if a crisp bag blew past. She didn't know how he'd react when confronted with people having picnics and road closed signs and tractors and trailers.

Abby's eyes locked onto the tractor which was the last hazard on the test. Stewards would be standing at various points to mark down a pass or fail.

"I think I'm just going to go for a little walk," Abby whispered suddenly, and wandered off looking distinctly shaky.

"It's for you." Guy left the brown parcel on the saloon table, swivelling it round so I could read the label. To the Six Pack. From Josh le Fleur. "Someone dropped it off five minutes ago – said it was urgent."

We gazed at the wrapping for ages and then Kate took the initiative, ripped off the string and pulled at one corner. Inside was a simple black box with a clasp. Kate prised it open and gasped in delight. On a velvet background, all in a line, were oval badges, navy blue and gold rimmed with a tiny riding hat and crop in the centre. They were beautiful.

"Here's a note." Sophie unfolded a piece of paper.

Dear girls,
    Every exclusive club needs a membership

badge. Hope these will suffice. Keep up your special work.

From one of your supporters, Josh.

It was amazing. Nobody had ever taken us this seriously before. In absolute reverence, Sophie carefully pinned the badges onto our riding shirts until there was just one left.

"I'd better find Abby," I said picking up the other badge and slipping it into my pocket. Thankfully Josh had thought of everybody.

"Number sixteen, number sixteen, kindly ride forward." The pony club District Commissioner had commandeered the loudspeaker and was frightening the ponies even more than the so-called hazards. The Sutton Vale members were having terrible problems keeping their ponies under control. They looked suspiciously like they had been fed oats. One tank-like pony had careered straight through the picnic hazard and was charging around with a tablecloth hanging from his stirrups.

Guy was trying to organize twelve riding school ponies to appear on time and looking presentable with the appropriate rider on board. Two whining girls in over-large back protectors were complaining that they'd put their names down to ride Rusty.

Rusty had just done a perfect test with Rachel, not batting an eyelid and earning top marks. Rachel was thrilled and started advising Kate who was panicking big time because Archie wouldn't move past the portable loo.

I'd left Monty in the stable, right till the last possible moment. Anything to keep him as calm as possible. Blossom stood idly switching flies and blowing herself up so that I couldn't tighten her girth. Abby was nervously chewing her nails, waiting for me to finish so she could change into my riding clothes.

"Oh no!" Sophie groaned out loud. Minstrel had just had a bucking fit and thrown Jodie into the pretend zebra crossing. "This is unbearable." She could hardly stand the tension any longer.

I felt as if the ground was rearing up at me, my throat suddenly desert-dry and throbbing. I'd just spotted Dad and Margaret walking casually towards the marked out course. And not alone. I'd recognize the short, blond couple anywhere – they were Monty's loan owners. They could only be here for one reason – to take him back. How could Dad do this to me? And on my birthday of all days. Hot, stinging tears built up at the back of my eyes.

I'd rarely seen Sophie so stirred up. "Dad, this is so unfair," she said, tripping after Mr Green who was stalking around, spreading gloom everywhere.

Rachel and Abby were leading Monty up from the stables. He was quietly observing all the activity, perfectly relaxed, walking like a famous racehorse, his mane and tail plaited, his hoofs oiled. He looked stunning.

"Dad, you can't go through with this. It's ridiculous."

Mr Green swung round and glared fiercely at his daughter, but we all knew it was a front – he adored her really, just wanted the best for her. That had always been the trouble. "Sophie, don't try and undermine my authority. I've made my decision and I'm not backing down. No, Sophie." She opened her mouth to answer back. "Just drop it. Please."

Abby sat on Monty, ramrod straight, her elbows carefully in at her sides. Only her nervous smile indicated that she was anything but calm.

"You can only do your best," I reassured her, reaching up and gripping her wrist. "You've already done your best. You've moved mountains to get this far. If he plays up you've got to get straight off. Don't even try to ride him." My voice tailed off. There was nothing left to say. Abby gave me a quick, bright little smile and pulled herself up to her full height in the saddle.

She was to do the road safety test first and as she came into the back field to tackle the hazards she was to stick up her thumb if everything had gone well.

Monty stood like an angel. I wrapped my arms round his solid neck, trying to breathe confidence into him. Dear, darling Monty. It was so important that Josh's training had worked. If it hadn't . . . I couldn't even bear to contemplate it. I turned away, tears pressing at the back of my eyes. Abby rode forward towards the first steward.

"Steph!" Dad's voice burst into my thoughts. He was coming towards me, waving, Margaret and the other couple tagging along, trying to keep up.

"Quick, hide me." I dived behind Emma and Kate who shuffled forward, shielding me from view. I couldn't talk to Dad now. In fact, after Monty went, I didn't think I'd ever be able to talk to him again.

"She's here!" Sophie was the first to spot Monty and Abby coming back into the field. Monty was walking with even steps, his nose tucked in, Abby was staring straight ahead, her jaw jutting out.

"Over here!" Sophie called. A cold tentacle of fear crept up my neck. Why hadn't she seen us? Then she stuck up her thumb. She was grinning.

"She's passed," Emma leapt in the air, swinging an arm round my neck.

"Has she? Really?" I could feel my face burning, my heart thudding. She was trotting now and two stewards were calling her number. This was the final hurdle – the pretend zebra crossing, the road-works, the tractor.

Monty stepped forward timidly.

"She needs to use more leg." Sophie stuck her knuckle in her mouth and started biting it.

Emma was standing on my foot but I didn't really notice. No amount of physical pain could compare to what was going on inside me.

"My nerves are in shreds," moaned Emma, screwing her eyes shut as Monty approached the roadworks.

"He's through." Rachel was the only one who could watch calmly.

"Steady! Careful!" Abby was trotting, rising too high, too fast . . .

"She's past the picnic site." For one awful moment Abby lost her balance and nearly fell off.

The tractor roared into life.

"Now we'll know," said Sophie, linking arms with me and Jodie. "He'll do it. I know he will. He's got to."

Over by the start rope Mr Green watched care-fully. Monty pricked up his ears, alert. I saw Abby patting his shoulder and talking to him with words of encouragement. I felt a stab of panic as he halted suddenly then moved forward. I could hardly bear it.

Abby sat up straight and shortened her reins. It was all down to Josh's training now. Monty thought for a moment, then miraculously he walked confidently past. He was the best pony in the world – a legend!

Abby let out a whoop of delight and rode back to the Six Pack who were clapping and cheering. It was brilliant. Monty was road-safe with a certificate to prove it.

"Stephanie!" Suddenly there was Dad pushing his way through. Happiness drained away. Monty was going back to his loan owners. They probably had the horsebox parked outside now. I managed a watery smile, all anger and resentment gone – I was just too exhausted.

"We've bought Monty!" he yelled, rushing up to me. "That's what you wanted, isn't it? For your birthday?"

The rest of the day was sheer bliss. I had loads of lovely presents from my friends and we ended up having a proper picnic with all the ponies gathered round munching on carrot sandwiches made by Kate. Monty knew he was the star attraction and kept pawing the ground, knocking over plastic cups of stewed tea. Buzby ate his road safety rosette which caused a huge laugh.

I couldn't stop looking at Monty's gorgeous, alert head. He was mine to keep, groom, ride, look after for ever.

Later on, when we were about to go home, I tracked down Abby for a very formal announcement. We wanted her to join the Six Pack as an official member.

"I'd best not." Abbey smiled nervously, unsure.

I was really taken aback.

"You see, I'm going back to live with Dad, just as soon as Mum sorts my stuff out."

The breath practically left my body. "I know I've been awful, really mean, but it's not like that any more. I love having you around – I've always wanted a sister."

Abby smiled, almost mischievous. "It's not that. I'm just missing my own mates, my own bedroom. I'll come back in the holidays. And you'd better send photos and write lots. I want to know all about Monty." She looked across to where he was staring out over the field gate, relaxed and happy. "Anyway," she said, nudging my arm, "I'm going to check out my local riding school, maybe form a Six Pack all of my own. What do you say?"

"I think that's an excellent idea." I knew that Abby wasn't just talking. She was the most determined person ever. "One thing's for sure," I said, thinking about all the horses and ponies and my friends at Brook House, "riding school life is just the best in the world."

Samantha Alexander
Riding School 4: Kate

Six very different girls – Jodie, Emma, Steph, Kate, Sophie and Rachel – bound together by their passion for horses.

"Are you all right?" Sophie touched my shoulder, concern traced all over her face. I was leaning against the stable wall, my breath coming in frantic gasps. "Only you look as if you've seen a ghost . . ."

The resurrection of an old ghost story is causing chaos at Brook House. Doors are being left open, taps suddenly turned on, bales of hay moved, and tack keeps disappearing. The horses are edgy and so are the riders – Kate sets out to solve the mystery.

Samantha Alexander
Riding School 5: Sophie

Six very different girls – Jodie, Emma, Steph, Kate, Sophie and Rachel – bound together by their passion for horses.

"You just can't help getting involved in my life, can you?" I could hear my voice rising, cracking with rage. For once Natalie just stared, speechless. "This was my chance," I shouted, "they asked me first. Me!"

Sophie cannot believe her luck when the pony magazine *In the Saddle* visits Brook House Riding School. She lands the star role in a photo story about a horse superstar. But her sister Natalie is determined to muscle in where she's not wanted.

Samantha Alexander
Riding School 6: Rachel

Six very different girls – Jodie, Emma, Steph, Kate, Sophie
and Rachel – bound together by their passion for horses.

*"Go boy, find help!" Rusty edged closer, refusing to leave. It
was getting dark. I couldn't spend a night on the fells – I
couldn't. "Rusty, you've got to find the others," I whispered.
Suddenly he seemed to understand.*

Excitement abounds when Brook House is nominated for
the Riding School of the Year Award. But everything goes
wrong for Rachel and she ends up deliberately defying
doctors' orders. Suddenly her life is in the balance and
Rusty is the only one who can save her.

Samantha Alexander
Hollywell Stables 1: Flying Start

Hollywell Stables – sanctuary for horses and ponies. It was
a dream come true for Mel, Ross and Katie . . .

A mysterious note led them to Queenie, neglected and
desperately hungry, imprisoned in a scrapyard. Rescuing
Colorado was much more complicated. The spirited
Mustang terrified his owner: her solution was to have him
destroyed.

But for every lucky horse at the sanctuary there are so
many others in desperate need of rescue. And money is
running out fast . . .

Samantha Alexander
Hollywell Stables 2: The Gamble

Hollywell Stables – sanctuary for horses and ponies. It was a dream come true for Mel, Ross and Katie . . .

It was a gamble. How could it possibly work? Why should one of the world's most famous rock stars give a charity concert for Hollywell Stables? But Rocky is no ordinary rock star and when he discovers that the racing stables keeping his precious thoroughbred are cheating him, he leads the Hollywell team on a mission to uncover the truth . . .